Salsa Stories

STORIES AND LINOCUTS BY

Lulu Delacre

SCHOLASTIC INC.

This book was originally published in hardcover by Scholastic Press in 2000.

ISBN 978-0-545-43098-2

12 11 10 9 8 7 6 5 4 3 2 1 12 13 14 15 16 17/0

Printed in the U.S.A. 40

This edition first printing, September 2012

The text type was set in Garamond 3.
The display type was set in Linoscript.
Book design by Marijka Kostiw

Este es sólo para tí,
querida Alicia.

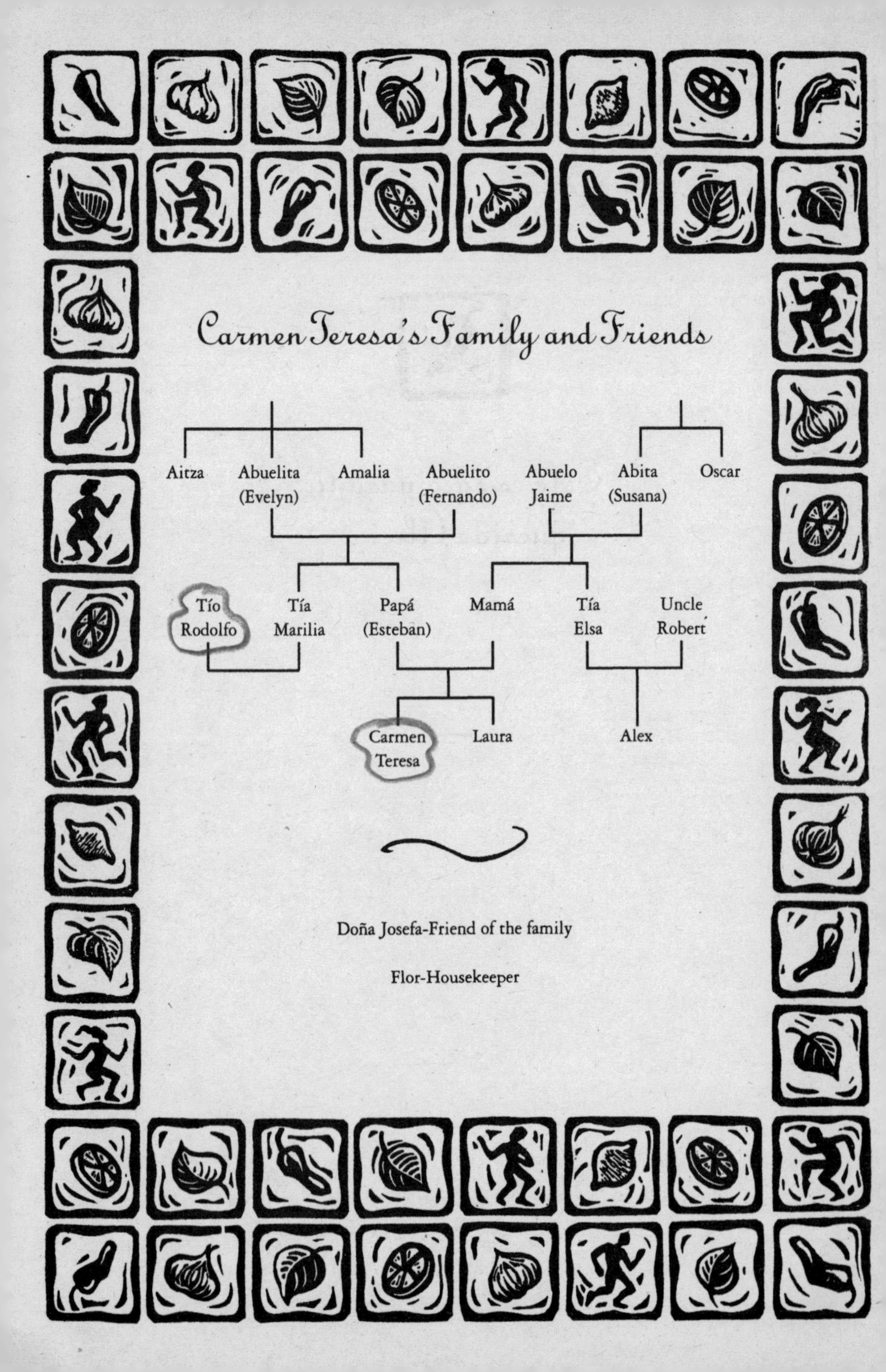
Carmen Teresa's Family and Friends
Aitza
Abuelita (Evelyn)
Amalia
Abuelito (Fernando)
Abuelo Jaime
Abita (Susana)
Oscar
Tío Rodolfo
Tía Marilia
Papá (Esteban)
Mamá
Tía Elsa
Uncle Robert
Carmen Teresa
Laura
Alex
Doña Josefa-Friend of the family
Flor-Housekeeper

Table of Contents

New Year's Day

"Esteban! Turn down the stereo," Mamá calls to Papá from the kitchen. She swirls the chicken in its marinade with one hand, then answers the telephone with the other.

Our house stirs with laughter and chatter as guests arrive, one by one. The cousins run noisily about our basement to the beat of salsa music that blares from speakers on two floors. In the dining room, Abuelito, Abuelo Jaime, Uncle Robert, and Papá click dominoes together, concentrating on each move of their game. They play with Abuelito's lucky dominoes, the ones he brought with him from Cuba forty years ago.

In the kitchen, my grandma Abita, our housekeeper Flor, and I rhythmically chop and slice. The rich, pungent scent of garlic crackling in olive oil rises from the stove. We are helping Mamá prepare the *sofrito* sauce for her *arroz con pollo.* This is the rice dish for which Mamá is famous among all our friends and family.

Flor and Abita chatter away in Spanish, as they

struggle to hold back tears from the chopped onion. Flor tells Abita about the trip she will soon make to Guatemala for Holy Week.

"I've been saving for over a year to visit my family," she says. Flor has saved not only for her ticket, but also for the gifts she will bring to everyone from America: new jeans, walkie-talkies, a small TV, and the latest toys.

Abita nods her approval.

Above the din of music, children's shouts, and clattering pots and pans, we miraculously hear the doorbell.

"Carmen Teresa, get the door!" my little sister Laura calls from the basement stairs.

"You get it — please!" I shout back. "I'm busy." I'm afraid that if I abandon my spot in the kitchen, I will lose it to someone else who is anxious to help. I love to cook, and when company comes, a good spot in Mamá's kitchen is hard to come by.

I watch Laura dash to open the door.

"Doña Josefa!" she calls out, then flies into the old woman's open arms.

"Feliz año nuevo, Laurita," Doña Josefa says, as she gives Laura a warm hug and a present. Doña Josefa is from Peru. She is one of the doctors from the free clinic where Mamá volunteers. Mamá always says Doña Josefa loves to dote on us since she has no children of her own.

Laura thanks her for the gift, then steals into the dining room to open it.

Doña Josefa finds me in the kitchen. She is holding a package wrapped in brown paper. Her leathery hands are a shade darker than the wrapping. She's about to place the package into my open hands, but stops herself when she notices they are covered in cilantro. She takes the package back to the entrance and puts it on a small table instead.

"For after you clean your hands, Carmen Teresa," she says.

The last to arrive are Tía Marilia and Tío Rodolfo. They've brought bottles of *coquito* and the latest hits from Rubén Blades and Willie Colón.

"Would you believe this?" Tía Marilia jokes, glancing at the guests. "All the men are enjoying themselves while the women slave in the kitchen. There are some old customs that not even life in the States can change!"

Tía Marilia is my favorite aunt. She has such a quick wit, and when she is around, there is laughter everywhere.

Suddenly, my sister tugs at my sleeve.

"Look, Carmen, look what I got!" Laura shows me a beautiful cloth doll that Doña Josefa gave her. "Let me see yours, what did you get?"

Curious to find out, I wash my hands and look for my gift. But it is not on the table where Doña Josefa left it. And no one is near the table except our little cousin Alex. When Laura sees him, she eagerly takes his hand and tries to play with him. But Alex has just learned to walk and he prefers to gleefully charge around the house.

"Laura!" calls Abuelita. "The cinnamon!"

Laura quickly forgets about Alex and my gift and runs to do her only and favorite job in the kitchen. She must sprinkle cinnamon over the cool *natilla.* Abuelita prepared the velvety cream for dessert and filled twenty-five small bowls with it. This dessert is Laura's favorite, and after carefully studying each bowl, she mischievously covers the fullest one with a blanket of the spice. That's her way of claiming it.

Mamá calls everyone to eat. We've set the platters on the kitchen counter and people stream in to serve themselves. Then they sit wherever they please at the dining room table, at the kitchen table, or in the living room.

Abuelito stands up to say grace. He can sometimes go on for quite a long time, for he loves to be the center of attention. And he always ends his prayer with the same old Spanish saying: "*¡Salud, dinero, amor, y tiempo para disfrutarlos!* Health, money, love, and time to enjoy it all!" he says. Everyone is very hungry by the time he finally gets to this part.

I take a huge mouthful of steaming *yuca* when Doña Josefa sits next to me.

"Did you like your gift?" she asks.

I quickly swallow and excuse myself to avoid the embarrassing situation of having to tell her I've misplaced it.

I look again on the entrance table and under it, but the package is gone. In whispers, I ask my parents and some relatives if they have seen it, but no one has. To avoid Doña Josefa, I duck into the kitchen where I find Tía Marilia and Tío Rodolfo. They've been lured to the center of the kitchen floor by the dance music that's become irresistible to them. Gracefully they twirl into each other's arms and show off their fiery moves. Inspired by her sister-in-law, Mamá pulls me to "the dance floor" to teach me some basic salsa steps. Reluctantly, I follow.

"Don't look at your feet," warns Mamá. "Just feel the rhythm of the music."

Across the room, I spot Laura next to Alex. I abandon the dance lesson to find out if she has seen my missing gift. Before I can ask, Alex topples the little rooster that was perched on the hand-carved nativity scene. And while Laura carefully rearranges the pieces, Alex has moved on to playing with something else. I peer over his shoulder to find he's trying to unwrap a brown package. *It's my gift!*

"Oh, Alex," I say. "Let me help you with that."

I let him unwrap the small parcel, then give him the wrapping paper to play with. He seems quite happy to noisily rustle and crinkle the paper.

My gift from Doña Josefa is a book filled with blank pages and covered with a red fabric sprinkled with daisies. Inside I find an inscription:

Dear Carmen Teresa,

When I was your age, I kept a journal in a book just like this one. I hope you'll find a treasured use for yours, as I did for mine.

Doña Josefa

"Show me!" demands Laura. A smug look comes over her face when she sees the book. She is pleased that it is not something she likes better than her doll.

Relieved to have found the gift, I run to Doña Josefa to thank her.

"What should I write in this book?" I ask her.

Doña Josefa's creased face lights up with her smile. "There are many things you can write," she says. "Perhaps you will want to keep a journal, like I did."

"Or," offers Abuelita, "you could write about things that have happened to you when you were younger."

"Yes. Or maybe, you could collect stories from our family and friends," suggests Mamá, "since everyone is here today."

"Stories — *ahh, ¡cuentos!*" calls Abuelito from his seat at the dining room table where he has been eavesdropping. "I have a great story for your book, Carmen Teresa. But first," he says in his deep voice, "Abuelita, bring me more of that wonderful *arroz con pollo,* please."

Abuelita nods to Flor, who quickly refills his plate.

Abuelito glows as everyone gathers around him to hear his tale.

"When you are finished, Señor," Flor adds, "I have a story for Carmen Teresa, too."

"*¡Ah! No, no, damas primero,*" says Abuelito. "Ladies first."

"Always a gentleman," replies Doña Josefa. "And who knows, maybe we'll all take a turn. Why don't you start, Flor?" As soon as we are comfortably settled around the dining room table, Flor begins her story.

A Carpet for Holy Week

Flor's Story

Ever since I was a little girl in Guatemala City, my family has made an *alfombra* for Holy Week. *Alfombras* are beautiful carpets handmade from colored sawdust and fresh flowers. Every Palm Sunday morning, we make an *alfombra* on the street right in front of our house. That week, dozens of processions walk by. Porters, who carry splendid statues of Jesus and Mary, follow the pathways of beautiful carpets that are spread throughout the neighborhood. We wait for one that will cross our carpet. At last it comes! And for us, it is like the Lord Himself has walked upon our carpet.

One Friday during Lent, when I was twelve, we had just finished Mamá's *bacalao a la vizcaína,* her delicious codfish stew, when Abuelo Marco asked me to do something I had only dreamed of doing.

"Flor," he said, smoothing his mustache that was now the color of his weathered straw hat. "Since you are the oldest grandchild, how would you like to make the design for the carpet this year?"

"Oh, Abuelo!" I shouted joyfully. Ever since I could walk, I had helped him with the carpet. When I was very young, I was only allowed to stamp on the saw-dust. Later, I was allowed to help dye it. And for the past few years, I carefully sifted out what was needed for its colorful border. But I had never had the honor of making the design. I couldn't wait to look through our well-worn collection of wooden stencils and pull out the ones I liked best.

I could feel the expectant stares of Abuelo, my par-ents, and my three little brothers as I sat on my chair, thinking. I had seen how Abuelo lovingly created new carpet designs by mixing patterns. I tried to remember sawdust carpets I had seen before and the many border stencils I knew we had stored. Then, I decided just what I wanted to do. I took some paper and a pencil, and started to draw. Abuelo Marco nodded in approval when I was finished.

"I think we'll have a beautiful carpet, Flor," he said.

The following day, Papá and all three of my brothers drove to the sawmill to get the sawdust. The owner of the sawmill gave away most of his sawdust just for making carpets for Holy Week. When Papá returned with twenty large sacks, we all helped carry them into the house. For the next several hours my mother and I stirred the sawdust in big vats of dye. We made batches of red, white, green, and black. The last thing I did that afternoon was to trace the new flying dove pattern on plywood. Papá cut out the stencil. I could already imagine the dove in the middle of a golden background surrounded by borders of flowers and geometric shapes.

By Thursday, we had everything ready to make the carpet. And on Palm Sunday at dawn we would assemble it right in front of our house. I couldn't wait.

But then something terrible happened.

When I woke up Saturday morning, the house was in chaos.

"You stay here!" I heard Papá shout. "I'll go see what happened!"

He ran out the door, leaving Mamá watching anxiously by the window. Doña Paca, our next-door neighbor, had heard the turmoil, and rushed over to help with my younger brothers. She was in the kitchen feeding them *torrejas.* They were too young to understand what was going on, but the syrupy warm bread kept them out of the way.

"Mamá, ¿qué pasa?" I asked sleepily. "What's going on?"

"Ay, Flor," Mamá wept softly as she put her rosary down. "It's Abuelo Marco," she said. "There's a fire in his apartment. Your father has gone to help."

While Mamá dragged herself to the sofa to continue her prayer, I ran to the window and threw the shutters open wide. Between the modern signs projecting from storefronts and the cascade of ferns hanging from the balcony next door, I could see a crowd gathering at the entrance of Abuelo Marco's building. A cloud of black smoke was escaping from his window and rising to the sky. Frozen in place, I bit my fingernails, my eyes fixed on the crowd. What if something bad had happened to Abuelo?

"Is Abuelo inside his apartment?" I asked Mamá. "Did you try to call him?" But Mamá was deep in prayer and did not hear me. Soothed by her repetitive Hail Marys, I continued to look for Abuelo. I even made up prayers of my own.

The sun outside was blinding and I squinted my eyes to see clearly. The firefighters were opening a path through the crowd. It was then that I saw Papá coming out of Abuelo's building. And a moment later Abuelo appeared by his side.

"Mamá! Mamá! Abuelo is alright!" I cried out.

"Ay, Santo Dios," Mamá sighed, kissing the cross of her rosary.

Soon Papá returned home with Abuelo. We greeted them with hugs and strong coffee. For the next few hours, the phone didn't stop ringing. A stream of neighbors, family, and friends came in to see how Abuelo was doing. All the while I helped by entertaining my brothers.

Nobody mentioned the carpet at all that afternoon, and I began to worry that we weren't going to assemble it tomorrow. It was difficult to hide my disappointment. It was difficult to hide how eager I was for Abuelo see how my first *alfombra* would turn out.

When the commotion finally died down, my grandfather took a long nap. Afterward he came into the living room, followed by Mamá and Papá. Holding onto his cane, he sank onto the checkered couch and gathered his grandchildren near him.

"Well, it looks like I'll be staying here with you for a while," Abuelo said, with a weary look on his face. "Everything inside my apartment is charred or burnt to ashes. But it doesn't matter. Who wants all those ancient things anyway?"

For a long moment nobody said anything. I thought it was unfair that he had lost everything — his old books and photographs, his furniture-making tools, and even his favorite rocking chair — all was gone. I couldn't imagine what it would be like to lose all my favorite things.

"The only thing that matters is that you are alive." Mamá finally broke the silence. "We'll love to have you here with us."

We all hugged him together.

"Abuelo," I asked, "is there something I can do?"

"*Nada,* Florcita," Abuelo smiled. "Not a thing." But after a pause he asked, "Do we have everything ready for tomorrow's carpet?"

"This is not a time to think about making an *alfombra,*" complained Mamá. "There are other more important things to take care of."

Fortunately, Abuelo Marco would not hear of any excuses. He was not about to break a tradition that he had loved since he was a little boy. Not for a fire — not for anything. So we all agreed we would make the carpet tomorrow as we had planned.

The following morning, my family was outside at the crack of dawn. My uncles opened sacks of sawdust and poured their contents inside a wooden frame. Amidst shrieks of delight, my three little brothers spread, stomped, and leveled the thick, golden foundation on which the design would be placed. Then, my

mother and I brought out big bowls of the dyed, moist sawdust we had prepared a few days before. Layer by layer, hour after hour, we sifted each color into the wooden stencils, taking pains not to step in what had already been made. Abuelo Marco sat on a chair nearby, watching as we worked. On the next street, several families worked on a two-block-long carpet they had been making since the night before.

Just as we finished, the bells of La Merced Church chimed loudly. Abuelo had gone inside to rest. It was then that I lovingly sifted something new into the carpet. Mamá came out and handed me a glass of cold *horchata.* Its bittersweet taste reflected my feelings. I drank it while we admired our work on the pavement.

"I like what you added to the design, Flor," said Mamá. "And I know Abuelo will like it, too."

After the fire, I had wanted to do something for Abuelo. So during the night I had cut two new stencils out of cardboard. One was the silhouette of an old man, the other was that of a flame.

A crowd of people gathered around us as we put the finishing touches on our *alfombra*. Papá sprayed the sawdust carpet with water once again, to protect it from the wind. Then he removed the wooden frame. The carpet's brilliant colors glowed in the morning sun.

Abuelo came out. As the sound of the tuba grew

louder, we knew the procession was coming near. Two long lines of men dressed in purple tunics carried an immense wooden platform on their shoulders. On it stood a statue of Jesus. Behind them, two lines of shawled women carried a platform with a statue of Mary. Burdened by the weight, the porters swayed from side to side as they solemnly walked forward.

Mamá, Papá, Abuelo, my brothers, and I gathered around our carpet and joined hands. I stood next to Abuelo, and I wondered if he liked what I had done.

"*Los cucuruchos,* the porters, they're coming!" said Abuelo, his voice filled with excitement. "They will finally step on the most beautiful *alfombra* our family has ever made."

A warm sensation deep inside me began to spread through my body like the sweet oozing syrup that soaked the *torrejas.* I felt the heat rise through my ears and color my cheeks. I watched as the porters first admired my design, and then slowly advanced across the carpet. They stepped on the green-and-white geometrical border. They stepped on the red-and-white flowered border. They stepped on the golden background where the white dove carried the black silhouette of an old man away from the red-and-yellow flames below it. Finally, they stepped on the two words I had written in black letters.

When the fragile carpet had vanished under the feet of the worshippers, I felt Abuelo squeeze my hand, and I looked up to meet his gaze. He had a broad smile on his face. It was then that I fully understood the importance of the words that I had written with black sawdust. *Gracias, Señor.*

Thank you, Lord.

Amen.

At the Beach

Abuelito's Story

I remember those evenings well when I was a young boy in Cuba, those balmy island nights before a trip to Guanabo Beach. The spicy aroma of *tortilla española* that Mami had left to cool would waft through the house as I lay in my bed. But I was always too excited to sleep. All I could think about was the soft white sand, the warm foamy water, and Mami's delicious *tortilla*. Ahhh. A day at the beach. It was full of possibilities.

One Saturday in May, I was awakened at the crack of dawn by sounds of laughter. My aunts, Rosa and Olga, had arrived with hammocks, blankets, and an iron kettle filled with Aunt Rosa's steaming *congrí*. And best of all, they had arrived with my cousins: Luisa, Mari, and little Javi. Uncle Toni had come, too.

When we were ready to leave, Papi, the only one in the family who owned a car, packed his Ford woody wagon with the nine of us. No one cared that we children had to squeeze into the back along with the clutter of pots and plates, food and bags, towels and blankets and hammocks. Soon the engine turned, and the car rumbled down the road into the rising sun.

Along the way, we drove past sugarcane fields and roadside markets. My cousins and I shouted warnings to the barking dogs and laughed at the frightened hens that scurried in every direction at the sight of our car. It seemed like a long time until the cool morning breeze that blew into the windows turned warm. And the growing heat made the aroma of Mami's *tortilla* all the more tempting.

"Lick your skin, Fernando," my older cousin Luisa told me. "If it tastes salty, that means we'll be there any time now."

She was right. My skin tasted salty. And soon — almost magically — the turquoise ocean appeared as we rounded a bend in the road. Papi pulled into the familiar dirt lot and parked under the pine trees. While the grown-ups unloaded the car, we eagerly jumped out and ran toward the sea, peeling off our clothes along the way.

"Remember, don't go too far!" Mami and Aunt Olga warned us sternly from the distance. I turned to see them picking up our scattered clothing.

When we reached the edge of the ocean, the water

felt cold. I waded farther in and went under to warm up quickly. When I emerged I saw Luisa, Mari, and little Javi, all standing still in the clear water. They were watching the schools of tiny gold-and-black striped fish rush between their legs. Then they swam over to join me and together we rode the big waves.

Later, Uncle Toni came in to play shark with us. We splashed, and swallowed the stinging sea water as he chased us above and under the waves. But after a while, we tired him out, and he went back to sit with the grown-ups.

I was getting very hungry, and for a moment I thought of returning with him to sneak a bite of Mami's *tortilla.* But then I had a better idea.

"Let's explore the reef!" I said.

"*¡Sí!*" everyone agreed. "Let's go!"

We all splashed out of the water and ran, dripping wet, across the sand. High above, the sun beat down on us.

When we got to the marbled rocks, Luisa looked concerned. "Our moms told us not to come this far," she said.

"I know the way well," I replied. "Besides, nobody will notice. They're too busy talking."

I looked in the distance and saw Mami and my two aunts in the shady spot they had picked. They had set

up a nice camp. The hammocks were tied to the pine trees, the blankets were spread over the fine sand. Papi and Uncle Toni played dominoes, while they sipped coffee and shared the *cucurucho de maní* they had purchased from the peanut vendor. They were having fun. No one would miss us for a long time.

"Watch out for sea urchins!" I warned as I led the group on our climb. The spiny black sea urchins hid inside the crevices and crannies of the rough boulders. It was very painful if you stepped on one. Luisa and Mari followed behind me. They were careful to only step on the rocks I stepped on. Little Javi came last. He stopped constantly to look at the *cobitos,* the tiny hermit crabs that scurried around on the rocks, and at the iridescent tropical fish that were concealed in the deepest tide pools. I had to keep checking behind me to make sure he didn't stray from our path.

Just then, I turned around to watch helplessly as Javi slipped on an algae-covered rock. *"¡Cuidado!"* I warned. But it was too late.

"¡Ay!" he shrieked, and then began to cry uncontrollably.

Cautiously, we all hurried back to help Javi. Luisa and Mari crouched down to examine his foot.

"He stepped on a sea urchin!" Mari cried. "Now what are we going to do?"

"We should have never followed you," Luisa lamented. "We'll all be punished."

At that moment I did not want to think of what the punishment would be. What if we couldn't have any of Mami's *tortilla*? All I knew was that we had to help Javi right away. I looked around and found a piece of driftwood.

"Luisa," I ordered. "Hold his leg still while I remove the urchin from his foot."

Luisa held Javi's leg still as Mari held his hand and tried to comfort him. But Javi's desperate cries were now drowning out the sound of the sea.

I pulled and tugged, but the urchin wouldn't budge. It was stuck to Javi's foot by the tips of its spines. Javi was scared and in pain. And we were too far from our parents to ask for help. What if we couldn't get Javi back? I struggled relentlessly until I was finally able to remove the spiny creature from his foot.

Gently, Luisa poured some sea water over Javi's foot. That was when she noticed there was still a piece of the sea urchin's spine lodged in it. Javi wasn't going to be able to walk back and he was much too heavy for us to carry. We had to remove that piece of spine so that he could walk on his own.

The sun burnt our backs as we all took turns trying to dislodge the sea urchin's spine.

"I have an idea," said Luisa suddenly. She removed her hair barrettes and held them like tweezers. Then, with the smallest movement, she pulled the broken spine out. With that solved, we started back.

I helped Javi walk on his sore foot. He wept and limped with every step. Our walk back seemed endless. As we got closer I realized that we would have to explain how it was that we went to the reef in the first place. I would surely end up with no *tortilla* if we told the truth.

"What will we do now?" Mari asked.

"We'll have to tell our parents what happened," said Luisa matter-of-factly.

"No!" I said emphatically. "We'll be punished for sure."

We walked the rest of the way in silence. The sound of crashing waves, children playing, and seagulls' calls became a background drone to Javi's cries.

When we finally reached our parents, Javi was crying louder than ever. Aunt Olga took one look at him and gasped. "*¡Niños!* Children! What's happened to Javi?"

Mari looked at Luisa. Luisa looked at me. Javi cried even louder.

"Well . . . ," I hesitated. By now everyone was staring at me. "We were walking along the beach looking for cockles and urchin shells," I began, "when I found a live sea urchin attached to a piece of driftwood. So I called the others. Javi came running so fast that he stepped on it by accident."

Luisa and Mari stared at me in disbelief. I didn't think they liked my story.

"Let me see your foot, Javi," Aunt Olga said, kneeling next to her son.

Mami and Aunt Rosa looked on as Aunt Olga examined Javi's foot closely. Then she gave him a big hug and a kiss. "He's fine," she said at last. "It looks like the children were able to pull it out."

And at this good news, Javi's tears disappeared and were replaced by a big broad smile. "I'm hungry," he said.

"Then let's have lunch," Aunt Olga suggested.

I was dumbfounded. Not only had they believed me, but we were also going to eat Mami's *tortilla*!

The men went back to their domino game. The women went back to their conversation as they busied themselves serving everybody. No one but me seemed to notice how quiet Luisa and Mari had grown.

Mami handed me a plate filled with my favorite foods. The *tortilla* smelled delicious. But I was unable to eat. I looked up at Luisa and Mari who were quietly picking at their food. I watched Mami as she served herself and sat next to my aunts. I looked at my plate again. How could I enjoy my food when I knew I had done something I wasn't supposed to do? There was only one thing I could do now. I stood up, picked up my plate, and went right over to Mami.

"What's wrong, Fernando?" Mami asked.

I looked back at Luisa and Mari and swallowed hard. Then, I handed Mami my untouched plate.

"You wouldn't have given me this if I had told you the truth," I said.

Mami looked puzzled. The whole group grew silent and watched me struggle. I was very embarrassed.

"It was my fault," Luisa said. "I should have stopped them."

"And I went along," said Mari.

"No, no, it was my idea to go to the reef," I said. Then I told everyone about our adventure at the reef. When I was finished, Mami looked at me with tear-filled eyes.

"You are right, Fernando," she said. "I should punish you for doing something you knew not to do. Somebody could have been seriously hurt."

"I know," I whispered, "and I'm sorry." But then the

glimmer of a smile softened Mami's expression. She slid her arm over my shoulders as she said, "You know, Fernando, anyone can make mistakes. But not everyone has the courage to admit it. *Gracias.* Thank you for telling the truth."

That afternoon, under the shade of the pine trees, the nine of us sat down on the old blankets for lunch. We had *congrí,* bread, and Mami's famous *tortilla española.* And do you know something? That day it tasted better than it ever had before.

The Night of San Juan

Abuelita's Story

Back in the 1940s, in Puerto Rico's walled city of Old San Juan, everybody knew everybody else. We neighborhood children played freely together on the narrow streets, while from windows and balconies adults kept a watchful eye on us. It was only my lonely friend José Manuel who was forbidden from joining us.

"Look, Evelyn," whispered Amalia. "He's up there again, watching us play."

Aitza and I looked up. There he was, sitting on his balcony floor. He peered sadly down at us through the wrought iron railing, while his grandma's soap opera blared from the radio inside. No matter how hard José Manuel tried, he could not convince his grandma to let him play out on the street.

"Too many crazy drivers! Too hard, the cobblestones! *¡Muy peligroso!*" His grandma would shake her head and say, "Too dangerous!"

Besides her fear of danger on the street, José Manuel's grandma kept to herself and never smiled, so most of us were afraid of her. That is, until my sisters and I changed all that.

"One day," Amalia suddenly announced, "I'm going to ask his grandma to let him come down and play." If anyone would have the courage to do that, it was my little sister Amalia. Even though she was only seven, she was also the most daring of the three of us.

We never knew what she would do next. In fact, at that very moment I could see a mischievous grin spreading across her freckled face as two elegant women turned the corner of Calle Sol. Once they strolled down the street in front of us, Amalia swiftly snuck up behind them and flipped their skirts up to expose their lace-trimmed slips.

"*¡Sinvergüenza!*" the women cried out. "Little rascal!"

We could hardly hold our laughter in. We all looked up to make sure none of the neighbors had seen her. If anyone had, we would surely have been scolded as soon as we got home. News traveled fast in our neighborhood.

Luckily, only José Manuel was watching us with amusement in his wistful eyes. Grateful for an audience, Amalia smiled at him, curtsied, and ran down the street toward the old cathedral with us chasing after her. I couldn't help but feel sorry for my friend as we left him behind.

There was hardly any sea breeze that day, and running in the humidity made us quite hot.

"Let's get some coconut sherbet," said Amalia, peeling her damp red curls away from her sweaty neck.

"*¡Sí, sí!*" we agreed, and we chattered excitedly about our plans for that night all the way to the ice-cream vendor's wooden cart by the harbor.

It was June twenty-third, and that night was the Night of San Juan. For this holiday, the tradition was to go to the beach, and at exactly midnight, everyone would walk backward into the sea. People say that doing this three times on the Night of San Juan brings good luck. I thought of my friend José Manuel. Perhaps if he did this with us, his luck would change, and his grandma would allow him to play with us outside on the street.

I thought about this as we bought our coconut sherbet and then ate it perched on the knobby roots of the ancient tree above the port. Excitement stirred in me while the distant ships disappeared over the horizon.

"How can we get José Manuel to go to the beach tonight?" I asked my sisters.

"Evelyn, you know very well his grandma will never let him go," Aitza said. "You know what she will say —"

"*¡Muy peligroso!*" Aitza and Amalia teased at once. "Too dangerous!"

It was getting close to dinnertime, and we knew we had to be home soon if we wanted our parents to take us to the beach that night. So we took the shortcut back across the main square. In the plaza, groups of men played dominoes while the women sat by the fountain and gossiped. Back on the street we heard the vegetable vendor chanting:

"*¡Vendo yuca, plátanos, tomates!*"

He came around every evening to sell his fresh cassava, plantains, tomatoes, and other fruits and vegetables.

Leaning from her balcony, a big woman lowered a basket that was tied by a cord to the rail. In it was the money that the vendor replaced with two green plantains. As we approached our street I saw José Manuel and his grandma out on the second floor. She gave José Manuel money and went back inside. He was about to lower his basket when I had an idea. Maybe there was a way we could ask him to join us.

"What if we send José Manuel a note in his grandma's basket inviting him to go to the beach with us tonight?" I offered.

"It will never work," Aitza said. "His grandma will not like it. We could get into trouble."

"Then we could ask her personally," I said.

"But what excuse could we use to go up there?" said Aitza. "Nobody ever shows up uninvited at José Manuel's house."

"Wait! I know what we can do," Amalia said, jumping up and down. "We'll tell him to drop something. Then we'll go up to return it."

Even though Aitza was very reluctant, we convinced her to try our plan. We wrote the note and asked the vegetable vendor to please place it in José Manuel's basket next to the vegetables. We impatiently waited on the corner as we watched. When he opened the note, he looked puzzled. He took the tomatoes he had purchased in to his grandmother. Soon he returned with his little red ball. He had just sat down to play when suddenly the ball fell from the balcony. It bounced several times, rolled down the hill, and bumped into a wall. Amalia flew after it. "I got it!" she called triumphantly, offering me her find.

With José Manuel's ball in my hand we climbed up the worn stairs of his pink apartment house. And while Aitza and I stood nervously outside his apartment trying to catch our breath, Amalia knocked loudly on the wooden door. With a squeaking sound it slowly opened, and there stood José Manuel's grandma wearing a frown as grim as her black widow's dress.

"¿Sí?" she said. "How can I help you?"

Aitza and I looked at each other. She looked as afraid as I felt. But without hesitation, Amalia took the little ball from my hand and proudly showed it to José Manuel's grandma. I wanted to run, but a glimpse of José Manuel's hopeful expression made me stay.

"This belongs to José Manuel," Amalia declared. "We came to return it." Amalia took a deep breath, then took a step forward. "We also wanted to know if he could come to the beach tonight with our family."

Aitza and I meekly stood behind Amalia.

"The beach?" José Manuel's grandma asked, surprised, as she took the little ball from Amalia's palm.

"Y-y-yes," I stuttered. "Tonight is the Night of San Juan, and our parents take us to the beach every year."

José Manuel's grandma scowled at us. How silly to think she would ever let him go. I suddenly felt embarrassed and turned to leave, pulling both sisters with me by their arms.

"Wait," we heard her raspy voice behind us. "Come inside for a *surullito de maíz.*"

It was then that I smelled the aroma of the corn fritters that was escaping from the kitchen. José Manuel's grandma was making *surullitos* for dinner.

"Oh, yes!" Amalia followed her in without a thought. And before we knew it, we were all seated in the living room rocking chairs next to José Manuel, eating the most delicious corn fritters that we dipped in garlicky sauce. Somehow, sitting there with José Manuel, his grandma seemed less scary. After we finished, José Manuel's grandma thanked us for our invitation and said she would let us know.

José Manuel smiled.

When we got home we found Mami waiting with her hands on her hips. She had just hung up the phone with José Manuel's grandma. She had reason to be upset. Not only were we late for supper, but in our excitement we had forgotten to ask for permission before inviting José Manuel to the beach. We all looked down, not knowing what to do or say.

"It wasn't my fault. It was Evelyn and Amalia's idea," volunteered Aitza, the coward.

"*Bendito,* Mami," I said. "Don't punish us, we forgot."

"Forgot?" Mami asked.

"*Sí,* Mami," we all said at once. "We are sorry."

"Actually it was very nice of you girls to invite him,"

said Mami. "But please remember to ask me first next time."

Late that night the whole family went to the beach as was our tradition on the Night of San Juan. But this time was special, for we had José Manuel with us.

The full moon shone against the velvet sky. The tide was high, and the beach swarmed with young revelers who, like us, had waited all year for this night's irresistible dip in the dark ocean. The moment we reached the water we all turned around, held hands, and jumped backward into the rushing waves. Amalia stumbled forward, Aitza joyfully splashed back, and so did I as I let go of my sister's hand. But my other hand remained tightly clasped to José Manuel's. When my friend and I took our third plunge into the sea, I wished good luck would come to him, and that from then on, his grandma would allow him to play with us out on the street. And as a wave lifted us high in the water, I suddenly knew this wish would come true.

Teatime

Abita's Story

I used to be a sickly child those years long ago in Buenos Aires. Once I had a severe virus that left me unable to eat or drink any dairy foods for eighty-nine days. Eighty-nine long days. I know because I counted each one carefully on my calendar. And I couldn't have been more pleased the day my doctor assured me that I could have milk again. That meant that at teatime that afternoon I would be able to have *alfajores.* Those were my favorite sandwich cookies, the kind that were filled with milk caramel. All day at school I thought of nothing else, and couldn't wait to get home.

Finally, the dismissal bell rang loudly and snapped me out of my sweet daydream. I leaped up from my seat, and put on my blue wool coat and matching beret and gloves to protect me from the chilly weather. Buenos Aires is always chilly in July. For while half of the world is warmed by the summer sun, Argentina is gliding through winter.

"See you Monday, Susana!" I heard my schoolmates

call from behind me as I crossed the courtyard. I barely had time to turn around and wave good-bye to them before I cut into the wind and hurried home to my mother and Abuela Elena. Our apartment house was only two blocks away from school, but the more I rushed to get there, the further away it seemed. I was trying to get home before my twin brother, Oscar, even though I knew he would run home ahead of me. That way he could sneak into the kitchen and take inventory of the afternoon sweets. At eleven years old, I might have been taller — but he was, without a doubt, faster. Particularly when sweets were involved.

Today's afternoon tea, *la hora del té*, was a special one. Aunt Cecilia and Aunt Morena were coming to join us. Of course, teatime was delicious every day of the week. But it was especially delicious when we had company. Only then would Abuela Elena buy *alfajores de dulce de leche*. And today, after eighty-nine days of deprivation, I would finally satisfy my craving. My mouth watered at the thought.

"Hola, querida," Abuela Elena greeted me, then took my coat and hung it next to Oscar's. He had, as I'd predicted, arrived before me. I washed my hands quickly and went to kiss my parents and aunts who had just sat down at the elegantly set table. After I took my place

next to Aunt Morena, Elvira appeared in her starched white cap and apron through the kitchen door, with a steaming silver pot of English tea.

"Leave it on the tea cart next to me, Elvira," said Mamá.

As soon as Elvira went back into the kitchen, Mamá prepared each individual cup with experienced grace. I saw her lace the perfumed tea with thin ribbons of cold milk and spoonfuls of sugar while I craned my neck to peek at the plate of sweets behind the centerpiece. But the large bouquet of roses hid them well.

Mamá served the tea to Oscar and me last. Then, as always, she passed the plate of tea sandwiches around. After that, she passed around a plate filled with buttered toast. And when everyone had their fill of tea sandwiches and toast, it was finally time for the sweets.

As Mamá lifted the serving dish with tiny brioches and sweet scones, I saw the unimaginable. I looked again in case I had seen it wrong. But I had not. In the middle of the sweets plate there was only one *alfajor!* Aunt Cecilia took the dish, chose a scone, and ceremoniously passed it on to Abuela who served herself a brioche. Neither of them touched the lone sandwich cookie. I could not take my eyes off of it. Papá took a

scone and handed me the rest. As I held the plate in my hands, time seemed to stop. My whole body ached for that *alfajor.* But one look at Mamá and it was clear I had no choice. Her silent gaze firmly warned me against improper manners at the table. I knew exactly what she was thinking: *Guests come first.* So reluctantly, I handed the plate to Aunt Morena. I knew she had a sweet tooth as big as mine, and I expected her to take what I had dreamed of eating for so long. But she didn't. Then, the plate had barely reached Oscar when the worst possible thing happened. With a single quick movement of his hand and a sneaky smile, Oscar raised the cookie to his lips — and gobbled it up!

I gave Mamá a stricken look.

"Elvira," Mamá called behind her. "Bring more *alfajores, por favor.*"

But when Elvira returned from the kitchen, she was empty-handed. "Señora," she whispered, "there are none left."

I stared, dumbfounded.

"What?" asked Mamá. "Did you not buy half a dozen?"

"We bought the last four at the bakery," said Abuela.

"That means there are three left!" I blurted out.

"They've disappeared, Niña Susana," Elvira apologized. "I looked everywhere in the kitchen and couldn't find them."

"I wonder what could have happened to them," Abuela mused.

Oscar, who had been quietly savoring the last bit of milk-caramel cookie, started to cough. He coughed until Abuela excused him and led him to his room. It looked fake to me. I figured he wanted to get away for some reason. But why? Abuela came in through the hallway and instantly disappeared into the kitchen.

My aunts kept talking with my father, as though nothing had happened. But I knew something interesting was going on behind the closed kitchen door. I had to find out what it was, so I excused myself and followed Abuela.

Abuela Elena was in front of the pantry sifting through bottles, cans, and boxes. As she was about to remove a pile of table linen, a small paper package from the bakery appeared in the corner of the shelf. It had a tear in it, and *alfajor* crumbs lay all around it.

"*¡Qué mala pata!*" exclaimed Elvira with a clap of her hands. "What bad luck!" She proceeded to pick up the torn package.

"What happened?" I asked.

"Your brother secretly ate two *alfajores* and hid the third one for later," said Abuela Elena, motioning to Elvira to throw away the package and its contents.

"And a mouse got to it before he did!" Elvira sighed as she wiped the shelf with a soapy rag. "It's too late to buy any more this evening."

I stood there frozen as I watched Elvira clear away all the crumbs from the precious *alfajor* and throw them into the garbage. The rage bubbling inside me soon gave way to numb disbelief. Abuela Elena tenderly took my hand and led me back into the dining room. With my well-learned good manners, I forced a smile and sat down to tea again.

The next morning at breakfast, I found Oscar's seat empty. Abuela told me he had been up all night with indigestion. In the early hours of the day he was quite weak. But as time went by he became hungry once again, and that meant he felt much better. That is, until Mamá told him that for the next eighty-nine days, whenever we had guests for tea, I was to have *his* share of *alfajores* — as well as mine.

Birthday Piñata

Uncle Robert's Story

One bright clear morning, right before my eighth birthday, Mami took me to my grandma Rosa's, just as she did every morning on her way to work.

"Apúrate, m'ijo," said Mami. "Hurry, or I'll miss my ride!"

Leaving a trail of red dust behind us, I ran to keep up with her as she pulled me along the narrow streets of our *barrio,* in the Mexican town of Juárez. Neighbors who trickled out of their houses to start their daily routines greeted us as we passed. But there was no time to stop and talk. Small pearls of sweat rose on Mami's brow and rolled down her carefully made-up face as we rushed along.

Today, as always, Mami had put on a freshly ironed dress, curled her light brown hair, and slipped her old plastic sandals onto her feet. She didn't want to ruin her high heels. So she would put them on just before she reached the Texas border.

When we finally arrived at Mama Rosa's, Mami

quickly bent down and offered me her cheek. "*Dame un beso,* Roberto, give me a kiss," she said, smoothing back my hair with her hand. "I get paid today. So when I pick you up we'll go to the market to buy the *piñata* I promised you."

"*¡Viva!*" I cheered, hugging her tight. I loved the *piñatas* my friends had on their birthdays, and I had always dreamed of having one of my own. Now, my wish would come true!

Mama Rosa, who had come out to greet us, smiled at my excitement. "And we'll make *chiles rellenos* for your birthday dinner, too," she added, squeezing my shoulders with her big warm hands.

"*Sí, chico,*" Mami said. "Didn't I tell you that if you got good grades, you would have a special dinner *and* a *piñata* for your birthday? Now, keep up the good work at school, and do what Mama Rosa says." Then she kissed her mother good-bye and left.

"Be careful at the border!" Mama Rosa called to Mami as she disappeared down the road.

Monday through Friday, Mami worked in Juárez's twin city, El Paso. She would catch a ride in a van with other women who, like her, worked as maids and nannies there. At the American border, she would tell the guard the same story: She was crossing the border to go shopping. She thought that being all dressed up made her story more believable. As soon as she was in El Paso, she would get on a bus for the long ride to the city's east side. Then she would get off the bus and walk the rest of the way to her final destination. Many other women lived all week in the houses where they worked. They would only return to their families on weekends. My mother was not one of them. She came home every evening to make dinner for us, to mend our clothing, and to check if I had done my homework. And I was glad to have her with me every night.

When it was time, Mama Rosa took me to school. And lucky me — to get there, we had to go by the market. In the distance I could see the vendors opening their stands and arranging their wares.

"Can we stop and look at the *piñatas* — PLEASE — Mama Rosa?" I begged.

"How many times have you seen them?" Mama Rosa laughed. But of course, she let me go.

Inside the dark market building we walked past the many stalls filled with fruits and vegetables, purses and handbags, and clothes. And then we came to the one I liked best—the big one that sold *piñatas*. Dozens of

them in all shapes and sizes hung from the ceiling. There were donkeys and horses, cats and dogs, rabbits and fish, and even a silver star. Dazzled by the brilliant colors of the tissue paper that covered them, I stared at each one, hypnotized. Then I looked in the corner to make sure my favorite one was still there — the huge red bull with multicolored ribbons tied to its horns. Standing next to him I could look right into his deep black paper eyes. He was as tall as I was. I was sure he could hold more treats than any other *piñata* there!

"Look!" I whispered to Mama Rosa. "The bull I want is still here."

"We'll see which one your Mami can buy," Mama Rosa said with a wink. "But now we must get you to school. Mami doesn't want you to be late."

"Don't worry," the vendor joked with me. "The *piñatas* will be waiting for you when you come back."

In the classroom I told my best friend Pablo about my *piñata.* He was as excited as I was. And all day long, I raised my hand to answer the teacher's questions, hoping to make the day go faster. But it went as slowly as ever.

That afternoon at Mama Rosa's I did my homework right away while I waited for Mami to return from her job. I kept thinking about my *piñata* and what we could fill it with. In the *barrio,* when someone had a *piñata,* it was hung out on the street, and all the children were invited to share in the fun. I prayed the vendor would not sell my bull before we got there.

When evening came, I sat on Mama Rosa's wooden front steps lost in my daydreams. The shadow of the saguaro cactus on the side of her house grew longer and longer until it faded into the darkness. Where was Mami? I never stayed at my grandma's this long. Would the market still be open after sunset? Behind me I heard Mama Rosa pacing in the kitchen. I was getting very hungry.

Suddenly, Papá appeared.

When he did not find us at home, he got worried and decided to come see if I was still at Mama Rosa's. Inside the house I saw them whisper to each other. Mama Rosa looked anxious as she set the table. The three of us sat down and had some *frijoles.* We ate the beans in silence.

It was late at night when Mami finally arrived. We all rose to greet her as she walked in the door. She looked frazzled.

"You won't believe the day I had!" she exclaimed.

She was out of breath. "This morning they stopped me at the border. They held me for hours, asking all kinds of questions. They asked what was I going to buy . . . how much was I going to spend . . . what stores was I going to . . . I was so nervous, I couldn't even answer. By the time they let me go, it was very late, and I thought I might lose my job. I was lucky Señora Smith didn't get mad. Then I worked late to make up for the time I lost." Mami collapsed next to me on the small couch where I sat, and her head sank into her hands. "I was careful to return after the change of border patrols," she said.

"I don't like it," Mama Rosa complained. "What if the guards filed a report? You could end up in jail. Can't you quit?"

"No," said Mami, weeping. "We need the money I bring home."

"It is true that with the money you bring we can buy many things we need," Papá said. "But it is not worth it if you get into trouble. We can do without some things."

"Like what?" Mami asked. "Roberto's school shoes? Groceries? Mama Rosa's medicine?

I rested my head on Mami's lap. It was almost midnight. She stroked my hair as she talked for a long time with Papá and Mama Rosa. Slowly their voices became fainter and fainter until they dissolved into my dreams.

The next morning, I woke up in my own bed. Papá must have carried me home. Seated at the foot of the bed Mami was singing *Las Mañanitas.* Still half asleep I realized it was my birthday.

"This evening we'll have your favorite meal," Mami said when she finished the birthday song. "Mama Rosa is coming to help me make you *chiles rellenos.*"

"*Gracias,* Mami," I whispered. I was about to ask if I was still getting my *piñata.* But when I remembered how upset Mami had been the night before, I thought it was better not to ask.

"Now get dressed, and after breakfast you'll go with Papá and help him with his errands. I need to clean the house."

I spent the morning of my birthday with Papá at the hardware store. He was buying materials he needed for a construction job. The store was close to the market, so while Papá payed, I ran to the *piñata* stand. The donkeys and the horses, the cats and the dogs, the rabbits and the fish, and the silver star dazzled more brilliantly than ever. But something was wrong. The corner where my huge bull had once stood was now empty.

My *piñata* was gone!

The burning desert sun was high when we got back home. Inside the kitchen, I found Mami roasting poblano chiles on the flat iron pan. When she finished, Mama Rosa filled them with cheese.

"Roberto," said Mami. "Go wash up and get me three, big ripe tomatoes from the garden. I need them for the *pico de gallo.*"

Slowly I went out to the garden. While I was excited about my birthday dinner, I knew that without my *piñata,* my birthday wouldn't be the same.

Outside, I found Papá talking with one of our neighbors who was attaching a rope to the roof of his house. Papá leaned over a large bag and slowly removed what was inside. At first I saw a horned head appear. Then I saw a big red body.

"Papá, Papá!" I ran up to him. "It's my *piñata*! The exact one I wanted!"

"I know," he said. "Mami and Mama Rosa bought it this morning."

I started to run to get Pablo, but stopped when I heard his shout from behind me. He raced toward us, followed by about twenty other children from the *barrio.* They all lined up single file to hit my birthday *piñata* with a wooden stick. When everyone was there, Papá put a blindfold on the first child in line. All the other children watched and chanted, *"Dale, dale, dale . . ."*

By the time the bull had lost a horn and a leg, it was finally my turn. Papá blindfolded me. *"¡Dale, Roberto!"* my friends cheered. "Hit it!" I aimed high and hit the *piñata.* I heard a muffled thud and took off my blindfold to see only a single orange had fallen.

"My turn!" cried Pablo. He gave two heavy blows, and with the second one, a shower of juicy oranges, hard candy, peanuts, and sugarcane pieces came pouring down from the *piñata*'s swaying shards. My *piñata* had more treats in it than any we had ever seen! Amid the laughter and shouting, all the children scrambled on the ground to pick up what they could. When I got up with my hands full, I saw Mami watching me tenderly.

The afternoon wore away, and one by one, my friends left. All except Pablo. Mama Rosa had invited him and his parents to join us for dinner. My uncles, aunt, and Pablo's parents chattered as they ate.

"Feliz cumpleaños, Roberto," Mami said as she handed me a plate with two freshly fried *chiles rellenos,* warm flour *tortillas, frijoles,* and *pico de gallo.*

"Victoria," Mama Rosa said. "Are you going back to work on Monday?"

"Sí, Mamá," Mami answered. "I have to."

"Don't you think you might get stopped again?" Mama Rosa asked anxiously.

As Pablo and I sank our teeth into the warm chiles oozing with melted cheese, Mami came to me and kissed me on the forehead. "How did you like your birthday?" she asked.

"It was the best birthday I ever had!" I answered.

Mama Rosa and Mami looked at each other, their eyes smiling with silent understanding.

"And that," Mami said, "is your answer."

The Lord of Miracles

Doña Josefa's Story

Many years ago on a misty October afternoon in Lima, Peru, I watched Mamá bake *turrón de Doña Pepa*. Even though she made it every year before the procession for the Lord of Miracles, I had never asked her why.

"Why do you bake *turrón* in October?" I asked. "Why is this the only time they sell it all over the city?"

"*¿Por qué, por qué?*" she sighed as she sprinkled the freshly-baked nougat with tiny colorful candies. "Always asking questions, Josefa. Why? It is because this is the month of the Lord of Miracles."

Not satisfied with her answer, I continued to ask more questions. Who was Doña Pepa? And why do so many people dress in purple around this time? Finally, I wore Mamá out and she said, "I really should tell you the beautiful story that goes with the nougat. After all, you are named after its creator, Josefina Marmanillo." Then, handing me a piece of the honey-glazed sweet, she led me to the balcony where we sat next to each

other. And as we watched the breathtaking procession down below, this is the story she told.

It all began in colonial times, when Lima was home to the Quechua Indians. It was also home to the Spanish colonists and to the *morenos,* who were brought from Africa as slaves. It was then that an old building with a thatched roof stood inside the city's stone walls. Some say it was a leprosarium. Others say it was a brotherhood of Indians and *morenos.* Yet there are those who believe that it was a barracks for African slaves. What is true, however, is that on a big adobe wall of this building, an Angolan slave had painted an unusually beautiful black image of Christ.

A few years later, in 1655, a powerful earthquake shook Lima. It demolished everything — from government palaces, mansions, and monasteries to the humblest of homes. Thousands of lives were lost to the mighty tremors. But in the wake of its destruction, survivors gathered on top of the rubble of the old building to witness a phenomenal sight. The fragile adobe wall where the *moreno* Christ had been painted stood perfectly intact!

Word of the event spread among the slaves, and the haunting image of the black Christ became a source of miracles for many. Some of the faithful are said to have been healed of incurable diseases. Others vowed to have been granted long-awaited favors. So in time, the painting became known as *el Señor de los Milagros.* By the 1700s, a church was built to house the image, and the purple-clad nuns from the convent next door became the caretakers of the shrine.

It was around this time that Josefina Marmanillo lived. Josefina was a slave woman who worked on a cotton farm in a coastal valley south of Lima. Known to all as Doña Pepa the *morena,* she spent long days in the farmhouse kitchen kneading, pounding, peeling, and slicing with her big wrinkled hands. And even in the strongest desert heat, she never failed to sing while she worked. She would stop only to laugh when one of the children of the house sneaked in to steal her scrumptious sweets.

One day, while working in the kitchen, a weakness overcame her. Later, she noticed her chores took longer to do. And soon, even the simplest task became impossible. Her cheerful laugh was silenced. And as her arms became paralyzed, her master freed her. For so many years Doña Pepa had thrived on caring for all the people that delighted in her wonderful cooking and baking. Now she was crippled.

That October, when Doña Pepa heard about *el Señor de los Milagros* and the procession that was to be held in His honor, her hopes soared, and she boarded a ship bound for the capital city. The *morena* believed that if she joined the religious caravan and followed the Christ's bier on her knees as a sacrifice to the Lord of Miracles, she might be cured.

It was a chilly day that October when the freed slave arrived in Lima. Above the city hovered the *garúa,* a damp, cold mist that blocked the sun. The city looked as mournful as the procession itself. Doña Pepa looked at the *moreno* Christ from the distance, then fell to her knees and joined the followers. She found herself surrounded by others who, like her, had placed their hopes in the Lord of Miracles. Enveloped by the soothing rhythm of continuous prayer, she accompanied the painting of Christ through long, cobblestone streets and hard dirt roads, until her long skirt was torn and her knees bled. She endured the pain for many long hours, and just as she felt she could not take any more, a tingling sensation suddenly returned to her fingertips. It crept up past her elbows, then went to her shoulders. Had her prayers been answered? Slowly, she clasped her hands together, then she pinched her forearms. She could move her arms and hands again! She fell to the ground and wept, for the *moreno* Christ had heard her.

"Ay, Señor de los Milagros," she whispered. "Whatever you ask of me, I shall do."

Doña Pepa spent the next few weeks trying to think of a way she could thank the Lord of Miracles. The answer finally came to her in a dream. She dreamed of orange-blossom honey perfumed with lemons and laced with aniseed. When she woke up the next morning, she ran to her tiny kitchen and invented a luscious nougat candy. As soon as it was ready, she filled the tray with the sweet confection and rushed to the courtyard of the *moreno* Christ's shrine where the poor gathered. There, she gave nougat to each man, woman, and child. At first, she told her story to all who asked her why she did this. Then she retold it to all who would listen. It is said that every October until her death, Doña Pepa baked large trays of the golden delicacy to feed to the needy. And as she told her story, she offered them hope for a miracle of their own.

Mamá said as she finished her story, "You know, my dear Josefa, Lima has witnessed hundreds of processions for the Lord of Miracles since they started in 1687. Year after year, you've seen how hundreds of thousands of believers cloaked in purple, like the first caretakers of the *moreno* Christ, come to profess their faith. And you've seen how in the path of the procession, buildings are lavishly adorned with purple garlands of flowers. You've heard the chants and the prayers that mingle with the fragrance of incense in the dim candlelight. And you've seen the gold-and-silver bier with the painted image of *el Señor de los Milagros* that is carried through Lima's streets. But of all the gifts of song, incense, and myrrh offered to the black Christ, none compare to the humble gift of the *morena.*

"And that is why to this day, Josefa, her delicious nougat is sold on every street corner of the city. It is to remind us what true faith in the Lord of Miracles can bring."

Aguinaldo

Tía Marilia's Story

When I was growing up in Puerto Rico, I went to a small, Catholic girls' school. Every December, Sister Antonia, our religion teacher, insisted that the sixth grade visit the nursing home in Santurce. Bringing Christmas cheer to the old and infirm was an experience she felt all sixth graders should have. But the year I was in fifth grade, Sister Antonia decided our class was mature enough to join the older girls and have that experience, too.

"I'm not going," I whispered to my friend Margarita.

"You have to, Marilia," she said. "Everyone has to go."

All of my classmates looked forward to the trip. Some, because they liked the rackety bus ride to anywhere. Some, because they could skip school for the day and that meant no homework. And others, because they believed that to do a sixth-grade activity in fifth grade was very special. But ever since my only grandma died in a nursing home, the thought of going back to one made me feel sad. I didn't want to go.

As I sat at my desk coloring the Christmas card that I was assigned to make for a resident, I tried to figure out how I could skip this field trip. Maybe they would let me help at the library. Maybe I could write a special book report at school while they were out. Or better yet, I could wake up ill and stay home from school. As soon as the recess bell rang, I ran over to the library to try out my first plan.

"*Hola,* Marilia," Señora Collazo greeted me.

"*Hola,* Señora Collazo," I said, smiling sweetly. "I came to ask you if I could stay here tomorrow to help you paint posters for the book fair. I really don't mind spending the whole day at the library."

"Aren't you going on a field trip tomorrow?" Señora Collazo asked.

"My class is going. But I could be excused if you need my help." The librarian thanked me and said that if I wanted to help I could join the other students who had already volunteered to stay after school to do the posters. Biting my lower lip, I left the library in a hurry. It was time to try my second plan.

Outside, seated on the polished tiles of the covered corridor, my friends were having a tournament of jacks. But I didn't join them. Instead, I marched right to the sixth-grade classroom. Sister Antonia was grading papers at her desk as I went in.

"Sister Antonia," I said softly.

"Yes, Marilia," Sister Antonia answered.

I stared for a moment at the buckles of my shoes. Then without looking up, I took a deep breath, swept back my black curls, and asked, "May I stay in school tomorrow to do an extra book report?"

"I'm afraid not, Marilia," Sister Antonia said firmly. "Tomorrow is our trip to the nursing home. Both the fifth and sixth grades are going. But if you want to do an extra book report, you can do it over the weekend."

I glanced across the room to the trays of *besitos de coco,* the coconut sweets that the sixth graders had prepared to bring to the nursing-home residents as an *aguinaldo. Aguinaldos,* surprise Christmas gifts, were fun to receive. But still, I wasn't going, so it wasn't my concern. I whispered thank you to the sister, and left.

That evening at dinnertime, I put my third plan into action. To my parents' surprise, I had two big helpings of rice and kidney beans, two helpings of Mami's *tembleque* for dessert, and three glasses of mango juice. I *never* ate so much. I figured that with all this food, I was sure to get indigestion. I went to bed and waited. I tossed and turned. I waited for several hours expecting a stomachache any second, but instead, the heavy meal made me tired and I fell sound asleep.

"Marilia, get dressed!" Mami called early the next morning. "We have to leave soon for school!"

How unlucky. I woke up feeling quite well. There was only one thing left to do, I ran to the bathroom, let the hot water run, and drank a full glass of it. Then I went back to bed.

"Marilia." Mami came in. "Get up! What is going on with you?"

"I feel warm, Mami," I mumbled.

Mami looked at me with concern. She touched my forehead and my neck. Then she left the room and in a few minutes came back with the thermometer in her hands. I opened my mouth and she slipped it under my tongue.

When the time was up, Mami pulled the thermometer out and read it.

"One hundred and six degrees?" she exclaimed. "That's impossible. You look perfectly fine to me."

After a little questioning, I confessed what I had done. I told Mami how much I didn't want to go on the field trip.

"You know, Marilia," she advised, "you might enjoy yourself after all. Besides, I've already promised Sister Antonia two trays of *tembleque* to bring as an *aguinaldo* to the residents of the home."

There was no way out. I had to go.

In the big lobby of the nursing home, paper streamers hung from the tall windows. The residents were scattered everywhere. Some were seated on the couches. Some were in wheelchairs. Some walked clutching onto their walkers. A nurse hovered over a group of men as she dispensed pills. Sister Antonia took out her guitar and at the sound of the first bar we began to sing a medley of carols. Several of the girls accompanied with *maracas, güiro,* and *palitos.* Meanwhile, the residents clapped and sang along while a sixth grader passed around our cards for us to give to them later. As I watched how happy our music made the residents, memories of my grandma rushed to me, making me dizzy with sadness. Suddenly, I saw that everybody was visiting with the residents. I was alone. I didn't feel like joining one of the groups. Maybe I could quietly slip away until the visit was over. I hoped it would be soon. Then I noticed a chair against the yellow wall. I sat there still holding the card I had made.

Across the room there was a frail old lady in a wheelchair. She was alone, too. I looked at my card again. It was rather pretty. I had painted it with shades of blue and gold. Maybe I could just hand it to her and leave. It might brighten her day. So gingerly, I crossed the lobby and stood next to her.

"Who is there?" the old lady asked as she coquettishly fixed her silver bun with the light touch of her manicured hand.

"My name is Marilia," I said. "I brought you a card."

"Dios te bendiga," the old woman said. "God bless you."

She reached for the card but her hand was nowhere near it. Her gaze was lost in the distance, and I knelt down to place the card in her hand. It was then that I saw the big clouds in her eyes. She was blind. *What was the use of a card if you couldn't see it?* I felt cheated. I stood up to go back to my chair.

"My name is Elenita," she said as I tried to slip away. "Tell me, Marilia, what does your card look like?"

I knelt down beside her and, in as vivid detail as I could, described the three wise men I had drawn. Then, Elenita's curious fingers caressed every inch of the card. She couldn't have enjoyed it more if she had seen it.

When the coconut sweets were passed around, she mischievously asked for two.

"I bet you are not supposed to eat one of these," she giggled.

"No," I replied. "Sister Antonia told us that the sweets were just for residents."

"Well," she whispered. "Nobody said I couldn't give you one of *mine*."

I liked Elenita. I placed the *besito de coco* in my mouth and relished it even more. Especially since I wasn't supposed to have it. I enjoyed being her partner in mischief. After that, she asked me if I liked music and if I knew how do dance.

"Ay," I said, "I love to listen to music and dance."

Then she told me how, when she was young, she had been a great dancer.

"I used to dance so well that men would line up for a chance to dance with me. I had many, many suitors at one time," she said. "I had suitors that serenaded me in the evening and others that brought me flowers. But I didn't go out with all of them. You have to be selective, you know."

Too soon we were interrupted by Sister Antonia. It was time to get on the bus and return to school. I didn't want to leave.

"Thank you for the card, Marilia," Elenita said. She opened her hand and gestured for me to give her mine. "I'll keep this card to remember you by."

"I'm sorry you can't see it," I said as I squeezed her hand. For a moment it felt as warm and giving as my own grandma's. "I wished I had brought you a better *aguinaldo.*"

"The best *aguinaldo,*" Elenita said, "was your visit, Marilia."

As I left, I felt light and warm and peaceful. On the bus ride back, I told my friend Margarita all about our visit. I couldn't wait to come back next year when I was in the sixth grade. I already knew what I would bring Elenita. I would make her a collage. That way she would be able to feel the many textures of my picture, even if she couldn't see it. And maybe I could make the picture of her dancing. I knew she had been very pretty when she was young.

"Are you going to wait until next Christmas to give her your collage?" Margarita asked.

I thought for a moment. "Maybe Mami could bring me back sooner," I said.

As I looked out the window, I remembered how good Elenita's hand felt to touch. It's funny how sometimes things change unexpectedly. Just that morning I didn't want to go at all. But then, I couldn't wait to visit my new friend again. We had gone to the nursing home to give *aguinaldos.* And what a very special *aguinaldo* I had been given — Elenita's friendship.

Carmen Teresa's Gift

"¡*Bueno!*" cheers Abuelito from the head of the table after the last story had been told. "Wonderful stories, all of them!"

"*¡Sí!* Oh, yes!" a chorus of voices answer Abuelito from around the room. "Wonderful stories."

Abuelito looks pleased. "Now tell us, Carmen Teresa, which of the stories will you write down first?"

I am about to answer, but everyone answers for me.

"She will record the stories in the order she heard them," Mamá says. "It's the only fair way."

"No, no," says Abuelita. "There are too many. She should write only the ones she likes best."

"I saw Carmen Teresa laughing while I told my story," Abita confides in Abuelita. "I'll bet she will choose mine." Abuelita nods in agreement.

Uncle Robert thinks I should write down everything I can remember. Tía Marilia generously offers to write hers. "It will make it easier for you," she assures me.

Suddenly, Flor appears from the kitchen with another tray of *natilla* and *flan de coco.* After everyone has taken seconds, she whispers to me that her story doesn't have to be included if there isn't room. But I can tell that she hopes there is.

"Carmen Teresa!" my sister Laura calls from across the table. She has already finished Alex's and her *natilla* and licks her spoon clean before she reaches for a third helping. But Mamá stops her.

"After you write those stories down in your book," Laura says sweetly, "I'll draw pictures to go along with them."

"Now, there is a fine idea!" says Abuelo Jaime. "You two can work on the book together."

By now, everyone has told me what they think I should do with my gift. Most of the children are no longer interested in the discussion and flee to the basement to play. Just as I am about to join the kids downstairs, Abuelito's deep voice stops me.

"Carmen Teresa!" he commands. "Let's get started right away. Sit next to me and we'll write my story together. Laura, you can start drawing the pictures."

"No." My voice comes out louder than I intend it to. Instantly, the room becomes silent.

"Carmen Teresa!" Mamá scolds.

"Why don't we let Carmen Teresa decide for herself what she wants to do with her gift," Doña Josefa suggests. "After all, the present was meant for her."

Everyone eagerly waits for me to speak. I know exactly what I want to do. I hug the blank book, and look at each one of the relatives and friends around me. Then I begin.

"In all of your stories, you all mentioned some kind of special food. I want to collect the recipes for all the foods you told about in my book. And I will add the recipes for the foods Mamá served here today."

"That is a delightful idea, Carmen Teresa," says Doña Josefa.

"Yes," agrees Abuelito, "and Abuelita can finally tell you how to make *tortilla española.*" He laughs as he squeezes Abuelita's hand. "She's taken all these years to learn how to make it just like Mami used to."

"I could also give you José Manuel's recipe for *surullitos,*" adds Abuelita. "It's as good as his grandmother's."

"But the best recipe for *alfajores argentinos,*" boasts Abita, "is the one I make."

As everyone chatters merrily about their recipes, Doña Josefa talks to me alone.

"I'm so pleased you liked my gift, Carmen Teresa," she says. "Each time you prepare one of these recipes, you will remember the story that was told with it. And each time someone tastes one of these dishes, they, too, might have a story to tell."

Content that I have finally found a way to make this

present my very own, I borrow Doña Josefa's fountain pen and open my book to the first page. Then, with great flourishes and curls, I write:

Carmen Teresa's Book of
Fantastic Family Recipes

Gently, I blow on the wet ink to dry it, and I close the book. And tomorrow, I will begin collecting my recipes.

Carmen Teresa's Book of

Fantastic Family Recipes

Mamá's Arroz con Pollo

Chicken with Rice

Puerto Rico

2½ lbs. skinless chicken thighs
juice of 2 limes
Adobo *seasoning**
1 oz. salt pork, diced
2 oz. cured ham, diced
2 tbs. olive oil
4 garlic cloves, peeled and crushed
1 lg. onion, peeled and chopped
2 lg. green peppers, seeded and chopped
1 tomato, chopped
pimento-stuffed Spanish olives
capers
3 cups long grain rice
3½ cups water
1½ cubes chicken bouillon
¼ cup tomato paste
2 envelopes Sazón *seasoning**
½ cup fresh cilantro, chopped
salt and pepper

*Available where Latin foods are sold

Coat the chicken with lime juice and sprinkle generously with Adobo seasoning. Set in refrigerator overnight.

In a *caldero,* a heavy pot, brown the pork and ham in olive oil over medium-high heat. Add garlic and marinated chicken. Reduce heat to moderate. Brown the chicken for 5 to 10 minutes then remove the chicken pieces and set them aside. Add onion, green peppers, and tomato to the pot, and sauté until tender. Replace the chicken, and add olives and capers to taste. Add rice, water, chicken bouillon cubes, tomato paste, Sazón seasoning, cilantro, and salt and pepper to taste. Stir well. Cover and bring to a boil. Then turn heat to low and cook for 20 minutes. Turn rice with a wooden spoon. Keep covered on the stove with the heat off for 10 to 15 minutes more. *Serves 6 to 8.*

Have an adult help you when frying or boiling.

Mamá's Yuca con Mojo Criollo

STEAMED YUCA WITH SAUCE

PUERTO RICO

YUCA

*2½ lbs. frozen yuca (also called cassava)**

water

salt

juice of one lemon

mojo criollo *sauce (see recipe below)*

*Available where Latin foods are sold

Place frozen yuca in a large pot. Cover with water and sprinkle with salt. Boil for at least 1 hour. Meanwhile, prepare *mojo criollo.*

When the yuca is very tender, remove it from the water with a slotted spoon, and arrange on a platter. Sprinkle with lemon juice, salt to taste, and pour *mojo criollo* on top. Serve immediately.

Mojo Criollo Sauce

4 lg. onions, peeled and sliced

6 garlic cloves, peeled and sliced

1 cup olive oil

4 bay leaves

1 tsp. peppercorns

In a large saucepan, sauté onions and garlic in olive oil until the onions are soft, but still white. Add bay leaves and peppercorns, and simmer covered for ½ hour. *Serves 8.*

Have an adult help you when frying or boiling.

Flor's Bacalao a la Vizcaína

Codfish Stew

GUATEMALA

*1 lb. dried, salted codfish fillets**

water

One 6-oz. can tomato paste

½ cup olive oil

¼ cup pimento-stuffed Spanish olives

1 tbs. capers

2 garlic cloves, peeled and crushed

1 bay leaf

4 medium potatoes, peeled and thinly sliced

2 medium onions, peeled and thinly sliced

*Available where Latin foods are sold

Cover codfish in water and soak for 4 hours, changing the water twice. Drain well. Place codfish in a pot with 8 cups of water, and boil for 15 minutes. Drain and let cool. Discard skin and bones, and then shred the flesh.

Mix tomato paste with 1 cup water and olive oil, and stir until paste is smooth. Add olives, capers, garlic, and bay leaf to the tomato mixture.

In a large frying pan, arrange alternate layers of tomato mixture, potatoes, codfish, and onions. Bring to a boil over medium-high heat and cover. Turn heat to low, and cook for 30 minutes or until potatoes are tender. Transfer to serving platter.

Serves 4 to 6.

Have an adult help you when frying or boiling.

Flor's Torrejas

Guatemalan Toast

GUATEMALA

Toast

½ lb. French bread
1 cup milk
ground cinnamon to taste
3 eggs, lightly beaten
vegetable oil, for panfrying

To prepare *torrejas,* cut bread into ½-inch-thick slices. Dip each slice in milk. Remove with a slotted spoon and place on a cookie sheet. Sprinkle both sides of the bread with cinnamon. Dip into beaten eggs and remove with a slotted spoon. Fry bread slices in hot oil until both sides are golden brown. Remove. Drain on absorbent paper towels and place several slices in each dessert bowl. Serve with syrup *(see recipe below)*.

SYRUP

2 cups sugar	*1 thin cinnamon stick*
1 cup water	*peel of 1 lime, grated*
¼ tsp. salt	

For the syrup, mix sugar, water, salt, cinnamon stick, and lime peel in a saucepan. Boil over high heat without stirring until syrup thickens slightly, about 20 minutes. Pour syrup over toast. Allow the syrup to cool a little before serving. Enjoy *torrejas* with a tall glass of milk. *Serves 4.*

Have an adult help you when frying or boiling.

Flor's Horchata

SESAME DRINK

GUATEMALA

1 cup sesame seeds	*½ cup sugar*
6 cups water	*ice*

Soak sesame seeds in 4 cups of water for 3 hours. Drain well. Crush seeds in a food processor or with a mortar. Add seeds to 2 cups of lukewarm water, mix, and squeeze mixture through a muslin cloth into a pot. Add sugar, mix, and refrigerate to chill. Stir well. Serve in a tall glass with ice. *Serves 4.*

Fernando's Tortilla Española

Spanish Omelet

Cuba

¼ cup olive oil

1 lg. onion, peeled and chopped

1¼ tsp. salt

1 Spanish chorizo*, *skinless and minced (optional)*

1 lb. new potatoes, washed and cut in small irregular shapes

6 lg. eggs

⅛ tsp. ground pepper

*Available where Latin foods are sold

Place oil, onion, ¼ tsp. salt, and *chorizo* (optional) in a 10-inch nonstick frying pan. Sauté for 10 minutes over low heat, stirring occasionally. Strain in a colander, reserving oil. Set onions aside and pour oil back into pan. Add potatoes and ¼ tsp. salt. Turn heat to high, then when mixture sizzles, cover and cook over low heat until potatoes are tender, about 25 minutes. Remove potatoes with a slotted spoon and set aside.

In a bowl, beat eggs with the pepper and ¾ tsp. salt. Stir in onions and potatoes. Turn heat to medium-high. Pour egg mixture into frying pan. Cook over medium-high heat for 2 to 3 minutes, then turn heat to low. Cook *tortilla* until surface is dry. Gently move pan back and forth to release the edges of the *tortilla.* Then, put a plate over the top of the pan. Using oven mitts, turn the pan over onto the plate. Once the *tortilla* is on the plate, slip it back into the pan to cook for 10 minutes on the other side. Remove from the pan and let cool before cutting into 1½-inch cubes. Serve at room temperature. *Makes about 32 appetizers.*

Have an adult help you when frying.

Amalia's Helado de Coco

Coconut Sherbet

Puerto Rico

One 14-oz. can unsweetened coconut milk
1½ cups sugar
⅛ tsp. salt
3½ cups water
peel of ⅛ lime, grated

Mix all ingredients well. Pour in a freezer container and freeze for several hours until the sherbet is half frozen. Remove from freezer and beat the sherbet to break up crystals. For a smoother texture, you can repeat this process. Freeze overnight or until firm.

Serves 10 to 12.

José Manuel's Surullitos de Maíz

Corn Fritters

PUERTO RICO

Corn Fritters

2 cups water

1¼ tsp. salt

1½ cups yellow cornmeal

1 cup grated Edam or Colby cheese

vegetable oil for deep-frying

Combine water and salt in a saucepan. Heat to boiling and remove from heat. Add cornmeal and mix thoroughly. Cook over moderate heat for about 10 minutes or until mixture separates from the bottom and sides of pan. Mixture will be thick and steam will rise from it. Remove from heat. Add cheese and mix well. Let cool slightly. Take mixture by the tablespoon, and roll it in the palms of your hands to form ½-inch-thick cylinders with rounded ends. Deep-fry in oil heated to 375° F. until golden brown. Remove and drain on absorbent paper. Serve warm with salsa. *Makes about 50.*

Have an adult help you when frying.

Salsa

½ cup mayonnaise

½ cup ketchup

3 peeled garlic cloves, crushed

Mix all ingredients together and serve as a cold dip for the warm *surullitos.*

Susana's Alfajores

Caramel Sandwich Cookies

Argentina

1⅓ cup cornstarch

¾ cup and 3 tbs. all-purpose flour

½ tsp. baking soda

2 tsp. baking powder

7 oz. butter, softened

½ cup and 3 tbs. sugar

3 egg yolks

peel of 1 lemon, grated

1 tsp. vanilla

dulce de leche *(see recipe below)*

powdered sugar

Preheat oven to 350° F. In small bowl, mix cornstarch, flour, baking soda, and baking powder. Set aside. In a food processor, mix butter with sugar. Mix in egg yolks, one by one. Add flour mixture by spoonfuls, mixing well after each addition. Finally, add lemon peel and vanilla. Mix well. Scrape sides of bowl and transfer the dough onto a floured surface. If dough is too soft, chill until easier to handle. With a floured rolling pin, roll the dough out to a ¼-inch thickness. Or, roll between two sheets of waxed paper. With a cookie cutter, make 2-inch diameter rounds. Place rounds on a cookie sheet. Bake for 10 minutes or until pale golden-brown. Let cookies cool. Make cookie sandwiches using *dulce de leche* as a filling. Sift a generous amount of powdered sugar on top of *alfajores.* *Makes about 16.*

DULCE DE LECHE

One 14-oz. can sweetened condensed milk *1 tsp. vanilla*

Place unopened can of sweetened condensed milk in a deep pan. Cover can with water. Bring to a boil. Boil for 2 hours, keeping the can under water at all times. Remove from pan. Let it cool completely. Open can and pour its contents into a small bowl. Stir in vanilla. *Makes enough filling for 16 alfajores.*

Have an adult help you remove the can from boiling water.

Mama Rosa's Chiles Rellenos

Stuffed Fried Peppers

MEXICO

12 cubanel or poblano peppers

Monterey Jack cheese, sliced into thick rectangular pieces

3 lg. eggs, whites and yolks separated

oil for deep-frying

In a *comal,* a heavy iron pan, roast peppers on all sides until the skin turns brown-black and begins to lift. Remove peppers from pan with tongs. While peppers are still warm, carefully peel off their skins. Make a 2-inch slit in each one and remove the seeds with a small spoon. Stuff each pepper with a piece of cheese. Set aside.

In a large bowl, beat egg whites until stiff. Gently fold in egg yolks. Dip peppers in beaten egg mixture and fry in hot oil. When peppers turn golden brown, remove with a slotted spoon and serve immediately. Enjoy *chiles rellenos* with *pico de gallo.*

Serves 12.

Have an adult help you when frying.

Victoria's Flour Tortillas

Mexican Pancakes

4½ cups all-purpose flour

1 tsp. salt

3½ tbs. canola oil

1 cup lukewarm water

In a large bowl, mix flour and salt. Cut in oil with a fork until mixture resembles coarse meal. Add water gradually and knead until dough forms a large ball. It should be elastic, but not sticky. Cover the ball with a towel for ½ hour.

Pinch off disks of dough 1 inch thick and 2 inches in diameter. Roll each one into a flat, thin circle. Heat a heavy iron pan until a drop of water sizzles in it. Cook *tortillas* until both sides are golden brown. Enjoy with meat filling, *pico de gallo,* shredded cheese, or by themselves. *Makes about 28.*

Roberto's Pico de Gallo

Mexican Relish

2 lg. ripe tomatoes, chopped

1 lg. onion, peeled and chopped

1 bunch of cilantro, stalks removed, leaves rinsed and chopped

1 jalapeño pepper, seeded and finely chopped

juice of 2 limes

Mix all ingredients together in a large bowl. Serve with warm flour *tortillas.*

Josefa's Turrón de Doña Pepa

Nougat Candy

PERU

Dough

2½ cups all-purpose flour	*8 oz. butter*
2 tsp. baking powder	*¼ cup aniseed herbal tea*
1 tbs. aniseed	*1 tsp. salt*
4 egg yolks	*¼ cup milk*

Preheat oven to 350° F. Mix flour, baking powder, and aniseed in a bowl. In another bowl, beat egg yolks. Add beaten egg yolks to flour mixture. Cut in butter with your hands until mixture resembles cornmeal. In a third bowl, mix aniseed tea, salt, and milk. Add this liquid mixture to the flour-and-egg mixture. Knead until you can form a ball with the dough. Let dough stand at room temperature for 1 hour.

Roll dough to form long cylinders ¼-inch thick. Cut into

4-inch lengths. Place the cylinder cookies on a greased cookie sheet and bake for about 20 minutes or until golden brown. Remove from oven and let cool.

Have an adult help you when baking.

HONEY

16 oz. Panela* *(Hard brown sugar)*	*peel of ½ orange, grated*
½ cup water	*1 cinnamon stick*
2 cloves	*juice of ½ lime*
juice of 1 lemon	

*Available where Latin foods are sold

Place all ingredients except the lime juice in a saucepan over medium heat. Carefully stir until *Panela* melts and the liquid becomes the consistency of honey, about 20 minutes. Add lime juice so mixture doesn't crystallize. Let cool.

ASSEMBLY

For the assembly, have your favorite sugar sprinkles on hand. When the honey has cooled to the point that it will stick to the cylinder-shaped cookies, arrange alternate layers of cookies and honey in a 9- by 13-inch dish. The cookies should be layered in a crisscross fashion and the last layer should be honey. Top with sprinkles or any kind of tiny, hard-candy pieces.

As soon as the *turrón* is completely cool, cut into small pieces.

Makes about 25 pieces.

Marilia's Besitos de Coco

COCONUT KISSES

PUERTO RICO

3¼ cups fresh frozen grated coconut, firmly packed*

1 cup brown sugar, firmly packed

8 tbs. all-purpose flour

¼ tsp. salt

4 tbs. butter, at room temperature

3 lg. egg yolks

½ tsp. vanilla

*Available where Latin foods are sold

Preheat oven to 350° F. Place grated coconut in a bowl. Add brown sugar, flour, salt, butter, yolks, and vanilla. Mix well. Grease a 9- by 13-inch glass baking dish. Take mixture by the tablespoon, shape into balls, and arrange in baking dish. Bake for about 35 minutes or until golden. Let cool in baking dish for 10 minutes. With a small spatula, remove *besitos* carefully and place upside down onto platter. Let cool completely and turn over.

Makes about 35.

Marilia's Tembleque

Coconut Dessert

PUERTO RICO

¾ cup sweetened coconut milk (shake can before measuring)

1½ cups water

½ cup cornstarch

¾ cup milk

¼ tsp. salt

cinnamon to taste

In a large bowl, mix together all ingredients except cinnamon. Pour mixture into a large pot. Place pot over medium-high heat. Stir constantly with a wooden spoon. When mixture begins to thicken, turn heat to low and stir until it is very thick and smooth, about 10 minutes. You should be able to see the bottom of the pan when running the spoon across it.

Spread mixture into a 9- by 13-inch glass baking dish. With a fork, draw swirls on top of the *tembleque.* Sprinkle with cinnamon. Let cool. Cover and refrigerate for several hours. Once *tembleque* is chilled, it should have the consistency of gelatin. Cut into squares and transfer to a serving platter.

Makes about 30 squares.

Abuelita's Natilla

CUSTARD

PUERTO RICO

4 egg yolks

¾ cup sugar

¼ tsp. salt

2 tbs. cornstarch

4 cups whole milk

2 tsp. vanilla

ground cinnamon

Using an electric hand mixer, beat the egg yolks in a large bowl. Continue beating and add sugar slowly. Mix in salt and cornstarch until ingredients are evenly distributed and you have a smooth mixture. Set aside.

Heat the milk in a large saucepan over medium heat. It should not boil. Transfer the milk into a glass measuring cup. Pour heated milk in a steady stream over the egg yolk mixture. Beat at low speed. Transfer the mixture into a large pot and place it over medium-high heat. Stir constantly with a wooden spoon. Once the mixture starts bubbling, turn heat to low and simmer until cream thickens, about 15 minutes. It should have the consistency of thick, chocolate syrup. Remove from heat and stir in vanilla. Pour into small bowls. Sprinkle generously with cinnamon. Once the *natilla* cools completely, cover bowls and refrigerate until cold. *Serves 4 to 6.*

Mamá's Flan de Coco

Coconut Flan

PUERTO RICO

1 cup sugar
One 14-oz. can sweetened condensed milk
One 12-oz. can evaporated milk
One 15-oz. can sweetened coconut milk
6 large eggs

Preheat oven to 350° F. Place sugar in a 9-inch fluted tube pan. Place the pan on the stove top over medium-high heat. Sugar will dissolve and turn caramel brown. After it has melted, wear oven mitts and gently rock the pan so that the bottom and sides become coated with caramel. The caramel does not have to reach the rim. Set aside.

Place condensed milk, evaporated milk, coconut milk, and eggs in a large bowl. Using an electric hand mixer, beat at medium speed until mixture is smooth. Pour into the caramelized pan.

The flan has to cook in a boiling-water bath. Pour water to cover the bottom of a deep pan that is larger than the tube pan.

The water has to be at least 1 inch deep. Place the filled tube pan in the water. Place both pans in oven. Cook for one hour or until a toothpick comes out clean. Take tube pan out of the water and remove from oven. Let flan cool completely. With a knife, gently loosen sides of flan. Turn flan over onto a large round platter and pour the caramel syrup remaining in the tube pan on top of the flan. *Serves 12 to 14.*

Have an adult help you caramelize the pan.

A Note from the Author

About the Recipes

The country mentioned before each recipe is meant to show where that particular variation of the recipe comes from. However, most of these recipes are popular in many other Spanish-speaking countries in addition to the country mentioned. For example, it is well known that *flan* is a common dessert in Spain, Mexico, Peru, Ecuador, Costa Rica, and Argentina, among others. But the coconut-flavored variation of *flan* is more specific to Puerto Rico. Perhaps it is less known that the flour *tortilla*, which is frequently associated with Mexico, is also a staple food of Guatemala, El Salvador, and Costa Rica.

All the recipes included have been tested in my kitchen. Many have been favorites of my family for generations.

Glossary

Abuela (ah-BWEH-lah): Grandmother

Abuelita (ah-bweh-LEE-tah): Grandmother (*Abuelita* is the diminutive term for *Abuela*)

Abuelito (ah-bweh-LEE-toh): Grandfather (*Abuelito* is the diminutive term for *Abuelo*)

Abuelo (ah-BWEH-loh): Grandfather

Aguinaldo (ah-gee-NAHL-doh): A small Christmas present

Alfajores de dulce de leche (ahl-fah-HOR-ays day DOOL-say day LEH-chay): Sandwich cookies filled with milk caramel

Alfombra (ahl-FOHM-brah): A carpet or rug

Apúrate (ah-POO-rah-tay): Hurry up

Arroz con pollo (ah-RROSS kohn POH-lyoh): Rice dish with chicken

¡Ay! (EYE): Oh!; used to express an emotion, such as surprise or pain

Ay, Santo Dios (EYE, SAN-toh DEE-ohs): Oh, Dear God

Bacalao a la vizcaína (bah-kah-LAH-oh ah lah viz-kah-EE-nah): A traditional codfish stew eaten during Lent

Barrio (BAH-ree-oh): District or quarter

Bendito (ben-DEE-toh): Blessed; dear

Besitos de coco (beh-SEE-tohs day KOH-koh): Coconut kisses, a dessert

¡Bueno! (BWEH-noh): Good!

Caldero (cal-DEH-roh): A small cauldron

Chico (CHEE-koh): Little boy

Chiles rellenos (CHEE-lays reh-LYEH-nohs): Roasted chili peppers that are stuffed with white cheese, then coated with a beaten egg mixture and fried

Chorizo (choh-REE-zoh): A spicy Spanish sausage

Cobitos (koh-BEE-tohs): Small hermit crabs

Comal (koh-MAHL): A heavy iron pan

Congrí (kohn-GREE): Cuban rice with black beans

Coquito (koh-KEE-toh): Holiday drink made with coconut milk and rum

Cucurucho de maní (koo-koo-ROO-choh day mah-NEE): A paper cone of roasted peanuts

Los Cucuruchos (los koo-koo-ROO-chohs): The porters

Cuentos (KWEN-tohs): Stories

¡Cuidado! (kwee-DAH-doh): Careful! Look out!

¡Dale! (DAH-lay): Hit it!

Damas primero (DAH-mahs pree-MEH-roh): Ladies first

Dame un beso (Dah-may oon BEH-soh): Give me a kiss

Dios te bendiga (dee-OHS tay ben-DEE-gah): God bless you

Doña (DOH-nyah): Title of courtesy and respect preceding a woman's first name

Feliz año nuevo (feh-LEEZ AH-nyoh NWEH-voh): Happy New Year

Feliz cumpleaños (feh-LEEZ koom-play-AH-nyohs): Happy birthday

Flan de coco (FLAN day KOH-koh): Coconut custard made with milk, sugar, and eggs

Frijoles (free-HOH-lays): Beans

Garúa (gah-ROO-ah): Drizzle

Gracias (GRAH-see-ahs): Thank you

Güiro (GWEE-roh): A percussion instrument played by scraping a stick along the notched surface of a gourd

Helado de coco (ay-LAH-doh day KOH-koh): Coconut-flavored sherbet

Hola (OH-lah): Hello

La hora del té (lah OH-rah del TAY): Teatime

Horchata (or-CHAH-tah): A chilled drink made of sugar, water, and crushed sesame seeds

Mamá (mah-MAH): Mama

Maraca (mah-RAH-kah): A rattle; a percussion instrument played by shaking a gourd filled with dry beans or small stones

M'ijo (MEE-hoh): Shortened form of *mi hijo*, which means "my son"

Mojo criollo (MOH-hoh cree-OH-lyoh): A sauce made with onion, garlic, olive oil, bay leaves, and peppercorns

Morenos (moh-RAY-nohs): Africans brought to Peru as slaves (*moreno* is the singular, masculine form and *morena* is the singular, feminine)

¡Muy peligroso! (MWEE peh-lee-GROH-soh): Too dangerous!

Nada (NAH-dah): Nothing

Natilla (nah-TEE-lyah): A creamy custard made with sugar, milk, egg yolks, and vanilla

Niña (NEE-nyah): Small girl

¡Niños! (NEE-nyohs): Children!

Palitos (pah-LEE-tohs): Sticks used to make sound by striking them against each other

Pico de gallo (PEE-koh day GAH-lyoh): Relish made with tomato, onion, cilantro, and jalapeño peppers

Piñata (pee-NYAH-tah): A decorated vessel, usually made of papier-mâché, that is filled with fruit, candy, and peanuts

¿**Por qué**? (por KAY): Why?

¡**Qué mala pata**! (kay MAH-lah PAH-tah): What bad luck!

Querida (keh-REE-dah): Darling or dear

Salsa (SAHL-sah): A style of Latin American music and dance; also, any kind of sauce

¡**Salud, dinero, amor, y tiempo para disfrutarlos**! (sah-LOOD, dee-NEH-roh, ah-MORE, ee tee-EHM-poh pah-rah dis-froo-TAHR-lohs): Health, money, love, and time to enjoy it all

Señor (say-NYOR): Mister or sir

El Señor de los Milagros (el say-NYOR day los mee-LAH-gross): Lord of Miracles

Señora (say-NYOR-ah): Missus

Sí (SEE): Yes

¡**Sinvergüenza**! (sin-vair-GWEHN-zah): Little rascal!

Sofrito (soh-FREE-toh): A seasoning sauce

Surullito de maíz (soo-roo-LYEE-toh day mah-YEES): Puerto Rican corn fritters

Tembleque (tem-BLEH-kay): A sweet dessert made with coconut milk

Tía (TEE-ah): Aunt

Tío (TEE-oh): Uncle

Torrejas (tor-RAY-hahs): Bread dipped in milk and egg that is pan-fried and served with homemade syrup

Tortilla (tor-TEE-lyah): A thin round cake of cornmeal or wheat flour

Tortilla española (tor-TEE-lyah ehs-pah-NYOH-lah): Potato omelet

Turrón (too-RROHN): A nougat dessert

¡**Vendo yuca, plátanos, tomates**! (VEN-doh YOO-kah PLAH-tah-nohs toh-MAH-tehs): Yuca, plaintains, tomatoes for sale!

¡**Viva**! (VEE-vah): Hurrah!

Yuca (YOO-kah): A fleshy rootstock plant; also called cassava

Acknowledgments

Many people inspired and guided me through the making of this book.

I'm very grateful to Roger Alexander Sandoval and José Rodolfo Rosales for their generous insight into Guatemalan traditions. I owe the pictorial information of Holy Week in Guatemala to my good friend Germán Oliver.

Rodolfo Perez and Lucía González shared their memories of growing up in Cuba. Olga Alonso shared not only her childhood anecdotes, but also her recipes. Thank you.

I also thank Iris Brown for shedding light onto the daily life of Old San Juan in the 1940s.

For her stories about her childhood in Buenos Aires, her constant encouragement, and for instilling in me a love of cooking, I must thank my mother, Marta Orzábal de Delacre. Nellie Carpio was a great help in the search for the perfect recipe for *alfajores.*

I will not forget my Mexican friend Victoria, whose inner strength I so admire and with whom I learned how to make *chiles rellenos* and *pico de gallo.*

It was Mayté Canto who introduced me to her Peruvian friend María Rosa Watson. María Rosa's enthusiasm for the legend and traditions associated with *El Señor de los Milagros* was irresistible. To her I owe the recipe for *turrón de Doña Pepa.*

I'm greatly indebted to Diana Oliver, who was so generous to share her wonderful recipes for *tembleque, flan de coco,* and *natilla.*

I thank Priya Nair and Monique Stephens for their great assistance with back matter. I also appreciate the valuable art direction of Marijka Kostiw, Dave Caplan, and David Saylor. For her editorial direction, dedication, insight, and commitment to my work, I thank my editor, Dianne Hess.

Finally, for their unconditional love, I should thank my husband, Arturo Betancourt, and my two daughters Verónica and Alicia. Thank you, Verónica, for critiquing my stories.

Salsa Stories

is also available in Spanish!

978-0-439-22649-3
CUENTOS CON SAZÓN
(SALSA STORIES)

And look for these other Latin American stories from Lulu Delacre!

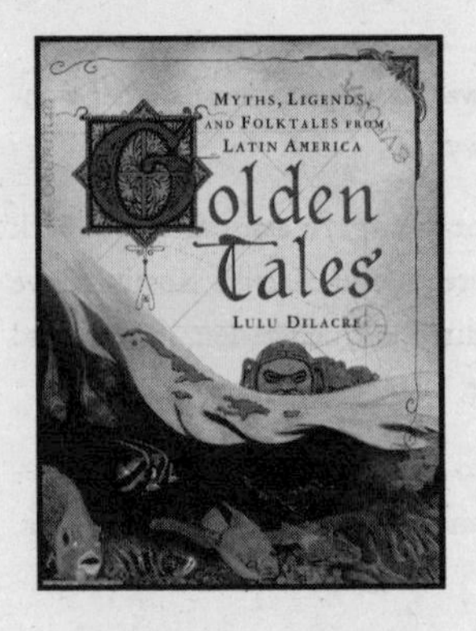

978-0-439-48187-8
GOLDEN TALES

978-0-590-45777-4
VEJIGANTE MASQUERADER

IDEA ART

Gregory Battcock is editor of several anthologies of criticism in the fine arts, including *The New Art, Minimal Art, The New American Cinema,* and *The New Music.* He is Special Correspondent for *Arts Magazine* and New York Correspondent for *Art and Artists.* Critical essays by Mr. Battcock have been published in *Art in America, Domus,* and *The Art Journal.* He teaches at William Paterson College in New Jersey and is general editor of the Dutton series called "Documents in Modern Art Criticism."

IDEA ART

A CRITICAL ANTHOLOGY

Edited by Gregory Battcock

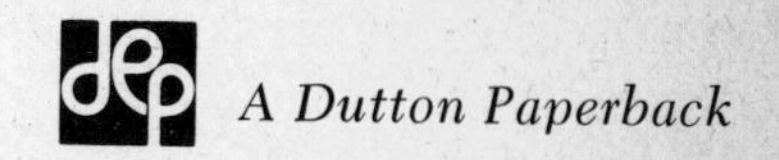

E. P. Dutton & Co., Inc. / New York / 1973

FIRST EDITION

Published simultaneously in Canada by Clarke, Irwin & Company Limited, Toronto and Vancouver.

SBN 0-525-47344-0

INDIVIDUAL COPYRIGHTS AND ACKNOWLEDGMENTS

Grateful acknowledgment is made to the following for permission to quote from copyright material:

Dore Ashton: "Monuments for Nowhere or Anywhere." Reprinted from *L'Art Vivant*, July, 1970, by permission of the author.

Jonathan Benthall: "The Relevance of Ecology." Reprinted from *Studio International*, December, 1969, by permission of the author.

Cheryl Bernstein: "The Fake as More." Printed by permission of the author.

Jack Burnham: "Problems of Criticism." Reprinted from *Artforum*, Vol. 9, No. 5, January, 1971, by permission of the author.

Joseph Kosuth: "Art After Philosophy, I and II." Reprinted from *Studio International*, October and November, 1969, by permission of the author.

Lucy Lippard: "The Art Workers' Coalition." Reprinted from *Studio International*, November, 1970, by permission of the author.

Ursula Meyer: "The Eruption of Anti-Art." Printed by permission of the author.

John Perreault: "It's Only Words." Reprinted from *The Village Voice*, May 20, 1971, by permission of the author.

Arthur Rose: "Four Interviews." Reprinted from *Arts Magazine*, Vol. 43, No. 4, February, 1969, by permission of the author.

Harold Rosenberg: "Art and Words." Reprinted from *The New Yorker*, March 29, 1969. Copyright © 1969 by The New Yorker Magazine, Inc.

Seth Siegelaub: "On Exhibitions and the World at Large: A Conversation with Seth Siegelaub." Reprinted from *Studio International,* December, 1969, by permission of the author.

Lawrence Weiner, Daniel Buren, Mel Bochner, Sol LeWitt: "Documentation in Conceptual Art." Reprinted from *Arts Magazine,* April, 1970, by permission of the authors.

Robert Hughes: "The Decline and Fall of the Avant-Garde." Reprinted by permission from TIME, The Weekly Newsmagazine; copyright © 1972 Time, Inc.

Les Levine: "Les Levine Replies." Printed by permission of the author.

ACKNOWLEDGMENTS

I should like to acknowledge my debt to the editors of *Studio International*, *Arts Magazine*, and *Artforum*, who were first to print some of the material reprinted in this book.

G.B.

CONTENTS

ILLUSTRATIONS

IDEA ART

INTRODUCTION

By 1970 it was clear that a new type of art was emerging in the New York and European art worlds. Quickly labeled Conceptual or Idea Art, the form encompassed an extraordinary variety of works. What they all seemed to have in common was a rejection of the "bourgeois" aspects of traditional art. Works of Idea Art frequently did not actually exist as objects. Rather, they remained ideas; frequently, what did exist was only some kind of documentation referring to the concept.

Initially, it appeared that this new art movement rejected the usual commercial, marketplace aspects of artmaking. Indeed, it was difficult to understand how such Conceptual works could be bought or sold; nor could they be "collected" in the usual sense. If Conceptual works opposed the idea of art as a consumer object, they also opposed traditional aesthetic orientations. The idea that Conceptual works would become a subject for qualitative speculation engaging the attention of the connoisseur was unimaginable. In addition, such matters of technique as color value, drawing, composition, and pictorial depth became all but useless when applied to the new form.

The Idea artists were mainly interested in exploring a new area of aesthetic speculation that seemed to represent a dramatic break from the usual activities of artmaking, looking, and appreciation. They were engaged in an emphatic rejection of the commercial and consumer aspects in art. At the same time many attempted to relate art activity to broad social, ecological, and intellectual concerns, as opposed to the making of objects designed according to firmly established criteria.

Therein lie, in a loosely and broadly defined way, the common bonds of this new and radical school of remarkably diverse art activity. The many differences found among the concepts of these artists indicate the absence of a formal, academic orientation such as one detects in the "schools" of Cubism or Abstract Expressionism.

Conceptualist works include a wide range of art activity. The efforts of the so-called Earth artists, represented mainly by Michael Heizer and Robert Smithson, come to mind. Such experiments involve the actual or proposed relocation of great quantities of earth and rocks. Such works are not, obviously, exclusively Conceptual. Yet, they too conform to the broad outlines noted above. But Earth works need not depend on thousands of tons of earth and equipment; a work by Lawrence Weiner involved the transportation of only a few pounds of dirt.[1]

Other artists have investigated possibilities in the area of disposable art. *Stock Exchange Transplant* (1970) involved the transportation of debris from the floor of the New York exchange to a new location;[2]

[1] *A Removal of an Amount of Earth from the Ground—The Intrusion into This Hole of a Standard Processed Material* (Public Freehold, 1967).

[2] Barry Bryant's penthouse (New York, Winter, 1969/70).

Michael Heizer: *Circumflex/Isolated Mass.* 1968. Massacre Lake, Nevada. 120′ x 1′ x 1′. Collection of Robert Scull.

Michael Heizer: #2/3 *Displaced-Replaced Mass.* 1969. Thirty-ton granite mass in cement depression. Silver Springs, Nevada. Collection of Robert Scull.

after several hours it was all removed and thrown away again. Still other artists attempted works that would be in a state of constant change; sooner or later they might totally disappear. Les Levine's *The Process of Elimination* (January, 1969), an experiment with pieces of white plastic on a vacant Greenwich Village lot, is but one example. Argentinian artist Uri Buru dumped quantities of dye into the East River and into public fountains in Kassel, Germany (*Documenta 5*, 1972).

Still other Conceptual artists have investigated the essential components of artistic communication. Joseph Kosuth and a group of English and American artists have explored printed systems; in this way Idea Art explores the realm of letters. And it also spills over into dance, music, and theatre. Probably the best example of Conceptual dance theatre has been provided by the dancer/choreographer Kenneth King. His dance programs frequently involve no actual dancing at all. At one program a film was projected. At another, a tape recording of the dancer musing over philosophical and semantic matters was the sole subject.

Dancer/choreographer Yvonne Rainer presented *Walk She Said* at the Whitney Museum of American Art, a work that emphasized the nonvisual. One reviewer remarked: "Though Ms. Rainer's logic is pictorial, her cerebral dependence on works and fairly traditional syntax is too well integrated into the work for her statement to be entirely visual." [3] This dance piece incorporated cinema and reading.

Idea Art has spilled over into cinema; a movie by Les Levine (*Movie for the Blind*, 1969) contains no

[3] Ellen W. Jacobs in *Changes*, July, 1972.

images. At *Documenta 5* in Kassel, Germany (1972), an artist offered a film consisting of several feet of film looped end-to-end that was projected out of a window into open space. Proposals from William Anastasi, including plans to film a wall in The Museum of Modern Art that would be projected onto that same wall, is yet another example. In the newer and rapidly expanding area of art/cinema/video is to be found an enormous potential for experiments within the area of Conceptual aesthetics.

The trend has profoundly affected many developments in contemporary music. It is not by accident that John Cage has become perhaps the leading "spiritual" symbol of Conceptual music. His writings and compositions were read and discussed by Conceptual artists before the "movement" had been identified. A study of the influence and relationship of Cage to contemporary art—both Minimal Art and Conceptual Art—would be a welcome contribution to the literature of the field. The annual New York Avant-Garde Festival, organized by cellist Charlotte Moorman, probably represents the most popular manifestation of certain Conceptual activities in the sound and performing areas.

The Conceptual form is broad and complex, and its initial impact has been widely felt. The design and emphasis of formal exhibitions in art museums have been altered, particularly in shows in which the audience experiences ideas and concepts rather than exercises critical faculties upon the design of objects. A listing of landmark exhibitions of this type must include the first such show organized by Seth Siegelaub, "0 Objects, 0 Painters, 0 Sculptures" (New York, January, 1969). Another, later exhibition organized in a similar way was Jennifer Licht's "Spaces" at The Museum of Modern Art in 1970. The Architectural League in New York encourages numerous such efforts.

As a result of these and other exhibitions, the usual lineup of paintings common to academic exhibition policy was challenged by provocative social and environmental exhibits that would have been unthinkable several years ago. One example was the large and controversial "Harlem on My Mind" show at The Metropolitan Museum of Art in 1970; a more recent example is the successful "The Domestic Landscape" show of Italian commercial design at The Museum of Modern Art in 1972.

The changes resulting from Conceptualist proclamations and provocations are being felt more slowly by the art magazines, the art schools, and particularly the university art departments. The last appear to be the slowest to catch on. It cannot be stressed too heavily how important the college art departments have become in distributing art ideas and providing energy to artmaking in general. However, the academic rigidity found within them, so greatly deplored during the Abstract-Expressionist years, seems more firmly entrenched than ever. The heavy emphasis of educational programs at almost all such schools upon the traditional mechanics of art has not abated. Yet if the real benefits of the Conceptualists' aesthetic provocations are to be exploited, then the very focus and goals of formal art training need serious realignment. Therein, it is to be hoped, lies a major reason for a book such as this. Its first purpose is to present in a direct way some of the action, diversity, and rationale behind these latest art developments. And it attempts to do so by presenting the student and educator with some of the original and important theoretical documents that helped set the direction of the new artistic emphasis.

Much has been said about the way that Idea Art rejects traditional artistic criteria. Such a rejection began well before the Conceptualists appeared actively upon the scene. The climate for new criteria began with the awareness that if art is to remain vital it must re-engage itself in the arena of cultural values. Cultural value changes, which were at one time a subject for the arts, are today primarily brought about (according to Allan Kaprow) "by political, military, economic, technological, educational, and advertising pressures."

No doubt some aestheticians will claim that value-changing is not an appropriate or even a historical concern for the arts. Yet I maintain that it is and usually has been. It need not be the major or exclusive concern; however, it remains clear that virtually all good and "lasting" art is linked to broader cultural developments. Frequently, the very form of such art is determined by cultural values. In fact, the two are inseparable. The very quality of some art, particularly within the Conceptual Art framework, is judged by how effectively it changes our cultural values. Specifically, a "good" Conceptual work is one in which some established aesthetic or cultural rule is effectively broken.

Idea Art is not a popular art. However, art should, to a much greater extent than it does now, involve the popular imagination and help determine cultural destiny and the identification and refinement of the ordinary. Therein lies the major reason for considerable objection to post-Modernist art (Pop, Minimal, and Conceptual). And that's why we must investigate Idea Art—not for what it is but, rather, for the ideas and changes that it motivates.

GREGORY BATTCOCK

MONUMENTS FOR NOWHERE OR ANYWHERE *

by Dore Ashton

Paralleling the largely conceptual trends toward nonvisual and nonexistent art worlds is a preoccupation with works constructed or proposed for open and public places. The phenomenon is explained by Dore Ashton as ". . . partly shaped to thwart the acquisitiveness and complacency of the bourgeois patron." Ashton observes that these artists ". . . share an impulse to move out into spaces that cannot be contained by single individuals." In fact, what these artists are doing is identified as an American artistic tradition, ". . . that of disavowing bourgeois standards for art."

Dore Ashton refers to the work of Oldenburg, Andre, Haacke, and Insley; in the final analysis she concludes that the ". . . definition of the monument will have to be revised when their work is done." She observes that the rejection of the monumental by many Conceptual artists is only temporary and ". . . will give way in the fact of the very real demand(s) for real symbols of an emergent new culture."

Dore Ashton has written criticism for The New York Times, Studio International, *and* ARTS *magazine. She is the author of* Modern Sculpture *and a collection of essays on Abstract Expressionism,* The Unknown Shore. *She heads the Department of Humanities at Cooper Union.*

*Reprinted from *L'Art Vivant*, July, 1970.

In the days when there was still a New York school, or so some critics thought, Willem de Kooning stated the situation succinctly: "The painter, it is true, was not always completely free. The things were not always of his own choice, but because of that he often got some new ideas."

Not long after, the younger artists found themselves increasingly unfree as the bourgeois consumer accelerated his smothering assault and they renewed an old American tradition: that of disavowing bourgeois standards for art. The most extravagant disclaimers appeared in the late 1950s, in the form of Happenings. Early in the 1960s, Claes Oldenburg summed it all up in his journal in a statement that is more wistful than ironic: "If I could only forget the notion of art entirely. I really don't think you can win. . . . The bourgeois scheme is that they wish to be disturbed from time to time, they like that, but then they envelop you, and that little bit is over, and they are ready for the next. . . ."

At that point where they threatened to envelop Oldenburg, he acted as have many other artists of his generation. He took himself out of the bourgeois salon; out of the museum, and into the public spaces. Or at least, into spaces grandly imagined to be beyond the realm of possibility. (Even there, he has seen a threat to envelop. After all, his tank mounted with a phallic lipstick is actually standing at Yale University.) Oldenburg's mockery in his projected monuments, as well as his serious social commentary, is probably intended to fulfill his early hope of disentangling himself from the bourgeois web. Such a project as his monument to immigration in which a reef would be placed in New York harbor and "wreck after wreck would occur until there was a huge pile of rusty and broken shiphulls in the middle of the bay" shows his serious intent and the ultimately polemical character of his aesthetic stance. His monuments, which are supposedly conceived of for specific places and occasions, are in reality schemes for a never-never land matched only by the irreality of the lands to which he flies incessantly nowadays in his itinerant public career.

Such itinerant careers as he and many others have made of late are partially shaped to thwart the acquisitiveness and complacency of the bourgeois patron. These artists have varied temperaments, just as any other group of artists, but they share an impulse to move out into spaces that cannot be contained by single individuals. They have abjured traditional ways of thinking about art and are in the earliest stages of self-definition. Some operate in the narrow interstices between art and science. Others are professional geometers of the visionary type. And others are ironists. What they share is a determination not to be contained by any definition, school, or country, and an indomitable restlessness. Their dreams are literally monumental, although the definition of monument will have to be revised when their work is done.

A monument to a Heraclitan such as Hans Haacke is of necessity fleeting. He wanders around the earth seeking natural situations in which he can intervene. He bases his endeavors on what he sees as "natural laws" which are articulated in interlocking systems. His analogues to these systems run from ambitious interventions with the laws governing vegetal growth to even more ambitious efforts to intervene with the mighty laws governing waterfalls. His monument to man's puny stature was eloquent when he stretched an ice-laden rope across the breadth of a powerful waterfall. He challenges, as do many other artists working in the outdoors, the very notion of monuments that has dominated our culture in the West.

The element of denunciation of the very idea of the enshrined monument is emphasized in the work of Carl Andre, whose works are extremely casual; are easily dismounted; and must be done by him *in situ*. These works, he claims, are "social facts," and he hints that his approach is fundamentally Marxist. In struggling against the bourgeois need to enshrine an object as a work of art, Andre must resort to words, encounters, and, paradoxically, commissions. The fragile signs of his presence, sparsely set out on lawns, in courtyards, and occasionally in museums, can scarcely be called monumental, and yet the imagination that forges poems to accompany them clearly envisions stupendous proliferations of "social facts."

Quite different is the impulse of Michael Heizer. He keeps returning to the primeval wilderness to leave monumental reminders of his manliness there. He tunnels through the summit of an isolated plateau, at the expense of enormous energy and finance, but he is unwilling to conserve the results of his endeavor. Weather will ultimately erase his traces which, by the logic of these monumental rebels against bourgeois values, justifies his position.

On the other hand, Will Insley, another dreamer of colossal monuments, has no intention of ceding his works to the natural logic of *force majeur*. He was trained as an architect and is intimately familiar with the tradition of visionary architecture emanating from the eighteenth century. In spirit he is far closer to

Jorge Borges or Kafka than to the writers such as Robbe-Grillet who more nearly correspond to the intentions of such artists as Haacke, Andre, or Oldenburg. But like them, he tries to move as far from the confined spaces of the bourgeois artists as possible. His reveries are on a scale that exceeds the practical conceptions of his society. "My work," he writes, "is a civilization/ fragment ruin clue/ remembered from the future/ if you could gather all the pieces/ they would fit together/ and reveal/ now hidden/ now mysterious/ a new meaning."

Insley's new meanings in drawings, diagrams, and models for vast sculptures on the prairies and tundras are to be culled from his vision of space—a vision that becomes more and more legible, and that is one of the few positive visions we have been offered lately. Like Oldenburg, who, in an unguarded moment, confessed his hunger for an "elevation of sensibility above bourgeois values," which could "restore the magic inherent in the universe," Insley is intent on realizing the projects of his mythicizing imagination. He speaks of poetry, mythology, and finding clues to his future archaeology. He explores what he calls "spaces within mind." But unlike Oldenburg and Andre, he does not trade in irony. He genuinely strives to evoke those spaces in visual objects. They must be far from New York, far from Paris, far from the impacted bourgeoisie. Those spaces of anywhere or nowhere are the most alluring to this authentically alienated artist.

It is not surprising that Insley's background is architecture. That is an art which, in the United States, has for a very long time been confined to reveries. The "project" for a monument is all too familiar to the architect who is trained to imagine great innovations and large-scale renovations, and who rarely if ever lives to see any of them enacted. His bondage to the monied patrons is ten times worse than the visual artist's, and he has all too often ceded his dreams to the terrible realities of his profession in the United States.

Conversely, the visual artist, intent on escaping the toils of the system, tends more and more to an architectural vision. The entire trajectory of the so-called Minimalist movement in sculpture was toward that end. Many sculptors have exhibited what they like to call "environmental" art, which attempts to incorporate the architectural features of the space with the work. The nostalgia for the great monuments of other cultures—Greece, Egypt, Rome, Mexico—is clear in the works of such artists as Insley, John McCracken, Robert Smithson, Tony Smith, Robert Morris, and countless others dealing with massive, simple, clearly architectonic structures.

If these men of imagination have been driven out of the traditions which sheltered painting and sculpture until very recently, it is obviously in large measure due to the nature of this whirlwind society. For them the social crisis is urgent, and they are constantly seeking for clues to the meanings of precipitous changes in Western culture. They, and many others, sense that new patterns are decisively emerging from what appears to be a hopeless cultural crisis.

Such new patterns will undoubtedly subsume the strikingly polemical aspects of much recent activity considered in the realm of the arts. Such paradoxes as a "conceptual art" will give way in the face of the very real demands for real symbols of an emergent new culture. Much of the rhetoric surrounding the monuments-for-anywhere deals with the lack of symbolism such works boast. Elaborate concepts will not satisfy the human hunger for meaning in art. Only monumental works of art in new modes will do that. The evolution seen in such collaborations as Experiments in Art and Technology clearly indicates that the new modes will seek increasingly to fashion complex works of aesthetic value. Both Robert Whitman and Billy Klüver are moving ever closer to a definable aesthetic and recently have called for a symposium on aesthetics—a gesture which would have roused infinite scorn only two years ago. If the anti-monument rhetoric of the monument-builders of today survives for more than a few hours tomorrow, we shall all be very surprised.

ART IN THE SERVICE OF THE LEFT?

by Gregory Battcock

In these notes on the recent aesthetic speculations of Herbert Marcuse (as they appear under the heading "Art and Revolution") in his new book *Counterrevolution and Revolt*, I have attempted to simplify what, perhaps, should not (or cannot) be simplified: I have attempted to streamline or, to use the corporate jargon, "highlight" Marcuse's thoughts and to relate them, wherever feasible, to contemporary trends in art; in so doing it will become necessary to de-elevate them from the realm of speculative pseudopolitical philosophy to a level where they will prove interesting to those who work in art. There is, then, considerable danger that I will be guilty of exactly what Marcuse cautions against. In his own words: "The common denominator for the misplaced radicalism in the cultural revolution is the anti-intellectualism which it shares with the most reactionary representatives of the Establishment."[1] While there are worse things than being accused of anti-intellectualism, I nevertheless hope to show that what Marcuse tends to find anti-intellectual may actually indicate efforts to invent new aesthetic forms, which, as a rule, take into account technological developments.

[1] Unless otherwise indicated, all quotations are from *Counterrevolution and Revolt* (Boston: Beacon Press, 1972).

It should also be pointed out that Marcuse argues consistently against a "social realist" type of art and seems to feel that art in the direct service of a revolution is to him just as pointless as certain types of avant-garde that dominate today's art scene. He writes: "Art . . . cannot change reality . . . cannot submit to the actual requirements of the revolution without denying itself." Such a belief falls squarely within the mainstream of twentieth-century aesthetic thought; it is neither capitalistic nor socialistic but, rather, commonly accepted by artists of all political persuasions. There is some new opinion, however, that questions whether this "aesthetic law" cannot, at least in some ways, be slightly bent. Marcuse argues that it cannot.

A Political Culture

Marcuse acknowledges that, in a direct sense, we are dealing with a "cultural revolution," and he defines the notion in two ways. Firstly, it implies that ideological developments (meaning, probably, art and social theory) are further along than practical developments in the basic institutional areas and secondly, that revolutionaries today generally aim ". . . at a total transformation of the entire traditional culture."

He notes that there is lots of interest in the political potential of the arts—a claim that he does not support with factual evidence and that some will doubt, saying instead that there really isn't much serious effort to use art as a political weapon—and he feels that the emphasis on art as political potential represents the need for some kind of effective way to communicate ". . . the indictment of the established reality" or, in effect, "the goals of liberation." In other words, we are still searching for a way to let people know and understand they are not free so they will desire freedom. This, essentially, is the problem for art.

If this communication is to come about at all, it will, according to Marcuse, involve a language that can be understood by people who have no interest in or desire to understand any language other than the language of oppression or, in Marcuse's words: ". . . a language that reaches a population which has introjected the needs and values of their masters and managers and made them their own. . . ." Since there is no way to invent a completely new political language, the only hope is to subvert the existing forms of communication. The existing forms that can best be intelligibly subverted are those that traditionally are in a state of constant change. In Marcuse's words: ". . . the possibilities of this subversion are naturally sought where the tradition itself has permitted . . . ," and while some culturalists will claim that all communicative forms—from beauty culture to advertising—are in a state of constant change (which is precisely why they remain so effective), Marcuse insists that there are, basically, only two such forms adaptable for subversion: they are the arts and folk (or popular ethnic) traditions, including slang.

Marcuse is mainly concerned with the fine arts in his recent writing. That's a shame because his thoughts on the folk or popular forms would, no doubt, make interesting reading. For example, he rejects his earlier writing on the political potential of the use of obscenity in language. He has moved farther toward an appreciation of the sensual areas, especially with his realization that the standardization of obscene language ". . . turns easily against sexuality itself." (Which is not necessarily true, of course, but no matter; it's a good thought.) He goes on to point out a most realistic dilemma: "If a radical says 'Fuck Nixon,' he associates the word for the highest genital gratification with the highest representative of the oppressive Establishment." Of course, fucking is not necessarily, for all people, the highest form of "genital gratification," but the point is clear, i.e., the word is too good for the likes of Nixon.

In this same vein, Marcuse observes that the radical who uses the word "shit" for the products of the establishment, in effect assumes ". . . the bourgeois rejection of anal eroticism." Such an application of Freudian and Marxist interpretation to contemporary "New Left" behavioral patterns is delightful, and one wishes there were more of them. However (or should one say "alas"), Marcuse returns to the subject of culture and the arts.

Unfortunately, he assumes a rather traditional aesthetic orientation that, I believe, is flatly rejected by many new artists. He seems unaware of the roles of satire, "put on," and humor and seems to reject flatly the possibility of art championing the ugly, or the trivial, or the banal, for example. This is not to claim he accepts the notion of the "beautiful" as the main subject for art. In fact, he rejects it implicitly in *An Essay on Liberation:* ". . . so much art is obviously not beautiful. . . ."

What a work of art can do is "transform the order prevailing in reality." This is, I think, Marcuse's main claim for art and with this in mind we can better understand Marcuse's broad (if not utopian) assertion that ". . . cultural revolution goes far beyond a revaluation in the arts: it strikes at the roots of capitalism in the individuals themselves."

The Target Is Bourgeois Culture

Typical middle-class culture is being attacked; at the same time it is inevitably changing anyway. In fact, it is doomed and already outdated. It will be destroyed not by the student rebellions or the new life-style movements but, surprisingly, by capitalism itself ". . . which made this culture incompatible with the requirements of its survival and growth."

The prevailing culture, or *bourgeois culture,* is actually made up of two cultures that are not necessarily compatible, the *material culture* and the *intellectual culture.* The former, the "life-style" of bourgeois materialism ". . . imposed repression for the sake of God and business." The latter, although frequently negating the material culture, was generally ineffective.

Marcuse cites, as evidence of the decline of *bourgeois culture,* the paradox of the need by the ruling class to perpetuate a "consumer" society while remaining dependent upon alienated labor. This point may appear outdated to some, who may question the validity of the alienated-labor concept. All his indices of the decline of *bourgeois culture* are equally debatable. He cites, for example, the ". . . co-option of libertarian subcultures which can enlarge the commodity market . . . ," the "decline of the father image," and the "destruction of the universe of languages." The last refers specifically to the introduction of "Orwellian language," which is basically the sort of official gobbledygook coming from Washington and other manipulative commercial agencies.

In a similar vein, Marcuse points out that whenever the ruling classes do adhere to traditional bourgeois values it is in a cynical and abusive way, i.e., "defending the Free World." Nevertheless the contradiction so far stated is, simply, if capitalism requires the overthrow of bourgeois culture, is not the cultural revolution defeating its own purpose by aiding capitalism rather than helping to prepare the groundwork for ". . . a radically anticapitalist culture?"

Rejection of Aesthetic Form

According to Marcuse the contradiction stated above is reflected in contemporary efforts to develop "anti-art" and "living" art forms. What is happening is that such forms represent efforts to unite the intellectual with the material culture, from which he has traditionally been separated. Major artworks of the bourgeois period (since the nineteenth century) illustrate the position of the intellectual who ". . . indicts, rejects, withdraws from the material culture of the bourgeoisie." Marcuse points out that the "higher" or intellectual culture ". . . dissociates *itself* from the world of commodities, from the brutality of bourgeois industry . . . from capitalist materialism." Thus art, the "aesthetic universe contradicts reality—a 'methodical,' intentional contradiction."

There is, of course, a "bourgeois art" that is different, in several ways, from higher intellectual art. Bourgeois artworks may be commodities yet Marcuse grants they represent authentic works. They do, however, possess particular class content ("the bourgeois, his decor and his problems dominate the scene") whereas the higher culture (of the bourgeois period) is an elite culture ". . . available and even meaningful only to a privileged minority." And such is the way things have always been. The problem then seems to be whether or not it is possible (or even desirable) to unite the two aspects of bourgeois culture and this, precisely, is what the anti-art and anti-form movements are all about, and why we have the current problem of rejection of aesthetic form. The cultural revolution, according to Marcuse, "aims far beyond bourgeois culture . . . it is directed against the aesthetic form as such."

At this point one is bound to ask "Why not?" Even Marcuse accepts certain basic arguments against aesthetic form. However, if he were able to accept certain bourgeois forms as art, rather than representing the destruction of aesthetic form, the dilemma referred to above would prove nonexistent: I refer especially to "rock" music—a form Marcuse rejects because, apparently, he doesn't like noise, and "rock" is too loud. As a cultural phenomenon "rock" certainly spans everything from idiot to intellectual.

Let's take a quick look at some arguments Professor Marcuse offers *against* aesthetic form.

Pro and Con

Ultimately Marcuse defends aesthetic form because it contains "anti-bourgeois qualities," and he claims that one task of the cultural revolution is to capture and transform such qualities. Briefly, his major arguments *against* aesthetic form state it ". . . is not adequately expressive of the real human condition," "it is divorced from reality," and basically it is a ". . . factor of stabilization in the repressive society." It is difficult to fault these elementary, frequently stated arguments, except that more could be added to the list. One could point out, for example, that aesthetic form is itself essentially a "Christian" notion that tolerates "non-aesthetic" form; that it requires refined (i.e., aesthetic) activity to remain distinct from work ethics; and lastly, that it elevates the artist to a ridiculous and altogether improper position (vis-à-vis the rest of the culture) that is both obsolete and hypocritical. The major argument *for* aesthetic form is that it contains "anti-bourgeois qualities," an argument that "seems to be called for" because aesthetic form has been placed in a threatened position by the "historical process in which the cultural revolution is placed."

The cultural revolution itself is coming to something of a dead end because it has assumed a rather contradictory role. It attempts to articulate and represent the ordinary nonrevolutionary feelings of the masses on the one hand, and on the other it promotes anti-forms. And what, according to Marcuse, are these counterrevolutionary anti-forms? They are "poems which are simply ordinary prose cut up in verse lines" and "paintings which substitute a merely technical arrangement of parts and pieces for any meaningful whole." Thus, in one fell swoop, Professor Marcuse has relegated virtually all contemporary art forms (cinema, literature, art, and music) to the realm of anti-form, thus inhibiting radical revamping of the bourgeois tradition. He claims that such forms are "incapable of bridging the gap between 'real life' and art"—a cliché we have been plagued with ever since Robert Rauschenberg claimed to have invented it.

It is, ultimately, the art and the soul "surrealist program" that Marcuse advocates. He claims the radical art forms of today—guerrilla theatre, rock music, anti-art—are not radical or even really revolutionary because, unlike the art of the Romantic and Classical periods, they lack the "negating power of art." By that he means such new forms lack the distance, the "transcendence which opposes art to the established order." In fact, such art actually "succumbs" to this order. At any rate it is not capable of real antagonism, cannot produce real, effective dissatisfaction, and will not lead to satisfactory authentic change. Of course, Marcuse is wrong on this, his major point. These forms do possess an educational energy that, in some ways, have been the most effective stimulators of the emerging cultural revolution. Incidentally, Marcuse supports this argument with a rather interesting twist.

He accepts the "rather profound uneasiness toward Classical and Romantic art" that he claims is a result of the fact that such art substitutes for the intellectual soul a real, living soul; and he says, almost unbelievably, that perhaps the extreme qualities of Classical and Romantic art ". . . strike us today as an all too *un*-sublimated, unrestrained expression of passion and pain" to the extent that we react with shame and embarrassment. He then proposes that such Classical art provides a "distance of reflection and contemplation" that new "anti-" and living art rejects.

Of course, not all new living art rejects such contemplation; though frequently, in order for it to reach a broader audience, it has reduced the contemplative distance somewhat. However, hysterical hair-pulling is not, of course, common to today's taste. Nevertheless, to suggest that human, real problems and feelings are not expressible in serious contemporary forms is debatable.

His explanation for the lack of deep feeling characteristic of new art is weak and, as it stands, not particularly convincing. There is, probably, a lot wrong with contemporary artistic developments, but it is not generally considered that "lack of deep feeling" is a particular problem. It is, according to Marcuse, a result of the intrusion of the ". . . totalitarian organization of society" into the ". . . inner and outer space where the extreme aesthetic qualities of art can still be experienced." To be sure, numerous epochs in the history of art have produced works that could be criticized as "lacking in deep feeling." However, as a rule, other qualities compensate for deep emotional content.

It's almost as if Professor Marcuse were pushing the maudlin and sentimental which, of course, isn't the case. Basically, his plea is for responsibility, commitment, and real sensual realization in art. Yet those contemporary art forms that do exploit such sentiment frequently aren't particularly good.

A Subversive Activity

Marcuse rightly insists upon the intrinsic subversive nature of art, and he writes "Permanent aesthetic subversion—this is the way of art." Yet he is careful to limit the nature of the "subversion" and accepts the inability of art (as we know it so far) to have much effect on political and/or social revolution. For example, he notes ". . . art cannot represent the revolution, it can only invoke it in another medium." It is curious that the "subversive" nature Marcuse sees in art in general he fails to see in certain types of art, such as those mentioned above. Minimal Art, electronic sound experimentation, and Conceptual choreographic efforts all remain subversive. Yet, according to Marcuse, they fall short of being acceptable as art. However, they have all helped us, by recognizing their specific subversive natures, to penetrate further and even enjoy the realm of the ordinary, the real, the popular, and the grotesque.

It seems redundant to point out at this late stage the fact that an artwork need not have revolution as its subject in order to be revolutionary. Equally, it is sometimes more interesting to engage in critical exercises pointing out the revolutionary and subversive content of *non-art* abstract communicative forms (like package design, printing types, or gasoline station architecture). Perhaps Marcuse would denigrate such endeavor as anti-intellectual.

Conclusion

Although Marcuse may not experience anything very "deep" or exhilarating or soulful from a film of Godard or Warhol, or a performance by The Rolling Stones, or a Conceptual presentation by Hans Haacke, to give only three examples, there are many persons who find such works intellectually and spiritually rewarding. Marcuse's traditional and relatively conservative taste in art may have led him to invent arguments against some new art forms that are not particularly illuminating.

The cultural theories of McLuhan, Cage, Fuller, and Skinner, among many other modern theorists, are ignored by Marcuse in favor of the old-line aestheticians; thus he overlooks technological and physical developments that surely have played an important role in determining the nature of contemporary visual speculation. In a similar vein, Marcuse is prone to interpreting the art of the past in purely aesthetic/ sensual terms and this may prove a narrow and inaccurate view. Social and/or political interpretation is not necessarily anti-intellectual. Even Marcuse himself demonstrates this on occasion.

Lastly, by insisting on an either/or rationale for the state of current art, Marcuse confuses the situation and makes it all but impossible, should one fully accept his theories, to move forward in art to a truly new scheme that exploits the knowledge of the present and at the same time offers the maximum in all areas of aesthetic experience.

THE RELEVANCE OF ECOLOGY *

by Jonathan Benthall

Without giving specific examples, or relating his explication to specific artists, trends, or works, Benthall examines the most essential condition for life itself—the balance between man and the nature that supports him—and sees important implications for art. Clearly, numerous artists, specifically those working in the Earth and Conceptual fields are motivated by just the stimuli Benthall identifies, which include, more or less ". . . a 'higher ecology' . . . a knowledge of exact physical ecology and a concern for the conservation of physical resources."

Benthall goes on to point out that "The artist, like everyone else, does not respond to abstract 'issues' but to the experience of being a certain person in a certain time and place." Thus, whether he consciously advocates ecological subjects or not, the artist, through his works, is inevitably affected by them.

The result of the influence of ecology upon an artist's performance is not, necessarily, immediately determinable because "His potential impact on society is in the longer term than that of social or political activists, and it is rarely direct or predictable." That the ecological influence is desirable is obvious: it is essential as a balance to the modern condition that finds man's ". . . quasi-

* Reprinted from *Studio International*, December, 1969.

divine powers . . . being usurped by politicians, bureaucrats, military strategists, and corporation men, against whose pressures only a minority of scientists and technologists are prepared to make a stand."

Thus we may assume that, in the long run, the artist may become something of a moral watchdog for an organizational system in which, in the words of Charles Reich, ". . . personal responsibility and personal awareness have been obliterated. . . . The ultimate evil is the result of carefully segmented acts; the structure itself guarantees an evasion by everyone of responsibility for the full moral act." [1]

Jonathan Benthall, graduate from Cambridge (England) in English literature, worked for some years as a systems engineer with IBM. He is organizer of the lecture series at the Institute of Contemporary Arts, London, and contributes a monthly column to Studio International *magazine.*

Generations have trod, have trod, have trod;
And all is seared with trade; bleared, smeared with toil;
And wears man's smudge and shares man's smell: the soil
Is bare now, nor can foot feel, being shod.

And for all this, nature is never spent;
There lives the dearest freshness deep down things . . .

(Gerard Manley Hopkins)

What have they done to the earth?
What have they done to our fair sister?
Ravaged and plundered and ripped her and bit her

[1] Charles A. Reich, "Reflections (Organization and the Law)," *The New Yorker*, June 19, 1971.

Stuck her with knives in the sight of the dawn and
Tied her with pincers and dragged her down.
(*The Doors*)

Hopkins' fine affirmation of the inexhaustibility of nature will now seem to many underguaranteed. In part one of this article, it was argued that the balanced ecological use of material resources will be hard to achieve for a society that lacks belief in nonmaterial ends. Most religions, if not all, are profoundly ecological in proposing a detailed and higher-than-material ordering of man's relationships with the living world and the inanimate world. One has only to think of the Christian symbolism of the lamb, the fish, bread and wine, the Nativity in a stable; or of the poetic strength of the Anglican burial service. Religion might be described as a transfigured ecology.

Nowadays most of us in the West live by a hotchpotch of humanist or utilitarian moral beliefs. Literature, with a few exceptions, has tended to reflect states of human centerlessness rather than map new centers of significance for human life. How *can* we make up our minds about the optimum ecological use of material resources—when most of us have no idea what, if anything, makes life worth living at all? Yet a social critic and anthropologist like Dr. Edmund Leach tells us that science has put man in the position of a god. Science (the argument goes) has now made possible many things that were in the past considered beyond man's control; so we must be quite calm and unsuperstitious, and make the wisest possible decisions about our future.

The actual situation is that man's quasi-divine powers are being usurped by politicians, bureaucrats, military strategists, and corporation men, against whose pressures only a minority of scientists and technologists are prepared to make a stand.

The delicacy of moral questions in a scientific context may be illustrated by the following sentence from a neurological paper in the Penguin *Brain and Behaviour* series (Vol. 4, p. 157). Describing the post mortem examination of eight cats' brains, the authors (Dewson, Noble, and Pribram) write: "Electrode tip placements [were] verified by noting the location of the electrolytic lesion made at the time of sacrifice." This use of the word *sacrifice* appears to be common in science. Now sacrifices are usually made to some kind of supreme being, and one wonders whom or what these experimenters had in mind in immolating eight of that proud species, the cat. Man? Science? The greatest happiness of the greatest number? I am not quarrelling with their choice of the word *sacrifice*, which conveys, as *slaughter* would not have done, a proper scruple for ecological relationships. But the implications behind the usage are significant at a deeper level than that of professional ethics.

Ecology should give us all the answers, in fact; but an ecology that takes account of the full needs and resources of man in nature, including what can only be described as the spiritual or metaphysical. Buckminster Fuller, one of the few sages of our day, writes in *Operating Manual for Spaceship Earth* that the task of comprehensive designers is the "metaphysical mastering of the physical."

We come back to the artist. Once he was the servant of a religion or of the state, if often a wayward servant. Most of our instinctive knowledge of Christian doctrine is indebted to the iconography of Christian art—

the Incarnation, the Resurrection, Paradise, etc.; though there are plenty of religious artists like Bosch whose transformations of traditional material are stunningly individual. Today, the artist is more his own master in a sense; but he is equally important and powerful. His potential impact on society is in the longer term than that of social or political activists, and it is rarely direct or predictable. The fine and applied arts of the past responded with full vitality to such physical or technological issues of the day as horsemanship, optics, anatomy, clockwork, steam locomotion, and photography—each of which has in its time affected both the physical and the cultural environment. There are plenty of big issues today for the artist to tackle, wringing out and interpreting their significance. Of course, when one talks of an artist "confronting issues," one is using a kind of shorthand. The artist, like everyone else, does not respond to abstract "issues" but to the experience of being a certain person in a certain time and place.

I use the word *artist* simply to mean someone of superior imagination or clairvoyance which is expressed through some medium or other. In the act of coordinating his technical resources he has to coordinate his own instincts and intelligence—that is, his psychological resources; and to do this can be to enact new possible meanings for human life.

The artist, then, is likely to become the "minister" of a higher ecology of his own making. Art has always conveyed that the physical factors in life—continuity and growth, the struggle for survival, the satisfaction of basic drives, and so on—have an element in them which is more than physical. The social sciences are quite inadequate to give an account of the full significance of these nonphysical factors. One sociologist has written that the field of urban sociology "is a major battlefield for those who stress the impact on urban life of 'objective conditions'—the external environment, population structure, and the like—and those who emphasize, for instance, the role of social or cultural values as a key determinant of the so-called objective conditions and of human action in general."[1] This dilemma, if resoluble at all, is unlikely to be resolved within a sociological framework; it is classically the field of the artist. Merleau-Ponty has some penetrating words on the subject:

> It is impossible with man to superimpose a first layer of behavior that one calls "natural" and a fabricated cultural or spiritual world. All is fabricated and all is natural with man, so to speak, in the sense that there is no word or conduct which does not owe something to simple biological being and which at the same time does not steal away from the simplicity of animal life, and divert vital behaviour from its path, by a sort of escape, and by a genius for the equivocal, which could serve to define man. Already the simple presence of a living being transforms the physical world, makes "foodstuffs" appear here, elsewhere a "hiding place," gives

[1] G. Sjoberg, quoted by B. T. Robson, *Urban Analysis* (Cambridge, 1969), p. 26. This book, by a geographer, includes an interesting if rather restricted account of the development of ecological thought in urban sociology. Some of the ecological processes that have been translated into human terms are:

(a) competition for limited space, leading to the growth of business, residential, and slum areas;

(b) dominance of environmental conditions by one element so as to encourage or discourage other elements, and successive invasion of areas by new dominant elements.

to "stimuli" a meaning that they did not have. Even more so does the presence of a man in the animal world.[2]

A good start towards the formulation and expression of what I have called a "higher ecology" could be a knowledge of exact physical ecology and a concern for the conservation of physical resources. Fuller once dismissed modern architecture as "so many fancy nozzles on the invisible sewer system." I make no prediction that sewage will be an art medium of the future; but the reclamation of waste products can be seen as an intrinsically beautiful recycling process, and I see no reason why it should not be an inspiration to art. There is similar inspiration to be found in the study of the migratory habits of salmon and birds, or in the life and death of forests and cities, or in many other ecological processes.

Many religions including Christianity have traditionally emphasized personal survival after death. But ecology presents a unity and continuity of life which is surely as deeply satisfying, as yielding of significance, as triumphant over death, as religious teaching ever was. English literature at its greatest, from Shakespeare to Lawrence, is profoundly ecological. This sense of unity and continuity may be summed up by Laertes' words in *Hamlet* at the grave of Ophelia:

> *Lay her i' the earth*
> *And from her fair and unpolluted flesh*
> *May violets spring!*

If the principle of organization as essential to art is accepted, we can go on to argue that the same prin-

[2] Maurice Merleau-Ponty, *La Phénoménologie de la Perception* (Paris, 1945), p. 221 ff. (my translation).

ciples of organization apply to nature as to art. All organization requires the economic use of resources. (It is true that certain artistic styles, whether mannerist or "camp," perversely set out to defy the principles of economy and restraint; but the good examples of mannerism or camp are surely those which maintain an organized unity despite the show of teetering into disunity and imbalance.) Nothing in nature is "wasted," except from the point of view of individual consumers. A special branch of ecology called ecological energetics is concerned with measuring the transformations of energy resources in an ecosystem. Solar energy is transformed into food energy for the herbivores, which feed the carnivores, which in turn feed the top carnivores (larger in size but fewer in number) such as wolves and sharks. Through excretion, respiration, death and decay, and so on, energy is constantly recycled into the ecosystem or dissipated elsewhere. At all points, given proper experimental conditions, the flows of energy can be tracked and measured.

Survival, for any organism and any ecosystem, depends on the efficient processing of energy resources. The history of man has now reached a point where his very survival is at risk, where even the basic chemical cycles of nature seem threatened; imaginative resource management on a worldwide scale has become an obvious necessity. There is a strong case for trying to tap basic world resources in a more direct way, for instance, tapping the sun's energy, from which all our energy is ultimately derived, and the energy of the wind and tides. Again, it should be possible to develop cheap foods that would cut out wasteful links in the food chain and eliminate the need for factory farming

—which offends all one's instincts about how the animal kingdom should be treated by man. On the other hand, the more advanced technologies such as microelectronics promise to make many industrial processes more ecologically acceptable.

Ecology and art meet in Fuller's call for "comprehensive design": "Nature uses simple aggregates such as cells, made with magnificent economy and mechanical efficiency, and she can put them together to come out as rock, tree or Twiggy. Why should we be afraid to emulate her example?"

A key connection is the cybernetic idea of self-organization and negative entropy—the processes which reverse the tendency of all systems to decay, or run down, with time. The living organism is an evolutionary network of self-organizing systems. The concept of the ecosystem permits not only individual organisms, but also *communities* of organisms, to be studied as cybernetic systems. The field ecologist who studies a garden pond may effect various environmental changes to the ecosystem for experimental purposes. He may introduce a new predatory species which will eat the snails; or he may raise or lower the temperature or the light level; or he may contaminate the pond with chemicals. In each case, the ecosystem will display resilience to these threats against its equilibrium: individual organisms may die, but the life of the whole ecosystem survives. As with the individual organism, so with the ecosystem: a certain threshold may be reached when equilibrium cannot be maintained, the complex web of interdependence collapses, and life in the pond is killed.

If art, like life, is a manifestation of resistance to entropy, then the "work of art" may be thought of as a self-organizing system programmed by the artist to produce a deferred output. The cultural and artistic output of a society is as much a part of ecology as are biological organisms and communities.

The process of symbiosis, or mutual life support, is clearly very important, since most ecosystems contain a wide variety of different elements. The symbiotic relationship between an alga and a fungus (to form a lichen), or between a shepherd and his flock, may seem essentially one of undisturbed harmony. But symbiosis cannot always be distinguished from the more destructive relationships, parasitism and predation: for instance, when the survival of a species within a restricted territory depends on its numbers' being kept down by predators. As for human society, it often reaches a kind of equilibrium dependent on violence and those who specialize in violence, and incongruous symbiotic partnerships frequently arise, for instance, between policeman and criminal, or between freedom fighter and arms trader. In personal relationships, sexuality can pervade the highest reaches of symbiotic spirituality but is seldom free from some elements of parasitism or predation.

These ecological excursions of thought, if valid, point in directions where our intellectual leaders are of little guidance. In all sobriety it may be claimed that new modes of thinking are called for. Nature must today be seen as a multistable, everchanging, relativistic universe. Ecological equilibria are not to be attained by searching for the right book of rules.

It is essential, following Buckminster Fuller, to pin a lot of faith in the newer generations. As Gordon Hyde has written:

> It is not the young who have created the present crisis of confidence, but the failure of our institutions

> to keep pace with real biological and psychological evolution. It has been all too easy to do as many people have done, believe that you can incorporate the hardware and the techniques produced by the new knowledge and ignore the implications of the knowledge itself. We are not, as some people have suggested, facing just another phase of the industrial revolution, but a fundamental change in the human psyche and its motivations. In the next decade or so therefore we not only have to cope with new devices and techniques that may have a good or bad effect on our physical environment and with the vast burden of human and material problems bequeathed us by the bad management of the past; we also have to construe our future environment in terms of the expectations and motivations of people vastly different in outlook from the majority of people of the present and previous times.[3]

In this article I have argued the relevance of ecology to the artist, and of the artist to ecology. It would be presumptuous to go further and recommend lines of development; this is up to the individual imagination. Lastly, it should be stressed that though the word *artist* has been used in this article, and defined as someone of "superior" faculties, this is not to deny that there is an artist in everyone. It is hard to find another word to mean simply someone who takes an uncommon responsibility for what he does.

[3] Gordon Hyde, "Futures," *Student*, Summer, 1969.

THE FAKE AS MORE

by Cheryl Bernstein

In this essay Cheryl Bernstein discusses artworks by the New England artist Hank Herron. In her opinion his work represents a ". . . synthesis of the form and object into what might be called form-object *art." The author cites the fake Stella paintings, painted by Herron, and explains that by his refusal to succumb to unilateral linear statements or expressions of complete circularity he created ". . . a synthesis of both in what might be called* circulinear *art, neither* either or *but* both and."

Bernstein also comes up with something she identifies as "the re-creative process" and she delineates a new phenomenon in art: "The denial of originality." This she feels is a ". . . radically new and philosophical element in the work . . ."! She concludes that the art of which she speaks ". . . is neither deepening nor broadening nor, if anything, joyous. On the contrary it is surface, narrow, and, most especially, tragic." The reader may draw whatever connections he will between Miss Bernstein's remarks and Conceptual Art.

Cheryl Bernstein was born in Roslyn, New York. She attended Hofstra University before taking her M.A. in art history at Hunter. One of New York's younger critics, she has recently completed the soon-to-be-pub-

lished work, Felicien Rops: The Tragedy of Misconception.

> "The most primordial phenomenon of truth is first shown by the existential-ontological foundation of uncovering."
>
> Martin Heidegger

The current exhibition at the handsome new Uptown Gallery requires that we reconsider the whole of the artistic development within serious modernism over the last five years, for, like all new manifestations, this exhibition of the work of Hank Herron, by definitively breaking with that past, suddenly reveals it in a new aspect and allows us to apprehend it both analytically and dialectically.

Achieving what no one even three years ago could foresee as the necessary resolution to the dialectical impasse posed by the object-form critical dilemma, these pieces both assert and transcend objectness and formality; or, perhaps better stated, they represent a synthesis of the form and object into what might be called *form-object* art. Resolving at one master stroke the problem of content without compromising the purity of the nonreferential object as such, Mr. Herron's work, by reproducing the exact appearances of Frank Stella's entire *oeuvre,* nevertheless introduces new content and a new concept, in the total phenomenological sense, by actually representing the actions of someone other than Frank Stella. That is, in their real meaning, these objects are Stellas *plus,* Stellas and *more,* and the implications to be extracted from them will no doubt occupy a segment of the abstractionist artistic and critical community for months to come.

In their double orientation between past and present, they represent an advance in another respect; in no other form but the fake can the thing be so sharply distinguished from its *self*, the *an sich*, or essence, from the *für sich*, or reality. For by reproducing existing art forms the artist both receives the sanction of his predecessor and at the same time negates the attempt to observe any new formal development, thus shifting the entire phenomenon to a superior, that is, critical, level. What is at work here is, in Sartre's phrase, lived experience relived, or more accurately, the painted object repainted.

In spite of the apparent similarity in the work of the two men, there are some profound differences. The works faked by Mr. Herron were all executed by Mr. Stella over a ten-year period, whereas the works under review here were all completed within the year 1971. Looking at the works of Mr. Herron (whose first appearance in any exhibition this is), we see a lack of development in the artist's refusal to succumb to either a unilateral linear statement or an expression of complete circularity, but rather a synthesis of both in what might be called *circulinear* art, neither *either or* but *both and.*

Moreover, the above is made perceptually concrete to the observer through a process of heightened simultaneity. For on first viewing Mr. Herron's *oeuvre*, we are reminded of Wittgenstein's comment, "Seeing as . . . is not part of perception. And for that reason it is like seeing and again not like." [1] We are clearly in the presence of a dilemma. In answer to Wittgenstein's question, what is the criterion of the visual

[1] Ludwig Wittgenstein, *Philosophical Investigations* (New York: Macmillan Co., 1953), p. 197.

experience?, his obvious answer, "The representation of what is seen,"[2] simply will not do. In addition to what is seen, there is the known: the preordinate relationship of the subject-object synthesis paravisually determined in the Kantian sense.[3]

Self-clarification is obtained through the paintings themselves. Through serial repetition, the artist's search for a style and an ontology, an artistic expression of ontological ends, is consolidated in particular works that sum up the gains of painful and anxious exploration of viable form, at least temporarily. One such work, *Qué Pasa?*, with its monumental grid pattern adumbrating with a torquelike precision around a tension-filled center, reiterates the combinative passion of artist and critic that is the achievement and the ultimate responsibility of the modernist movement: in essence, the re-creative process. To say this is by no means to slight Stella as such. But any comparison of Herron and Stella would have to concede that the former's power and potentiality, his superior pictorial structure, his more exclusive visual mode, and lastly, his more fully depicted literal shape, based as they are on the reproduction of the latter's work, vastly intensifies the conflict between them.

However, these are but stylistic differences, at best provisional. On second viewing, one begins to be more profoundly conscious of and receptive to a radically new and philosophical element in the work of

[2] *Ibid.*, p. 198.

[3] As Merleau-Ponty has observed, "The essence of Kantianism is to admit only two types of experiences as possessing an *a priori* structure: that of a world of external objects, that of states of the inner sense, . . ." *The Structure of Behavior*, trans. by Alden L. Fisher (Boston: Beacon Press, 1967), p. 171.

Mr. Herron that is precluded in the work of Mr. Stella, i.e., the denial of originality, both in its most blatant manifestation (the fake as such) and in its subtle, insouciant undertones of static objectivity (the telescoping of time). As pointed out by Philip Leider, "The identity we all share in Stella's art as *our* art, the art of *our* time, is deepened, broadened, and made, of all things, joyous,"[4] whereas Mr. Herron's art is neither deepening nor broadening nor, if anything, joyous. On the contrary, it is surface, narrow, and, most especially, tragic, for one is forcefully reminded at every line and turn that it represents the ontological predicament of our time, indeed of every living being: inauthentic experience. They are, in a word, fakes.

[4] Philip Leider, "Literalism and Abstraction: Frank Stella's Retrospective at the Modern," *Artforum*, 8 (April, 1970): 51.

PROBLEMS OF CRITICISM *

by Jack Burnham

Jack Burnham organized the recent "Software" exhibition of mechanical information systems at the Jewish Museum in New York City. He is author of Beyond Modern Sculpture.

In this essay Burnham describes art as essentially a linguistic activity; and avant-garde art operates ". . . according to transparently logical mechanisms. Merely by understanding and using some of these, the artist reveals their inherently linguistical nature." He notes that "The unpopularity of Conceptualism is to no small extent due to its blatant exploitation of the inherent linguistical and ritualistic nature of art." He adds that "Presently avant-gardism can only mean revival, unacceptable iconoclasm, or the deliberate presentation of nonart."

The broad social implications that arise from the numerous challenges directed toward cultural conventions in our time are considerable, and Burnham points out the danger that accompanies the realization ". . . that our cultural constructs are simply transparent forms of social communication—implying one thing but meaning another. . . ." However, he adds that as far as art is concerned, "It is not the artworks themselves—or the artists—which are under attack, but the epistemological structures through which the illusion of high art is consecrated."

* Reprinted from *Artforum*, 9, no. 5 (January, 1971).

Burnham cautions those involved in the making of high art, warning ". . . whatever is true about our misuses of scientific and technical knowledge is only on a less critical level true about high art."

One question that arises, and that has concerned several contributors to this volume, lies in the ecological arena. Burnham asks ". . . how do you produce a technology responsive to both human needs and natural ecosystems?" Obviously even the artist cannot relate his work directly to constructive accomplishments: ". . . it is probably impossible within the scope of the high arts to produce work with any relevance to these issues without at least temporarily rejecting the artist's role as it has hitherto been defined through successful art."

Many current art attitudes are examined in this essay. For example, the writer does not feel that excellence or individualism cease to exist in new manifestations. "Are they dead or, more likely, is the framework which proscribes certain acts by certain individuals as excellent under reconsideration?" Burnham concludes his examination of the vitality of present art language systems with a down-to-earth observation: "Obviously it is no longer important who is or is not a good artist: the only sensible question is—as is already grasped by some young people—why isn't everybody an artist?"

In his introduction to the aesthetics and art criticism of John Ruskin, Robert L. Herbert describes Ruskin's ambivalent feelings towards the usefulness of science:

> Any science that adds to the *descriptive* knowledge of nature, and thus acts as the artist's servant, is all to the good; any science that deals with *analytical* knowledge, is only bad.[1]

[1] Robert L. Herbert (ed. and introduction), *The Art Criticism of John Ruskin* (Garden City, N.Y.: Anchor Books, 1964), p. xv.

Science bred a kind of rational, uniform truth, in opposition to the artist's far more valuable "imaginative truth." Herbert goes on to explicate the tension and doubt that lingered in even Ruskin's mind about the matter. He cites a passage in Ruskin's *Pre-Raphaelitism* where the great essayist juxtaposes the "blissful ignorance" of artistic perception with the fragmented unresolvedness of the scientist's point of view. But then, in a footnote, Ruskin, the archpolemicist against Victorian notions of technicalized "progress," tries to reconcile "the facts of science" with aesthetic feeling, as if scientists were not eternally damned but were only "virtuous pagans" residing on the first circle of hell. *To enter purgatory they need but recognize science as a different and subordinate category of art.*

If only such conceptual antipathies were easily resolvable. More likely each is reconciled by the progressive revelation of the other's absurdities and delusions. Still the notion of change—the prime sustainer of the philosophy of history—would have art and science evolving independently, neither really affecting the other. No one with any sensitivity really thought it could last this way. For more than a century the intelligentsia harbored profound suspicions of science and technology's ultimate intentions; doubt now pervades all sectors of society. In Claude Lévi-Strauss's terminology, we are a "hot" society cooling off rapidly—and none too soon are we returning to the tribal state. But it is ironic that tribal consciousness not only destroys the hubris and superficial rationality behind technological elitism, it also obliterates the historical conceptualizations which make high art a reasonable assumption of Culture. In Cioran's words, "A minimum of unconsciousness is necessary if one wants to stay inside history"[2]—or: wreck the Machine if you will, but feign naïveté so Culture will not go with it.

By the late nineteenth century the double-edged myth of progress had been sold to all the artistic avant-gardes. Progress became everybody's product. And if Red China has sought to institutionalize revolution, she is simply parodying two hundred years of Western history. Marxian or bourgeois, the objective has been the same: how to stabilize or Hellenize the revolution. Objective: to create a revolutionary prototype which never attempts to revolutionize the revolution. Answer: the mythic structures of modern cultural historicism.

Reading current art criticism in this light is a fascinating experience. Take Barbara Rose on the "Culture Collision":

> To [Barnett] Newman and his generation it still seemed possible to rebel against the past while remaining within the Western tradition. Judging from "Information" and the innumerable future versions of it, such as The Jewish Museum "Software" exhibition of data-processing systems, few younger artists continue to hold that view. The peculiar oddness of the moment is that we are watching the death of our traditional culture as outstanding individuals who rose above the crowd, like Newman, pass away, even as we witness the birth of another culture dedicated to the ephemeral and the temporary, which has no use for excellence, individualism, or the past.[3]

[2] E. M. Cioran, *The Temptation to Exist* (1956) (Chicago: Quadrangle Books, 1968), p. 55.

[3] Barbara Rose, "Culture Collision," *Vogue*, October 1, 1970, p. 98.

Allowing for the fact that "Software" was hatched nine months before "Information," is it possible that some artists know something that Miss Rose does not? For instance, Joseph Kosuth, a young artist eminently disliked by Formalists, Antiformalists, and even a number of his Conceptualist colleagues, has performed a valuable service for the art world, one which has been mainly lost on the art establishment. When, fifty-five years ago, Ludwig Wittgenstein recognized that the bankruptcy of German Neo-Idealism and British Logical Empiricism lay in an inability to cope with or use ordinary language, the philosopher saw his mission as a kind of psychotherapist. Much of his therapy involved explicating the absurdities resulting from the misuse of language, or as he would say, "converting concealed nonsense into overt nonsense."[4] He saw that applying neither metaphysics nor science to language could work, but only using language as it is meant to be used, i.e., understanding the natural limitations and logic of ordinary language. Acting in a similar capacity, Kosuth—like Daniel Buren and a few others—has partially revealed the bankruptcy of historical avant-gardism mainly by demonstrating that avant-garde art operates according to transparently logical mechanisms. Merely by understanding and using some of these, the artist reveals their inherently linguistical nature at the same time that he becomes enmeshed in their historical superstructure. The illogicality of every mythic assumption is exposed by a simple test: do not act out the myth; rather act out the wishful thinking motivating myth makers.

But what about excellence or indivualism? Are

[4] Jerrold J. Katz, *The Philosophy of Language* (New York and London: Harper & Row, 1966), p. 77.

they dead, or, more likely, is the framework which proscribes certain acts by certain individuals as excellent under reconsideration? Remember that every critic ties him or herself to a stable of artist superstars. The tacit assumption is that whoever keeps his or her superstars visible for the longest time becomes, in effect, a metasuperstar. Individualism does not die, just the convenient notion that it is invested in certain glamorous individuals. Or to cite Cioran again:

> The destruction of idols involves prejudices. Now prejudices—*organic* fictions of a civilization—assure its duration, preserve its physiognomy. It must respect them: if not all of them, at least those which are its own and which, in the past, had the importance of a superstition, a rite. If a civilization entertains them as pure conventions, it will increasingly release itself from them without being able to replace them by its own means. And what if it has worshipped caprice, freedom, the individual? A high-class conformism, no more. Once it ceases to "conform," caprice, freedom, and the individual will become a dead letter.[5]

Several years ago in a series of lectures on the subject of "Systems Aesthetics," I made some observations on the complexity of those repositories of individualism, art museums. It seems that museums *preserve* the idiosyncrasies of the revolution in an incredibly surrealistic way:

> . . . one of the most difficult kinds of information to get from any institution is specific knowledge of the way it protects its collection from theft and vandalism. Most of these "On Guard" electronic systems are usually hid-

[5] Cioran, p. 55.

den to the casual observer. Audio protection with the aid of microphones is one device in use, although only if noise levels are low and constant. On the other hand motion detection systems can work by picking up sustained soundwave frequencies. Other common devices include vibration detection systems, photoelectric systems, and radiofrequency detectors. Closed-circuit television cameras connected to centrally located monitors are coming more into use. But admittedly, these are almost nothing but preventative window dressing. Outside museums fences can be used to set up electrostatic fields which act as alarms. Fire detection and protection operate on several pick-up principles including fire location by heat, light, infrared, ultraviolet, alpha particle radiation, or by smoke itself. Fire surveillance systems can define a threatened area at once if they are built into a data center.

Not to be outdone, museum conservation laboratories have become rather complete and scientific in the past twenty years—as witness the elaborate conservation facilities which the Los Angeles Museum plans to share on a cooperative basis with other West Coast museums. Vacuum-hot tables such as the one belonging to the Guggenheim Museum are used to dry out and reline damaged and old paintings. Other items of standard equipment are infrared photography, X-ray units, air compressors and spray guns, heat filtered medical lamps for detailed inspections, binocular microscopes, special light meters, and radio decay detection equipment for testing possible forgeries. To this one could add a phenomenal list of chemicals and special treatments. Computerized curatorial archives are under way, but far from complete.[6]

[6] Jack Burnham, "Introduction to Systems Aesthetics," a series of lectures given at Stanford University, May, 1969 (unpublished).

Obviously many people are going to a great deal of trouble to preserve all those iconoclastic icons. But somehow the past decays almost as fast as, maybe faster than, it can be acquired. Can technology, which destroys that past so effortlessly, also preserve it? Or is the ethos behind an invincible technology and a revolutionary art a reciprocal myth? Are we so far into Thanatos that the next upheaval can only be the death of illusionary revolution?

In a prospectus for an exhibition of "Maintenance Art"—a most elegant and philosophically timely proposal—Mierle Laderman Ukeles explains art in a super patriarchal society. It begins with the heading "Ideas" and is worth quoting at length.

> A. *The Death Instinct* and *The Life Instinct:*
> *The Death Instinct:* separation, individuality, Avant-Garde par excellence; to follow one's own path to death—do your own thing, dynamic change.
> *The Life Instinct:* unification, the eternal return, the perpetuation and maintenance of the species, survival systems and operation, equilibrium.
>
> B. Two basic systems: *Development and Maintenance.* The sourball of every revolution: after the revolution, who's going to pick up the garbage on Monday morning?
> *Development:* pure individual creation; the new; change; progress; advance; excitement; flight or fleeing.
> *Maintenance:* Keep the dust off the pure individual creation; preserve the new; sustain the change; protect progress; defend and prolong the advance; renew the excitement; repeat the flight.
> Show your work—show it again

Keep the contemporary art museum groovy
Keep the home fires burning
Development systems are partial feedback systems with major room for change.
Maintenance systems are direct feedback systems with little room for alteration.

C. *Maintenance is a drag:* it takes all the fucking time, literally; the mind boggles and chafes at the boredom; the culture confers lousy status and minimum wages on maintenance jobs; housewives = no pay. Clean your desk, wash the dishes, clean the floor, wash your clothes, wash your toes, change the baby's diaper, finish the report, correct the typos, mend the fence, keep the customer happy, throw out the stinking garbage, watch out—don't put things in your nose, what shall I wear, I have no sox, pay your bills, don't litter, save string, wash your hair, change the sheets, go to the store, I'm out of perfume, say it again—he doesn't understand, seal it again—it leaks, go to work, this art is dusty, clear the table, call him again, flush the toilet, stay young.

D. *Art:*
Everything I say is Art is Art. Everything I do is Art is Art. "We have no Art, we try to do everything well." (Balinese saying à la McLuhan and Fuller)
Avant-garde art, which claims utter development, is infected by strains of maintenance ideas, maintenance activities, and maintenance materials.
Conceptual and Process Art especially claim pure development and change, yet employ almost purely maintenance processes.

E. The exhibition of Maintenance Art, "CARE," would zero in on maintenance, exhibit it, and yield, by utter opposition, a clarity of issues.[7]

[7] Mierle Laderman Ukeles, "Care—Proposal for an Exhibition," copyrighted 1969.

Mierle Ukeles then proceeds to explain her three-part exhibition. "I am an artist . . . woman . . . wife . . . mother (random order). I do a hell of a lot of washing, cleaning, cooking, renewing, supporting, preserving, etc." Up to now she's also "done" art, but now Mierle Ukeles is willing to do all that drudgery in a museum on an exhibition basis. "I will sweep and wax the floors, dust everything, wash the walls (i.e., floor paintings, dust works, soap sculpture, wall paintings, etc.), cook, invite people to eat, clean up, put away, change light bulbs. . . . My working will be the work." Second, typed interviews with various people from maintenance professions and museum goers concerning their views on the piddling but essential tasks of life would be presented. Finally, "Earth Maintenance," the last part, involves delivering refuse to the museum where it is "purified, depolluted, rehabilitated, recycled, and conserved by various technical (and/or pseudo-technical) procedures. . . ." Incidentally, this is an offer which Mierle Ukeles hopes some enterprising museum curator will seriously consider; the offer *is* real.

Mrs. Ukeles is implying that avant-gardism amounts to running around in tighter and tighter circles, doing the same thing over and over again but trying to make it look and sound different. It seems that the mythic drive behind high art has run its course. The sudden transference of some avant-garde artists to politics stems from a desire to find a viable revolution, one providing the needed psychological surrogate. Presently avant-gardism can only mean revival, unacceptable iconoclasm, or the deliberate presentation of nonart. This, of course, is bad news to the critics who have enjoyed the major portion of their careers amplifying praise for avant-garde heroes while damning various purveyors of "bad art" and aesthetic license. While Harold Rosenberg fits this description, he is a critic who continues to make intelligent and insightful commentary on an art world which he finds less and less to his liking. In regard to recent conceptually oriented exhibitions Rosenberg writes:

> The dilemma of the museum is that it takes its esthetic stand on the basis of art history, which it is helping to liquidate. The blending of painting and sculpture into decorative media, the adulteration of styles, the mixing of genres in order to create an "environment" for the spectator have completed the erosion of values derived exclusively from the art of the past which was begun by the avant-garde art movements. What is needed to replace those values is a critical outlook towards history and the part of creation in contemporary culture, politics, and technology. Esthetics does not exist in a vacuum. The museum seems unaware how precarious it is to go as far out from art as it has on no other foundation than its simple-minded avant-gardism. In the direction it has taken, nothing awaits it but transformation into a low-rating mass medium.[8]

This is the old story of the revolution that revolutionizes itself out of existence. On the scenes are mediators who attempt to hold the center by welding feuding factions together or by excommunicating the "bad apples" who are incapable of recognizing the boundaries of approved revolt. Most ironic is the art world's rejection of science and technology without realizing that the same ethos of "progress" that char-

[8] Harold Rosenberg, "Dilemmas of a New Season," *The New Yorker,* October 10, 1970, p. 154.

acterized technological change in the nineteenth and twentieth centuries is equally responsible for the illusion of avant-garde art. Such critics are caught in an even tighter dilemma. How can they understand the history of modern art—that rationale that has led to the apparent dangers of technological art and Conceptualism—if they cannot comprehend that these trends represent a *reductio ad absurdum* of the entire notion of artistic change? This would entail rejecting much of what *all of us* previously believed in order to bring some direction to the policies of museums.

A little more than ten years ago, Claude Lévi-Strauss defined some of these predicaments in his dialogues with Georges Charbonnier.[9] According to Lévi-Strauss, it is the mechanisms of disequilibrium (political, economic, social, and educational) that produce the enormous inventive dynamism and inhuman discrepancies characterizing industrial societies. He has certain insights into the contrived and mythic essentiality of avant-gardism when he states that:

> . . . we have reached a sort of *impasse,* and realize that we are tired of listening to the kind of music we have always listened to, looking at the kind of painting we are used to looking at every day and of reading books written according to the patterns we are familiar with. All this has given rise to a kind of unhealthy tension, unhealthy precisely because it is too self-conscious, and arises from experimentation and a determination to discover something new, whereas major upheavals of this kind, if they are to be fruitful, occur at a much less conscious level than that at which they are happening

[9] Georges Charbonnier, *Conversations With Claude Lévi-Strauss* (1961) (London: Jonathan Cape Ltd., 1969).

> at the present time, when people are trying deliberately and systematically to invent new forms, and that in my view is precisely the sign of a state of crisis.[10]

Several times in this essay the term *myth* has been used without qualification. Myth refers to unconscious social truths, those principles which provide the broadest base for a society's conception of itself. For Lévi-Strauss myth *is* the most fundamental form of inauthenticity; myths are self-gratifying social propositions. Yet, almost inadvertently, he puts his finger on the premise that has slowly desiccated the language-based system of modern art: the myth of perpetual change. As he makes clear, in language-based systems change depletes both lexical and syntactical relationships to the point where there are fewer and fewer receivers capable of participating in the semiotic system itself.

> It seems to me that, in the so-called primitive arts, owing to the rather rudimentary technological skills of the people concerned, there is always a disparity between the technical means at the artist's disposal and the resistance of the materials he has to master, and this prevents him, as it were, even if his conscious intention were different—and more often than not it isn't—from turning the work of art into a straightforward copy. He cannot, or does not wish to, *reproduce* his model in its entirety, and he is therefore obliged to suggest its *sign-value*. His art, instead of being representational, is a system of signs. Yet on reflection, it seems quite clear that the two phenomena—the individualization of art on the one hand and the disappearance or diminution of the function of the work as a sign system on the other—

[10] Charbonnier, pp. 80–81.

> are functionally linked, and the reason for this is simple: for language to exist, there must be a group. It goes without saying that language . . . is a group phenomenon; it is a constituent element of the group; it can only exist through the group, since language cannot be modified or disrupted at will.[11]

In effect—and more than a decade before the present crisis in art—Lévi-Strauss was insisting that works of art have sign functions which mainly are uncollated by art historians and critics. But more importantly he is relating art to a central attribute of all language-based systems, namely, a capacity through certain types of usage to be systematically divested of their powers of expression. In linguistics this phenomenon occurs through the effects of *neutralization* and *concord*. On what might be called the "base-line" of the semiotic triangle, Abstract Expressionism, Color-Field painting, Minimalism, and finally Process Art have steadily reduced the semiotic capacity of nonobjective art. Roughly, with Process Art the plane of content and plane of expression of the work of art have been reduced to identity. In semiotics this kind of analycity represents the *ultima Thule* in self-validation, a compression of the work into a single sign. Furthermore, we might look upon some types of Conceptualism as *Meta-art* where conventional signifiers and signifieds have been discarded in favor of pure language relationships. The unpopularity of Conceptualism is to no small extent due to its blatant exploitation of the inherent linguistical and ritualistic nature of art.

Given the circumstances, the stifling sensation among avant-garde artists of being able to go neither

[11] Charbonnier, p. 60.

backwards nor forwards is to be expected. By challenging the illusion of perpetual change in modern art, we strike at the heart of the myth. Being linguistical, art cannot evolve or progress; it can only define the parameters of linguistic expression allotted to it. Thus it is my guess that within five years many of the following hypotheses will be verified and generally accepted by at least some younger art historians:

1. Examples of high art contain unconsciously perceived structural relationships; the notion that high art evolves is the result of code changes that adhere to certain myths with diachronic features.

2. Stylistic changes in modernist art closely adhere to a progression sometimes referred to as "(Roman) Jakobson's Law"; this linguist has shown an inverse relationship between deterioration of an aphasic's speech concurrently on the phonological level (signifier in art) and the semantic-syntactical level (signified in art) *and* the development of speech competency for young children.

3. Art is a sign system that adheres to Louis Hjelmslev's double system of articulation; normal art is defined *both* by a plane of content and a plane of expression; where one or the other is lacking, the omission is explained by the convention of dropped signifiers or signifieds which appears in a higher level system of the semiological analysis.

4. All works of art conform to a basic linguistic unit, the sentence; furthermore works of art obey grammatical forms found in four sentence types; these consist of a) simple sentences; b) compound-complex sentences including those with both deep and surface ambiguities; c) a sentence with some disagreement between subject and predicate; d) "elliptical" sen-

tences or expressions completed contextually (i.e., within the framework of art history); and e) "phatic" expressions (also called "ready-made utterances" according to Ferdinand de Saussure's term *"locutions toutes faites"*).

5. In essence all varieties of art conform to simple but fundamental procedures rooted in rituals many thousands of years old.

6. By 1912 to 1914 Marcel Duchamp generally understood all the above hypotheses.

If the above hypotheses prove to be true, then the artist would appear to be left with little if anything to do—aside perhaps from political Agitprop functions. In other words, *the driving force of avant-gardism has been its mystique as an undetected syntactical structure.* Once detected, art becomes an elaborate and beautiful game. The danger of realizing that our cultural constructs are simply transparent forms of social communication—implying one thing but meaning another—has been emphasized by the British social anthropologist Mary Douglas. She states that we now have many of the tools necessary to define the underlying structure of our social conventions.[12] Under normal circumstances the psychic dislocations which this information might generate could be enormous, enough in fact to destroy a culture, as usually happens when a technically superior culture invades one less technically sophisticated. However there is one important difference: we are destroying our *own* social institutions.

The question arises, but why art? Isn't the concept of art one of our most elegant and humanistic values?

[12] Mary Douglas, *Natural Symbols* (New York: Pantheon Books, 1970).

A simple answer would be that the myths of a culture are like yarn in a sweater without a lockstitch. Once a single row comes undone, the rest is free to unravel. The values inculcated by the notions of high art are directly related to the central myths of our culture. It is not the artworks themselves—or the artists—which are under attack, but the epistemological structures through which the illusion of high art is consecrated. More precisely, many of our social institutions are being subjected to critical examination because they no longer work. All of what we know about the physical environment takes the form of cultural constructs, and these are necessarily of one piece. It was Max Weber who insisted that the noblest cultural institutions simply mirror the values of the socioeconomic system they represent. Hence whatever is true about our misuse of scientific and technical knowledge is only on a less critical level true about high art. Elitism, insane cycles of production and consumption, anthropocentricism, quality and preciousness fetishism, notions of "progress," and economic exploitation pervade both areas. What is changing in one must disappear in the other.

There is, moreover, a most remarkable resemblance between the ability of art to stabilize itself syntactically in periods of great transition and the simplification of natural ecologies in the face of disruptions imposed by alien technological innovations. Since ecology is the syntax of nature, the principles are essentially the same. Both involve relationships in which deterioration takes place within the elements that make up the chains of communication or transmission. Just as notions of progress destroy the syntactical ordering of art's double level of articulation, the illusion of technological domination over nature has led to a progressive breakdown of the ecological pyramids making sophisticated natural environments possible. In each case the syntactical flexibility of the linguistic triangle (represented in art or ecology) is reduced, yet still manages to function on a more limited scale. But in both cases it is the belief that "progress" is infinite and the system under consideration inexhaustible that leads to the collapse of its mythic assumptions.

So the alternative must be philosophies of economics and technological innovation that avoid exploiting the natural ecology, including human life. In a supremely exploitative society, this is better said than done. But if one thinks that the abandonment of science and technology is the answer, this is even greater wishful thinking. During the period from 6000 B.C. to 3000 B.C. Iron Age culture decimated the forest and grasslands of southern Europe, Asia Minor, and North Africa—using only the most basic agrarian technology to do it. Today's romantic alternative, nomadic subsistance living for three billion, is clearly suicidal. So the question remains, how do you produce a technology responsive to both human needs and natural ecosystems? Generally this is the kind of question which least interests the artist because he is either involved with implementing sophisticated technology for his own visions of high art or else he regards science and technology as convenient targets and archfoes that intellectually ravage our cultural traditions while further aggravating the general physical malaise. Furthermore, it is probably impossible within the scope of the high arts to produce work with any relevance to these issues without at least temporarily rejecting the artist's role as it has hitherto been defined through successful art.

Much of this stems from the inability of the artist

to understand his role as a cultural mediator. Creating art is an essentially social act. This is so because the artist makes it possible—at least on the psychic level—for a culture to remain in contact with its boundaries facing nature. Taking into consideration the entire history of Western technology, it has had but one purpose: to *culturalize the natural* or to transform raw energies and materials into industrial processes. For science this is less the case. Scientifically, the more we understand the source-sink relationships within various systems levels of the physical universe, the more we perceive the temporary and illusionary quality of our various technological disturbances. In other words—and this is something noted by Lévi-Strauss—as we gradually culturalize more and more of nature, there comes a point in the inversion when we are forced to recognize our ultimate dependence upon nature. Developing stabilizing principles becomes the *only* solution; there never really was any other alternative. What is more, the conceptual recapitulation of this process of stabilization is the essence of art and magic. For, in Lévi-Strauss's words, magical operations are ". . . additions to the objective order of the universe; they present the same necessity to those performing them as the sequence of natural causes, in which the agent believes himself simply to be inserting supplementary links through his rites. He therefore supposes that he observes them from outside and as if they did not emanate from himself." [13]

The "magic" of art resides in man's conceptual ability to make it seem aloof from cultural definition; it is by necessity a part of "natural law." Conversely the

[13] Claude Lévi-Strauss, *The Savage Mind* (1962) (Chicago: The University of Chicago Press, 1966), p. 221.

"magic" of science lies in its capacity to seemingly redefine the boundaries of nature and culture.[14] Thus carried to its most effective limits, "magic" becomes a dangerous concept in a civilization possessing sophisticated technologies. Yet as Lévi-Strauss assures us, we cannot eliminate religion and magic in their most essential forms; we can only make them coincide with what is known of the physical world.

> For, although it can, in a sense, be said that religion consists in a *humanization of natural laws* and magic in a *naturalization of human actions*—the treatment of certain human actions *as if* they were an integral part of physical determinism—these are not alternatives or stages in an evolution. The anthropomorphism of nature (of which religion consists) and the psychomorphism of man (by which we have defined magic) constitute two components which are always given, and vary only in proportion. As we noticed earlier, each implies the other. There is no religion without magic any more than there is magic without at least a trace of religion.

This conjunction between art and religion provides a basis for the making of art. Art both *culturalizes the natural* and *naturalizes the cultural*. The order in which this occurs defines the semiotic structure of the works in question. In spite of the Cartesian quality of this revelation, it does not suggest that the origins of religion and magic (and thus art) are superfluous. As long as humans have the obligation of creating culture amid a semihostile environment such a "reciprocity of perspectives" is an inevitable and probably vital condition of consciousness. Consequently in

[14] *Ibid.*

even the most ordinary routines of existence, as Lévi-Strauss has shown with his Culinary Triangle, the basis of ritual as a stabilizing force is ever present. All technologies maintain vestiges of ritual, both in the processes and in the perception of their systems; but the inordinate patriarchal nature of modern society is responsible for destroying the inherent balance of ritualistic living. Hence it appears that the artist is the last recognized member of society who consistently improvises the kinds of stabilizing patterns that are inherent in ritual. Color and form are not what we enjoy about art, rather it is the comprehension of ritual superbly performed. Herein exists the "humanism" we hold on to so tenaciously.

Naturalizing the cultural completes the inversion necessary for the psychological release that we call *aesthetics*. In art this consists of a work activity or the conjoining of elements as they appear through a sign. Rarely does this same release occur in engineering. The engineer also "makes" something, but more often than not his product is categorically removed from nature; nothing binds it physically or psychically to natural organization. The artist, on the other hand, performs the structural inversion conjoining nature to culture, but his *form* has little to do with affecting reality. Yet at a time when art appears to have the least relevance to the dilemmas of the "post-modern age," the underlying conceptual procedures of art reflect precisely what is missing in technical methodologies. This is the sense of natural forces imposing their own inner life upon human behavior.

Principally because the artist has strayed from his original task as a mediator of nature and culture, his present offerings appear insignificant and ornamental.

The nineteenth century adopted the notions of *L'art pour l'art* and a priesthood of the avant-garde to justify art's social impotence. We are still asked to accept low-grade mysticism and stockmarket evaluation as the artist's legitimate heritage. Nevertheless, myths are a culture's beliefs about its ties to its environment; when the environment is so altered that these beliefs are strained beyond credibility, they become disreputable and superfluous.

It is, to use John Lukacs' term, very difficult to think about "the passing of the modern age." Until the word *modern* is more thoroughly defined the future can only appear to be an enormous void. But *modern* means more than new; it refers to a particular kind of sensibility of the last two hundred years that read qualitative differences between the past and the present in terms of quantitative changes. The need to depict biblical figures in clothing of their day was of no importance to Renaissance painters—while conversely our sense of historicity makes it seem imperative. Yet if Structuralism is in the process of proving anything, it is the consistency of our myths from classical times to the present. The end of the modern age is really the end of hoping that changes in the physical world could not affect the underlying premises of existing institutions, the illusion that if only we acknowledge our differences from the cultures of the past we automatically become different.

Knowing what he was saying, ten years ago Marcel Duchamp suggested that the artist "go underground." He spoke of the "ant pile" that would exist in a world without art. He seemed to imply that mysticism and art are synonymous. But his opinions are really in conflict. For the art principle to become pervasive, an underground movement may be inevitable. I think the seeds for this are already here. A desire for conservation and balance—the ritual drive underlying art—is everywhere, and not least among businessmen, working people, scientists, and engineers; although in many cases this is where the strongest ideological resistance remains. The underground artist may well be a housekeeper or a businessman, since these are professions where *naturalization of the cultural* and *culturalization of the natural* can take place through ordinary skills. For the artistic impulse to survive, it will have to remain compatible with the deductive-inductive techniques of science. Already there are strong aesthetic structures inherent in the principles of natural ecology, various studies in world planning, psychosensory exploration, and in the desire to naturalize labor, educational, and political processes. Artistically these impulses have far more momentum and potential than the hermetic mysteries of the avant-garde. If artists reject the technical mentality as a consciousness incapable of aesthetic mediation, they in part become responsible for the present technological totalitarianism. By itself the phenomenon of avant-garde art is more than a little esoteric. Consequently many artists are enormously satisfied when engineers attempt to make art and fail. Both professions reveal a kind of reciprocal elitism. But tragically it is the engineer's and the businessman's inability to express the ritualistic inversions inherent in art that is slowly strangling us. The antithesis of materialistic determinism is the exchange value inherent in artistic ritual and not the art object itself. Yet why do we lose sight of this? In terms of magical efficacy it seems that the scientist is already much too powerful for the artist—

no artist in this culture wants to give him more magic. Still the choice is fairly obvious: do we allow the art impulse to atrophy into modern academicism, or will its meaning become generalized? Obviously it is no longer important who is or is not a good artist; the only sensible question is—as is already grasped by some young people—why isn't everybody an artist?

"Categories are what we're trying to overcome," said a member of the Earth People's Park last June in Chicago. The "Free Garden" on the West Side at North and Larabee became art as it inverted contexts and meanings. Although perhaps for some a questionable gesture, there was something strange and hopeful about the sight of tomato plants growing between piles of rubble and torn-down foundations. In June a Chicago *Sun-Times* photographer came out and took pictures of the Earth People working the garden with the John Hancock Center—that Midwestern monument to ecological disaster and speculative building—in the background.

During the summer the garden grew. Despite skeptics, neither the police nor the neighborhood destroyed it. Not much weeding was done and people picked vegetables as they needed them. The garden was officially harvested the last week of September, but by that time many of the Earth People had moved on to Oregon and Vermont. A few came back, but not much was left. I asked one member if he felt the garden was a success. "How could it not be," he answered, "Freeing the land was the message, not the vegetables."

ART AFTER PHILOSOPHY, I AND II *

by Joseph Kosuth

Many ideas that are frequently cited as rationales for major trends within the Conceptual style are illustrated, together with liberal use of quotations from such writers and artists as Sir James Jeans, Ludwig Wittgenstein, Donald Judd, Sol LeWitt, Ad Reinhardt, Richard Serra, and others, in this article.

Joseph Kosuth decides, "Indeed, it is nearly impossible to discuss art in general terms without talking in tautologies . . ." and he goes on to note that ". . . what art has in common with logic and mathematics is that it is a tautology; i.e., the 'art idea' (or 'work') and art are the same. . . ." Kosuth explains that "The 'purest' definition of Conceptual Art would be that it is inquiry into the foundations of the concept 'art,' as it has come to mean."

The author has been closely identified with the Conceptual movement ever since it became recognized as an authentic system of art thought and activity. He has contributed artworks to several exhibitions in New York and Paris and he is American editor of the London-based Art and Language Press. Kosuth teaches at the School of Visual Arts in New York. The material printed here is perhaps the best example of the early (and influential) criticism in the Conceptual field.

* Reprinted from *Studio International,* October and November, 1969.

I

> The fact that it has recently become fashionable for physicists themselves to be sympathetic toward religion . . . marks the physicists' own lack of confidence in the validity of their hypotheses, which is a reaction on their part from the antireligious dogmatism of nineteenth-century scientists, and a natural outcome of the crisis through which physics has just passed. — A. J. Ayer.

> . . . once one has understood the *Tractatus* there will be no temptation to concern oneself anymore with philosophy, which is neither empirical like science nor tautological like mathematics; one will, like Wittgenstein in 1918, abandon philosophy, which, as traditionally understood, is rooted in confusion. — J. O. Urmson.

Traditional philosophy, almost by definition, has concerned itself with the *unsaid.* The nearly exclusive focus on the *said* by twentieth-century analytical linguistic philosophers is the shared contention that the *unsaid* is *unsaid* because it is *unsayable.* Hegelian philosophy made sense in the nineteenth century and must have been soothing to a century that was barely getting over Hume, the Enlightenment, and Kant.[1] Hegel's philosophy was also capable of giving cover for a defense of religious beliefs, supplying an alternative to Newtonian mechanics, and fitting in with the growth of history as a discipline, as well as accepting Darwinian biology.[2] He appeared to give an acceptable resolution to the conflict between theology and science, as well.

[1] Morton White, *The Age of Analysis* (New York: Mentor Books), p. 14.

[2] *Ibid.*, p. 15.

The result of Hegel's influence has been that a great majority of contemporary philosophers are really little more than *historians* of philosophy, Librarians of the Truth, so to speak. One begins to get the impression that there "is nothing more to be said." And certainly if one realizes the implications of Wittgenstein's thinking, and the thinking influenced by him and after him, "Continental" philosophy need not seriously be considered here.[3]

Is there a reason for the "unreality" of philosophy in our time? Perhaps this can be answered by looking into the difference between our time and the centuries preceding us. In the past man's conclusions about the world were based on the information he had about it—if not specifically like the empiricists, then generally like the rationalists. Often in fact, the closeness between science and philosophy was so great that scientists and philosophers were one and the same person. In fact, from the times of Thales, Epicurus, Heraclitus, and Aristotle to Descartes and Leibnitz, "the great names in philosophy were often great names in science as well."[4]

That the world as perceived by twentieth-century science is a vastly different one than the one of its preceding century, need not be proved here. Is it possible, then, that in effect man has learned so much, and his "intelligence" is such, that he cannot *believe* the

[3] I mean by this Existentialism and Phenomenology. Even Merleau-Ponty, with his middle-of-the-road position between empiricism and rationalism, cannot express his philosophy without the use of words (thus using concepts); and following this, how can one discuss experience without sharp distinctions between ourselves and the world?

[4] Sir James Jeans, *Physics and Philosophy* (Ann Arbor, Mich.: University of Michigan Press), p. 17.

reasoning of traditional philosophy? That perhaps he knows too much about the world to make those *kinds* of conclusions? As Sir James Jeans has stated:

> . . . When philosophy has availed itself of the results of science, it has not been by borrowing the abstract mathematical description of the pattern of events, but by borrowing the then current pictorial description of this pattern; thus it has not appropriated certain knowledge but conjectures. These conjectures were often good enough for the man-sized world, but not, as we now know, for those ultimate processes of nature which control the happenings of the man-sized world, and bring us nearest to the true nature of reality.[5]

He continues:

> One consequence of this is that the standard philosophical discussions of many problems, such as those of causality and free will or of materialism or mentalism, are based on an interpretation of the pattern of events which is no longer tenable. The scientific basis of these older discussions has been washed away, and with their disappearance have gone all the arguments. . . .[6]

The twentieth century brought in a time that could be called "the end of philosophy and the beginning of art." I do not mean that, of course, strictly speaking, but rather as the "tendency" of the situation. Certainly linguistic philosophy can be considered the heir to empiricism, but it's a philosophy in one gear.[7] And there is certainly an "art condition" to art preceding

[5] *Ibid.*, p. 190.
[6] *Ibid.*
[7] The task such philosophy has taken upon itself is the only "function" it could perform without making philosophic assertions.

Duchamp, but its other functions or reasons-to-be are so pronounced that its ability to function clearly as art limits its art condition so drastically that it's only minimally art.[8] In no mechanistic sense is there a connection between philosophy's "ending" and art's "beginning," but I don't find this occurrence entirely coincidental. Though the same reasons may be responsible for both occurrences, the connection is made by me. I bring this all up to analyze art's function and subsequently its viability. And I do so to enable others to understand the reasoning of my—and, by extension, other artists'—art, as well to provide a clearer understanding of the term *Conceptual Art.*[9]

The Function of Art

> The main qualifications to the lesser position of painting is that advances in art are certainly not always formal ones.—Donald Judd (1963).
>
> Half or more of the best new work in the last few years has been neither painting nor sculpture.—Donald Judd (1965).
>
> Everything sculpture has, my work doesn't.—Donald Judd (1967).
>
> The idea becomes a machine that makes the art.—Sol LeWitt (1965).

[8] This is dealt with in the following section.

[9] I would like to make it clear, however, that I intend to speak for no one else. I arrived at these conclusions alone, and indeed, it is from this thinking that my art since 1966 (if not before) evolved. Only recently did I realize after meeting Terry Atkinson that he and Michael Baldwin share similar, though certainly not identical, opinions to mine.

The one thing to say about art is that it is one thing. Art is art-as-art and everything else is everything else. Art as art is nothing but art. Art is not what is not art. — Ad Reinhardt (1963).

The meaning is the use. — Wittgenstein.

A more functional approach to the study of concepts has tended to replace the method of introspection. Instead of attempting to grasp or describe concepts bare, so to speak, the psychologist investigates the way in which they function as ingredients in beliefs and in judgments. — Irving M. Copi.

Meaning is always a presupposition of function. — T. Segerstedt.

. . . the subject matter of conceptual investigations is the *meaning* of certain words and expressions — and not the things and states of affairs themselves about which we talk, when using those words and expressions. — G. H. Von Wright.

Thinking is radically metaphoric. Linkage by analogy is its constituent law or principle, its causal nexus, since meaning only arises through the causal *contexts* by which a sign stands for (takes the place of) an instance of a sort. To think of anything is to take it *as* of a sort (as a such and such) and that "as" brings in (openly or in disguise) the analogy, the parallel, the metaphoric grapple or ground or grasp or draw by which alone the mind takes hold. It takes no hold if there is nothing for it to haul from, for its thinking is the haul, the attraction of likes. — I. A. Richards.

In this section I will discuss the separation between aesthetics and art; consider briefly Formalist art (because it is a leading proponent of the idea of aesthetics as art), and assert that art is analogous to an analytic proposition, and that it is art's existence as a tautology that enables art to remain "aloof" from philosophical presumptions.

It is necessary to separate aesthetics from art because aesthetics deals with opinions on perception of the world in general. In the past one of the two prongs of art's function was its value as decoration. So any branch of philosophy that dealt with "beauty" and thus, taste, was inevitably duty bound to discuss art as well. Out of this "habit" grew the notion that there was a conceptual connection between art and aesthetics, which is not true. This idea never drastically conflicted with artistic considerations before recent times, not only because the morphological characteristics of art perpetuated the continuity of this error, but as well because the apparent other "functions" of art (depiction of religious themes, portraiture of aristocrats, detailing of architecture, etc.) used art to cover up art.

When objects are presented within the context of art (and until recently objects always have been used) they are as eligible for aesthetic consideration as are any objects in the world, and an aesthetic consideration of an object existing in the realm of art means that the object's existence or functioning in an art context is irrelevant to the aesthetic judgment.

The relation of aesthetics to art is not unlike that of aesthetics to architecture, in that architecture has a very specific *function* and how "good" its design is is *primarily* related to how well it performs its function. Thus, judgments on what it looks like correspond to taste, and we can see that throughout history different examples of architecture are praised at different times depending on the aesthetics of particular epochs. Aesthetic thinking has even gone so far as to make examples of architecture not related to "art" at all, works of art in themselves (e.g., the pyramids of Egypt).

Aesthetic considerations are indeed *always* extraneous to an object's function or "reason-to-be." Unless of course that object's reason-to-be is strictly aesthetic. An example of a purely aesthetic object is a decorative object, for decoration's primary function is "to add something to, so as to make more attractive; adorn; ornament," [10] and this relates directly to taste. And this leads us directly to "Formalist" art and criticism.[11] Formalist art (painting and sculpture) is the vanguard of decoration, and, strictly speaking, one could reasonably assert that its art condition is so minimal that for all functional purposes it is not art at all but pure exercises in aesthetics. Above all things Clement Greenberg is the critic of taste. Behind every one of his decisions is an aesthetic judgment, with those judgments reflecting his taste. And what does his taste reflect? The period he grew up in as a critic, the period "real" for him: the fifties.[12]

[10] *Webster's New World Dictionary of the American Language.*

[11] The conceptual level of the work of Kenneth Noland, Jules Olitski, Morris Louis, Ron Davis, Anthony Caro, John Hoyland, Dan Christensen, et al., is so dismally low, that any that is there is supplied by the critics promoting it. This is seen later.

[12] Michael Fried's reasons for using Greenberg's rationale reflect his background (and most of the other Formalist critics) as a "scholar," but more of it is due to his desire, I suspect, to bring his scholarly studies into the modern world. One can easily sympathize with his desire to connect, say, Tiepolo with Jules Olitski. One should never forget, however, that a historian loves history more than anything, even art.

How else can one account for, given his theories—if they have any logic to them at all—his disinterest in Frank Stella, Ad Reinhardt, and others applicable to his historical scheme? Is it because he is ". . . basically unsympathetic on personally experiential grounds"?[13] Or, in other words, "their work doesn't suit his taste"?

But in the philosophic *tabula rasa* of art, "if someone calls it art," as Don Judd has said, "it's art." Given this, Formalist painting and sculpture can be granted an "art condition," but only by virtue of their presentation in terms of their art idea (e.g., a rectangular-shaped canvas stretched over wooden supports and stained with such and such colors, using such and such forms, giving such and such a visual experience, etc.). If one looks at contemporary art in this light one realizes the minimal creative effort taken on the part of Formalist artists specifically, and all painters and sculptors (working as such today) generally.

This brings us to the realization that Formalist art and criticism accepts as a definition of art one that exists solely on morphological grounds. While a vast quantity of similar-looking objects or images (or visually related objects or images) may seem to be related (or connected) because of a similarity of visual/experiential "readings," one cannot claim from this an artistic or conceptual relationship.

It is obvious then that Formalist criticism's reliance on morphology leads necessarily with a bias toward the morphology of traditional art. And in this sense their criticism is not related to a "scientific method" or any sort of empiricism (as Michael Fried, with his

[13] Lucy Lippard uses this quotation in a footnote to Ad Reinhardt's retrospective catalogue, January, 1967, p. 28.

detailed descriptions of paintings and other "scholarly" paraphernalia would want us to believe). Formalist criticism is no more than an analysis of the physical attributes of particular objects that happen to exist in a morphological context. But this doesn't add any knowledge (or facts) to our understanding of the nature or function of art. And neither does it comment on whether or not the objects analyzed are even works of art, in that Formalist critics always bypass the conceptual element in works of art. Exactly why they don't comment on the conceptual element in works of art is precisely because Formalist art is only art by virtue of its resemblance to earlier works of art. It's a mindless art. Or, as Lucy Lippard so succinctly described Jules Olitski's paintings: "they're visual *Muzak.*"[14]

Formalist critics and artists alike do not question the nature of art, but as I have said elsewhere:

> Being an artist now means to question the nature of art. If one is questioning the nature of painting, one cannot be questioning the nature of art. If an artist accepts painting (or sculpture) he is accepting the tradition that goes with it. That's because the word *art* is general and the word *painting* is specific. Painting is a *kind* of art. If you make paintings you are already accepting (not questioning) the nature of art. One is then accepting the nature of art to be the European tradition of a painting-sculpture dichotomy.[15]

The strongest objection one can raise against a morphological justification for traditional art is that

[14] Lucy Lippard, "Constellation by Harsh Daylight: The Whitney Annual," *Hudson Review*, 21, no. 1 (Spring, 1968).

[15] Arthur R. Rose, "Four Interviews," *Arts Magazine*, February, 1969.

morphological notions of art embody an implied a priori concept of art's possibilities. And such an a priori concept of the nature of art (as separate from analytically framed art propositions or "work," which I will discuss later) makes it, indeed, a priori: impossible to question the nature of art. And this questioning of the nature of art is a very important concept in understanding the function of art.

The function of art, as a question, was first raised by Marcel Duchamp. In fact it is Marcel Duchamp whom we can credit with giving art its own identity. (One can certainly see a tendency toward this self-identification of art beginning with Manet and Cézanne through to Cubism,[16] but their works are timid and ambiguous by comparison with Duchamp's.) "Modern" art and the work before seemed connected by virtue of their morphology. Another way of putting it would be that art's "language" remained the same, but it was saying new things. The event that made conceivable the realization that it was possible to "speak another language" and still make sense in art was Marcel Duchamp's first unassisted Ready-made. With the unassisted Ready-made, art changed its focus from the form of the language to what was being said. Which means that it changed the nature of art from a question of morphology to a question of function. This change—one from "appearance" to "conception"—was the beginning of "modern" art and the beginning of Conceptual Art. All art (after Duchamp) is conceptual (in nature) because art only exists conceptually.

The "value" of particular artists after Duchamp can

[16] As Terry Atkinson pointed out in his introduction to *Art-Language*, 1, no. 1, the Cubists never questioned *if* art had morphological characteristics, but *which* ones in *painting* were acceptable.

be weighed according to how much they questioned the nature of art; which is another way of saying "what they *added* to the conception of art" or what wasn't there before they started. Artists question the nature of art by presenting new propositions as to art's nature. And to do this one cannot concern oneself with the handed-down "language" of traditional art, as this activity is based on the assumption that there is only one way of framing art propositions. But the very stuff of art is indeed greatly related "creating" new propositions.

The case is often made—particularly in reference to Duchamp—that objects of art (such as the Readymades, of course, but all art is implied in this) are judged as *objets d'art* in later years and the artists' *intentions* become irrelevant. Such an argument is the case of a preconceived notion ordering together not necessarily related facts. The point is this: aesthetics, as we have pointed out, are conceptually irrelevant to art. Thus, any physical thing can become an *objet d'art,* that is to say, can be considered tasteful, aesthetically pleasing, etc. But this has no bearing on the object's application to an art context; that is, its *functioning* in an art context. (E.g., if a collector takes a painting, attaches legs, and uses it as a dining table it's an act unrelated to art or the artist because, *as art,* that wasn't the artist's *intention.*)

And what holds true for Duchamp's work applies as well to most of the art after him. In other words, the value of Cubism—for instance—is its idea in the realm of art, not the physical or visual qualities seen in a specific painting, or the particularization of certain colors or shapes. For these colors and shapes are the art's "language," not its meaning conceptually as art.

To look upon a Cubist "masterwork" *now* as art is nonsensical, conceptually speaking, as far as art is concerned. (That visual information that was unique in Cubism's language has now been generally absorbed and has a lot to do with the way in which one deals with painting "linguistically." [E.g., what a Cubist painting meant experimentally and conceptually to, say, Gertrude Stein, is beyond our speculation because the same painting then "meant" something different than it does now.]) The "value" now of an original Cubist painting is not unlike, in most respects, an original manuscript by Lord Byron, or *The Spirit of St. Louis* as it is seen in the Smithsonian Institution. (Indeed, museums fill the very same function as the Smithsonian Institution—why else would the *Jeu de Paume* wing of the Louvre exhibit Cézanne's and Van Gogh's palettes as proudly as they do their paintings?) Actual works of art are little more than historical curiosities. As far as *art* is concerned Van Gogh's paintings aren't worth any more than his palette is. They are both "collector's items." [17]

Art "lives" through influencing other art, not by existing as the physical residue of an artist's ideas. The reason that different artists from the past are "brought alive" again is because some aspect of their work becomes "usable" by living artists. That there is no "truth" as to what art is seems quite unrealized.

What is the function of art, or the nature of art? If we continue our analogy of the forms art takes as being art's *language* one can realize then that a work of art

[17] When someone "buys" a Flavin he isn't buying a light show, for if he was he could just go to a hardware store and get the goods for considerably less. He isn't "buying" anything. He is subsidizing Flavin's activity as an artist.

is a kind of *proposition* presented within the context of art as a comment on art. We can then go further and analyze the types of "propositions."

A. J. Ayer's evaluation of Kant's distinction between analytic and synthetic is useful to us here: "A proposition is analytic when its validity depends solely on the definitions of the symbols it contains, and synthetic when its validity is determined by the facts of experience." [18] The analogy I will attempt to make is one between the art condition and the condition of the analytic proposition. In that they don't appear to be believable as anything else, or be about anything (other than art), the forms of art most clearly finally referable only to art have been forms closest to analytical propositions.

Works of art are analytic propositions. That is, if viewed within their context—as art—they provide no information whatsoever about any matter of fact. A work of art is a tautology in that it is a presentation of the artist's intention, that is, he is saying that that particular work of art *is* art, which means, is a *definition* of art. Thus, that it is art is true a priori (which is what Judd means when he states that "if someone calls it art, it's art").

Indeed, it is nearly impossible to discuss art in general terms without talking in tautologies—for to attempt to "grasp" art by any other "handle" is merely to focus on another aspect or quality of the proposition, which is usually irrelevant to the artwork's "art condition." One begins to realize that art's "art condition" is a conceptual state. That the language forms that the artist frames his propositions in are often "private"

[18] A. J. Ayer, *Language, Truth, and Logic* (New York: Dover Publications), p. 78.

codes or languages is an inevitable outcome of art's freedom from morphological constrictions; and it follows from this that one has to be familiar with contemporary art to appreciate it and understand it. Likewise one understands why the "man in the street" is intolerant to artistic art and always demands art in a traditional "language." (And one understands why Formalist art sells "like hot cakes.") Only in painting and sculpture did the artists all speak the same language. What is called "Novelty Art" by the Formalists is often the attempt to find new languages, although a new language doesn't necessarily mean the framing of new propositions: e.g., most kinetic and electronic art.

Another way of stating, in relation to art, what Ayer asserted about the analytic method in the context of language would be the following: The validity of artistic propositions is not dependent on any empirical, much less any aesthetic, presupposition about the nature of things. For the artist, as an analyst, is not directly concerned with the physical properties of things. He is concerned only with (1) the way in which art is capable of conceptual growth and (2) how his propositions are capable of logically following that growth.[19] In other words, the propositions of art are not factual, but linguistic in *character*—that is, they do not describe the behavior of physical or even mental objects; they express definitions of art, or the formal consequences of definitions of art. Accordingly, we can say that art operates on a logic. For we shall see that the characteristic mark of a purely logical inquiry is that it is concerned with the formal consequences of

[19] *Ibid.*, p. 57.

our definitions (of art) and not with questions of empirical fact.[20]

To repeat, what art has in common with logic and mathematics is that it is a tautology; i.e., the "art idea" (or "work") and art are the same and can be appreciated as art without going outside the context of art for verification.

On the other hand, let us consider why art cannot be (or has difficulty when it attempts to be) a synthetic proposition. Or, that is to say, when the truth or falsity of its assertion is verifiable on empirical grounds. Ayer states:

> . . . The criterion by which we determine the validity of an a priori or analytical proposition is not sufficient to determine the validity of an empirical or synthetic proposition. For it is characteristic of empirical propositions that their validity is not purely formal. To say that a geometrical proposition, or a system of geometrical propositions, is false, is to say that it is self-contradictory. But an empirical proposition, or a system of empirical propositions, may be free from contradiction and still be false. It is said to be false, not because it is formally defective, but because it fails to satisfy some material criterion.[21]

The unreality of "realistic" art is due to its framing as an art proposition in synthetic terms: one is always tempted to "verify" the proposition empirically. Realism's synthetic state does not bring one to a circular swing back into a dialogue with the larger framework

[20] *Ibid.*
[21] *Ibid.*, p. 90.

of questions about the nature of *art* (as does the work of Malevich, Mondrian, Pollock, Reinhardt, early Rauschenberg, Johns, Lichtenstein, Warhol, Andre, Judd, Flavin, LeWitt, Morris, and others), but rather, one is flung out of art's "orbit" into the "infinite space" of the human condition.

Pure Expressionism, continuing with Ayer's terms, could be considered as such: "A sentence which consisted of demonstrative symbols would not express a genuine proposition. It would be a mere ejaculation, in no way characterizing that to which it was supposed to refer." Expressionist works are usually such "ejaculations" presented in the morphological language of traditional art. If Pollock is important it is because he painted on loose canvas horizontally to the floor. What *isn't* important is that he later put those drippings over stretchers and hung them parallel to the wall. (In other words what is important in art is what one *brings* to it, not one's adoption of what was previously existing.) What is even less important to art is Pollock's notions of "self-expression" because those *kinds* of subjective meanings are useless to anyone other than those involved with him personally. And their "specific" quality puts them outside of art's context.

"I do not make art," Richard Serra says, "I am engaged in an activity; if someone wants to call it art, that's his business, but it's not up to me to decide that. That's all figured out later." Serra, then, is very much aware of the implications of his work. If Serra is indeed just "figuring out what lead does" (gravitationally, molecularly, etc.), why should *anyone* think of it as art? If he doesn't take the responsibility of it being art, who can, or should? His work certainly appears to be empirically verifiable: lead can do, and be used for, many physical activities. In itself this does anything but lead us into a dialogue about the nature of art. In a sense, then, he is a primitive. He has no idea about art. How is it then that we know about "his activity"? Because he has told us it is art by his actions *after* "his activity" has taken place. That is, by the fact that he is with several galleries, puts the physical residue of his activity in museums (and sells them to art collectors—but as we have pointed out, collectors are irrelevant to the "condition of art" of a work). That he denies his work is art but plays the artist is more than just a paradox. Serra secretly feels that "arthood" is arrived at empirically. Thus, as Ayer has stated:

> There are no absolutely certain empirical propositions. It is only tautologies that are certain. Empirical questions are one and all hypotheses, which may be confirmed or discredited in actual sense experience. And the propositions in which we record the observations that verify these hypotheses are themselves hypotheses which are subject to the test of further sense experience. Thus there is no final proposition.[22]

What one finds all throughout the writings of Ad Reinhardt is this very similar thesis of "art-as-art," and that "art is always dead, and a 'living' art is a deception."[23] Reinhardt had a very clear idea about the nature of art, and his importance is far from recognized.

Because forms of art that can be considered syn-

[22] *Ibid.*, p. 94.

[23] Ad Reinhardt's retrospective catalogue (The Jewish Museum, January, 1967), written by Lucy Lippard, p. 12.

thetic propositions are verifiable by the world, that is to say, to understand these propositions one must leave the tautological-like framework of art and consider "outside" information. But to consider it as art it is necessary to ignore this same outside information, because outside information (experiential qualities, to note) has its own intrinsic worth. And to comprehend this worth one does not need a state of "art condition."

From this it is easy to realize that art's viability is not connected to the presentation of visual (or other) kinds of experience. That that may have been one of art's extraneous functions in the preceding centuries is not unlikely. After all, man in even the nineteenth century lived in a fairly standardized visual environment. That is, it was ordinarily predictable as to what he would be coming into contact with day after day. His visual environment in the part of the world in which he lived was fairly consistent. In our time we have an experientially drastically richer environment. One can fly all over the earth in a matter of hours and days, not months. We have the cinema, and color television, as well as the man-made spectacle of the lights of Las Vegas or the skyscrapers of New York City. The whole world is there to be seen, and the whole world can watch man walk on the moon from their living rooms. Certainly art or objects of painting and sculpture cannot be expected to compete experientially with this?

The notion of "use" is relevant to art and its "language." Recently the box or cube form has been used a great deal within the context of art. (Take for instance its use by Judd, Morris, LeWitt, Bladen, Smith, Bell, and McCracken—not even mentioning the quantity of boxes and cubes that came after.) The difference between all the various uses of the box or cube form is directly related to the differences in the intentions of the artists. Further, as is particularly seen in Judd's work, the use of the box or cube form illustrates very well our earlier claim that an object is only art when placed in the context of art.

A few examples will point this out. One could say that if one of Judd's box forms was seen filled with debris, seen placed in an industrial setting, or even merely seen sitting on a street corner, it would not be identified with art. It follows then that understanding and consideration of it as an artwork is necessary a priori to viewing it in order to "see" it as a work of art. Advance information about the concept of art and about an artist's concepts is necessary to the appreciation and understanding of contemporary art. Any and all of the physical attributes (qualities) of contemporary works, if considered separately and/or specifically, are irrelevant to the art concept. The art concept (as Judd said, though he didn't mean it this way) must be considered in its whole. To consider a concept's parts is invariably to consider aspects that are irrelevant to its art condition—or like reading *parts* of a definition.

It comes as no surprise that the art with the least fixed morphology is the example from which we decipher the nature of the general term *art*. For where there is a context existing separately of its morphology and consisting of its function one is more likely to find results less conforming and predictable. It is in modern art's possession of a "language" with the shortest history that the plausibility of the abandonment of that "language" becomes most possible. It is understandable then that the art that came out of Western painting and sculpture is the most energetic, questioning (of its nature), and the least assuming of all the general "art" concerns. In the final analysis, however, all of the arts have but (in Wittgenstein's terms) a "family" resemblance.

Yet the various qualities relatable to an "art condition" possessed by poetry, the novel, the cinema, the theatre, and various forms of music, etc., are those aspects of them most reliable to the function of art as asserted here.

Is not the decline of poetry relatable to the implied metaphysics from poetry's use of "common" language as an art language?[24] In New York the last decadent stages of poetry can be seen in the move by "Concrete" poets recently toward the use of actual objects and theatre.[25] Can it be that they feel the unreality of their art form?

> We see now that the axioms of a geometry are simply definitions, and that the theorems of a geometry are simply the logical consequences of these definitions. A geometry is not in itself about physical space; in itself it cannot be said to be "about" anything. But we can use a geometry to reason about physical space. That is to say, once we have given the axioms a physical interpretation, we can proceed to apply the theorems to the

[24] It is poetry's use of common language to attempt to *say the unsayable* that is problematic, not any inherent problem in the use of language within the context of art.

[25] Ironically, many of them call themselves "Conceptual Poets." Much of this work is very similar to Walter de Maria's work and this is not coincidental; de Maria's work functions as a kind of "object" poetry, and his intentions are very poetic: he really wants his work to change men's lives.

> objects which satisfy the axioms. Whether a geometry can be applied to the actual physical world or not, is an empirical question which falls outside the scope of geometry itself. There is no sense, therefore, in asking which of the various geometries known to us are false and which are true. Insofar as they are all free from contradiction, they are all true. The proposition which states that a certain application of a geometry is possible is not itself a proposition of that geometry. All that the geometry itself tells us is that if anything can be brought under the definitions, it will also satisfy the theorems. It is therefore a purely logical system, and its propositions are purely analytic propositions. — A. J. Ayer [26]

Here then I propose rests the viability of art. In an age when traditional philosophy is unreal because of its assumptions, art's ability to exist will depend not only on its *not* performing a service — as entertainment, visual (or other) experience, or decoration — which is something easily replaced by kitsch culture, and technology, but, rather, it will remain viable by *not* assuming a philosophical stance; for in art's unique character is the capacity to remain aloof from philosophical judgments. It is in this context that art shares similarities with logic, mathematics, and, as well, science. But whereas the other endeavors are useful, art is not. Art indeed exists for its own sake.

In this period of man, after philosophy and religion, art may possibly be one endeavor that fulfills what another age might have called "man's spiritual needs." Or, another way of putting it might be that art deals analogously with the state of things "beyond physics" where philosophy had to make assertions. And art's

[26] Ayer, p. 82.

strength is that even the preceding sentence is an assertion and cannot be verified by art. Art's only claim is for art. Art is the definition of art.

II

> The disinterest in painting and sculpture is a disinterest in doing it again, not in it as it is being done by those who developed the last advanced versions. New work always involves objections to the old. They are part of it. If the earlier work is first rate it is complete.—Donald Judd (1965)

> Abstract art or non-pictorial art is as old as this century, and though more specialized than previous art, is clearer and more complete, and like all modern thought and knowledge, more demanding in its grasp of relations.—Ad Reinhardt (1948)

> In France there is an old saying, "stupid like a painter." The painter was considered stupid, but the poet and writer very intelligent. I wanted to be intelligent. I had to have the idea of inventing. It is nothing to do what your father did. It is nothing to be another Cézanne. In my visual period there is a little of that stupidity of the painter. All my work in the period before the *Nude* was visual painting. Then I came to the idea. I thought the ideatic formulation a way to get away from influences. —Marcel Duchamp

> For each work of art that becomes physical there are many variations that do not.—Sol LeWitt

> The main virtue of geometric shapes is that they aren't organic, as all art otherwise is. A form that's neither geometric or organic would be a great discovery.—Donald Judd (1967)

The one thing to say about art is its breathlessness, lifelessness, deathlessness, contentlessness, formlessness, spacelessness, and timelessness. This is always the end of art.—Ad Reinhardt (1962)

Note: The discussion in the previous article does more than merely "justify" the recent art called Conceptual. *It points out, I feel, some of the confused thinking which has gone on in regards to past—but particularly—present activity in art. This article is not intended to give evidence of a "movement." But as an early advocate (through works of art and conversation) of a particular kind of art best described as* Conceptual *I have become increasingly concerned by the nearly arbitrary application of this term to an assortment of art interests—many of which I would never want to be connected with, and logically shouldn't be.*

The "purest" definition of Conceptual Art would be that it is inquiry into the foundations of the concept "art," as it has come to mean. Like most terms with fairly specific meanings generally applied, Conceptual Art is often considered as a *tendency.* In one sense it is a tendency of course because the "definition" of *Conceptual Art* is very close to the meanings of art itself.

But the reasoning behind the notion of such a tendency, I am afraid, is still connected to the fallacy of morphological characteristics as a connective between what are really disparate activities. In this case it is an attempt to detect stylehood. In assuming a primary cause-effect relationship to "final outcomes," such criticism bypasses a particular artist's intents (concepts) to deal exclusively with his "final outcome." Indeed most criticism has dealt with only one very superficial aspect of this "final outcome," and that is the apparent "immateriality" or "anti-object" similarity amongst most "conceptual" works of art. But this can only be important if one assumes that objects are necessary to art—or to phrase it better, that they have a definitive relation to art. And in this case such criticism would be focusing on a negative aspect of the art.

If one has followed my thinking (in part one) one can understand my assertion that objects are conceptually irrelevant to the condition of art. This is not to say that a particular "art investigation" may or may not employ objects, material substances, etc., within the confines of its investigation. Certainly the investigations carried out by Bainbridge and Hurrell are excellent examples of such a use.[27] Although I have proposed that all art is finally conceptual, some recent work is clearly conceptual in intent whereas other examples of recent art are only related to Conceptual Art in a superficial manner. And although this work is an advance—in most cases—over Formalist or "Anti-formalist" (Morris, Serra, Sonnier, Hesse, and others) tendencies, it should not be considered Conceptual Art in the *purer* sense of the term.

Three artists often associated with me (through Seth Siegelaub's projects)—Douglas Huebler, Robert Barry, and Lawrence Weiner—are not concerned with, I do not think, Conceptual Art as it was previously stated. Douglas Huebler, who was in the "Primary Structures" show at The Jewish Museum (New York),

[27] *Art-Language*, 1, no. 1.

uses a nonmorphologically artlike form of presentation (photographs, maps, mailings) to answer iconic, structural sculpture issues directly related to his Formica sculpture (which he was making as late as 1968). This is pointed out by the artist in the opening sentence of the catalogue of his "one-man show" (which was organized by Seth Siegelaub and existed only as a catalogue of documentation): "The existence of each sculpture is documented by its documentation." It is not my intention to point out a *negative* aspect of the work, but only to show that Huebler—who is in his mid-forties and much older than most of the artists discussed here—has not as much in common with the aims in the *purer* versions of Conceptual Art as it would superficially seem.

The other men—Robert Barry and Lawrence Weiner—have watched their work take on a Conceptual Art association almost by accident. Barry, whose painting was seen in the "Systemic Painting" show at The Guggenheim Museum, has in common with Weiner the fact that the "path" to Conceptual Art came via decisions related to choices of art materials and processes. Barry's post-Newman/Reinhardt paintings "reduced" (in physical material, not "meaning") along a path from two-inch square paintings, to single lines of wire between architectural points, to radio-wave beams, to inert gases, and finally to "brain energy." His work then seems to exist conceptually only because the material is invisible. But his art does have a physical state, which is different than work which only exists conceptually.

Lawrence Weiner, who gave up painting in the spring of 1968, changed his notion of "place" (in an Andrean sense) from the context of the canvas (which could only be specific) to a context which was "general," yet all the while continuing his concern with specific materials and processes. It became obvious to him that if one is not concerned with "appearance" (which he wasn't, and in this regard he preceded most of the "Antiform" artists) there was not only no need for the fabrication (such as in his studio) of his work, but—more important—such fabrication would again invariably give his work's "place" a specific context. Thus, by the summer of 1968, he decided to have his work exist only as a proposal in his notebook—that is, until a "reason" (museum, gallery, or collector) or, as he called them, a "receiver" necessitated his work to be made. It was in the late fall of that same year that Weiner went one step further in deciding that it didn't matter whether it was made or not. In that sense his private notebooks became public.[28]

Purely Conceptual Art is first seen concurrently in the work of Terry Atkinson and Michael Baldwin in Coventry, England; and with my own work done in New York City, all generally around 1966.[29] On Kawara, a Japanese artist who has been continuously traveling around the world since 1959, has been doing a highly conceptualized kind of art since 1964.

On Kawara, who began with paintings lettered with one simple word, went to "questions" and "codes," and paintings such as the listing of a spot on the Sahara Desert in terms of its longitude and latitude,

[28] I did not (and still do not) understand this last decision. Since I first met Weiner, he defended his position (quite alien to mine) of being a "Materialist." I always found this last direction (e.g., *Statements*) sensical in *my* terms, but I never understood how it was in his.

[29] I began dating my work with the *Art as Idea as Idea* series.

is most well known for his "date" paintings. The "date" paintings consist of the lettering (in paint on canvas) of that day's date on which the painting is executed. If a painting is not "finished" on the day that it is started (that is, by twelve midnight) it is destroyed. Although he still does the date paintings (he spent last year traveling to every country in South America), he has begun doing other projects as well in the past couple of years. These include a "One-hundred year calendar," a daily listing of everyone he meets each day (*I met*), which is kept in notebooks, as is *I went*, which is a calendar of maps of the cities he is in with the marked streets where he traveled. He also mails daily postcards giving the time he woke up that morning.

On Kawara's reasons for his art are extremely private, and he has consciously stayed away from any publicity or public art-world exposure. His continued use of "painting" as a medium is, I think, a pun on the morphological characteristics of traditional art, rather than an interest in painting "proper."

Terry Atkinson and Michael Baldwin's work, presented as a collaboration, began in 1966 consisting of projects such as a rectangle with linear depictions of the states of Kentucky and Iowa, titled *Map to not include: Canada, James Bay, Ontario, Quebec, St. Lawrence River, New Brunswick* . . . and so on; conceptual drawings based on various serial and conceptual schemes; a map of a thirty-six-square-mile area of the Pacific Ocean, west of Oahu, scale three inches to the mile (an empty square). Works from 1967 were the "Air Conditioning" show and the "Air show." The "Air show" as described by Terry Atkinson was, "A series of assertions concerning a theoretical usage of a column of air comprising a base of one square mile and of unspecified distance in the vertical dimension."[30] No particular square mile of the earth's surface was specified. The concept did not entail any such particular location. Also such works as *Frameworks, Hot-cold,* and *22 sentences: the French army* are examples of their more recent collaborations.[31] Atkinson and Baldwin in the past year have formed, along with David Bainbridge and Harold Hurrell, the Art & Language Press. From this press is published *Art-Language* (a journal of Conceptual Art),[32] as well as other publications related to this inquiry.

Christine Kozlov has been working along Conceptual lines as well since late 1966. Some of her work has consisted of a "Conceptual" film, using clear Leder tape; *Compositions for audio structures*—a coding system for sound; a stack of several hundred blank sheets of paper—one for each day on which a concept is rejected; *Figurative work*, which is a listing of everything she ate for a period of six months; and a study of crime as an art activity.

The Canadian Iain Baxter has been doing a "Conceptual" sort of work since late 1967. As have the Americans James Byars and Frederic Barthelme; and the French and German artists Bernar Venet and Hanne Darboven. And certainly the books of Edward Ruscha since around that time are relevant too. As are *some* of Bruce Nauman's, Barry Flanagan's, Bruce McLean's, and Richard Long's works. Steven Kaltenbach's *Time capsules* from 1968, and much of his

[30] Terry Atkinson, pp. 5–6.

[31] All obtainable from Art & Language Press, 84 Jubilee Crescent, Coventry, England.

[32] Of which the author is the American editor.

work since, is relatable. And Ian Wilson's post-Kaprow "Conversations" are Conceptually presented.

The German artist Franz Walther in his work since 1965 has treated objects in a much different way than they are usually treated in an art context.

Within the past year other artists, though some only related peripherally, have begun a more "Conceptual" form of work. Mel Bochner gave up work heavily influenced by Minimal Art and began such work. And certainly some of the work by Jan Dibbets, Eric Orr, Allen Ruppersberg, and Dennis Oppenheim could be considered within a Conceptual framework. Donald Burgy's work in the past year as well uses a Conceptual format. One can also see a development in a *purer* form of "Conceptual" art in the recent beginnings of work by younger artists such as Saul Ostrow, Adrian Piper, and Perpetua Butler. Interesting work in this "purer" sense is being done, as well, by a group consisting of an Australian and two Englishmen (all living in New York): Ian Burn, Mel Ramsden, and Roger Cutforth. (Although the amusing pop paintings of John Baldessari allude to this sort of work by being "conceptual" cartoons of actual Conceptual Art, they are not really relevant to this discussion.)

Terry Atkinson has suggested, and I agree with him, that Sol LeWitt is notably responsible for creating an environment which made our art acceptable, if not conceivable. (I would hastily add to that, however, that I was certainly much more influenced by Ad Reinhardt, Duchamp via Johns and Morris, and by Donald Judd than I ever was specifically by LeWitt.) Perhaps added to Conceptual Art's history would be certainly early works by Robert Morris, particularly the *Card File* (1962). Much of Rauschenberg's early work such as his *Portrait of Iris Clert* and his *Erased de Kooning Drawing* are some important examples of a Conceptual kind of art. And the Europeans Klein and Manzoni fit into this history somewhere, too. And in Jasper Johns' work—such as his "Target" and "Flag" paintings and his ale cans—one has a particularly good example of art existing as an analytical proposition. Johns and Reinhardt are probably the last two painters that were legitimate *artists* as well.[33] Robert Smithson, *had* he recognized his articles in magazines as being his work (as he could have, and should have) and his "work" serving as illustrations for them; his influence would be more relevant.[34]

Andre, Flavin, and Judd have exerted tremendous influence on recent art, though probably more as examples of high standards and clear thinking than in any specific way. Pollock and Judd are, I feel, the beginning and end of American dominance in art; partly due to the ability of many of the younger artists in Europe to "purge" themselves of their traditions, but most likely due to the fact that nationalism is as out of place in art as it is in any other field. Seth Siegelaub, a former art dealer who now functions as a curator-at-large and was the first exhibition organizer to "specialize" in this area of recent art, has had many group exhibitions that existed no *place* (other than in the

[33] And Stella, too, of course. But Stella's work, which was greatly weakened by being painting, was made obsolete very quickly by Judd and others.

[34] Smithson of course did spearhead the Earthwork activity—but his only disciple, Michael Heizer, is a "one idea" artist who hasn't contributed much. If you have thirty men digging holes and nothing develops out of that idea you haven't got much, have you? A very large ditch, maybe.

catalogue). As Siegelaub has stated: "I am very interested in conveying the idea that the artist can live where he wants to—not necessarily in New York or London or Paris as he has had to in the past—but *anywhere* and still make important art."

THE ART WORKERS' COALITION *

by Lucy Lippard

In January, 1969, several artists and critics met at the Hotel Chelsea in New York City to discuss ways in which members of the art community could become more responsive in political and social matters and at the same time remain true to their artistic instincts.[1] *The results of this and hundreds of subsequent meetings are still influencing the purpose and activities of art and educational institutions everyplace.*

The Art Workers' Coalition was the organization that emerged from these meetings. Many changes that have directly affected the very structure of our major artistic institutions were initially proposed by this loosely organized group.

In the notes that follow, Lucy Lippard discusses one of the most significant projects of the Coalition—an open hearing for artists, dealers, critics, and students held at the School for Visual Arts; she relates the event to broad social and administrative provocations that are of concern to everybody in the art field.

Lucy Lippard is one of our most distinguished art critics. Her books include Pop Art *as well as a collection of essays on Surrealism. A volume of her criticism,* Changing, *has been published in the Dutton series called "Documents in Modern Art Criticism."*

* Reprinted from *Studio International*, November, 1970.

[1] The first several meetings of the group consisted of the following: Takis, Tsai, Hans Haacke, Willoughby Sharp, John Perreault, Farman, and Carl Andre.

On April 10, 1969, some three hundred New York artists and observers thereof filled the amphitheatre of the School of Visual Arts for an "Open Public Hearing on the subject: What Should Be the Program of The Art Workers Regarding Museum Reform, and to Establish the Program of an Open Art Workers' Coalition." The last time such a large and various group had got together for nonaesthetic reasons concerned the Artists Tenants Association's threatened loft strike in 1961, which did not take place. The hearing was preceded by a list of thirteen demands to the Museum of Modern Art and demonstrations supporting them which emphasized artists' rights: legal, legislative, and loosely political; they were the product of the newly named Art Workers' Coalition (temporarily and simultaneously the Artists' Coalition). The AWC was conceived on January 3, 1969, when the kinetic artist Takis (Vassilakis) removed a work of art, made by him but owned by the Museum of Modern Art, from the museum's "Machine" show, on the grounds that an artist had the right to control the exhibition and treatment of his work whether or not he had sold it. Not a revolutionary proposition, except in the art world.

Despite the specific subjects announced for the Open Hearing, taped and later published verbatim by the AWC, the real content of the night was the airing of general complaints about The System, keynoted by Richard Artschwager's use of his two minutes to set off firecrackers instead of talk. The picture of frustrated violence that emerged from this motley cross-section of the art community (seventy artists, architects, filmmakers, and critics, a number of them black, spoke) surprised the establishment at which it was aimed. As well it might, since art-world complaints are made loudly, but in the relative privacy of studios and bars, rarely in public. Those who voiced them were immediately accused of opportunism by some of those who remained closet protestants. A number of speakers considered the Museum of Modern Art an unworthy object of artists' attention, but a grudging consensus agreed it was the best place to start if only because it is the seat (in all senses) of power; not enough people, time, and energy were available then to tackle all the museums at once and MOMA qualified by its rank in the world, its Rockefeller-studded Board of Trustees with all the attendant political and economic sins attached to such a group, its propagation of the star system and consequent dependence on galleries and collectors, its maintenance of a safe, blue-chip collection, and, particularly, its lack of contact with the art community and recent art, its disdain for the advice and desires of the artists that filled its void. The demands made in February, 1969, were boiled down from thirteen to eleven in June, and revised slightly as the nine-plus below to apply to all museums in March, 1970:

A. WITH REGARD TO ART MUSEUMS IN GENERAL THE ART WORKERS' COALITION MAKES THE FOLLOWING DEMANDS:

1. The Board of Trustees of all museums should be made up of one-third museum staff, one-third patrons and one-third artists, if it is to continue to act as the policy-making body of the museum. All means should be explored in the interest of a more open-minded and democratic museum. Artworks are a cultural

heritage that belong to the people. No minority has the right to control them; therefore, a board of trustees chosen on a financial basis must be eliminated.

2. Admission to all museums should be free at all times and they should be open evenings to accommodate working people.

3. All museums should decentralize to the extent that their activities and services enter black, Puerto Rican, and all other communities. They should support events with which these communities can identify and control. They should convert existing structures all over the city into relatively cheap, flexible branch-museums or cultural centers that could not carry the stigma of catering only to the wealthier sections of society.

4. A section of all museums under the direction of black and Puerto Rican artists should be devoted to showing the accomplishments of black and Puerto Rican artists, particularly in those cities where these (or other) minorities are well represented.

5. Museums should encourage female artists to overcome centuries of damage done to the image of the female as an artist by establishing equal representation of the sexes in exhibitions, museum purchases, and on selection committees.

6. At least one museum in each city should maintain an up-to-date registry of all artists in their area that is available to the public.

7. Museum staffs should take positions publicly and use their political influence in matters concerning the welfare of artists, such as rent control for artists' housing, legislation for artists' rights, and whatever else may apply specifically to artists in their area. In particular, museums, as central institutions, should

be aroused by the crisis threatening man's survival and should make their own demands to the government that ecological problems be put on a par with war and space efforts.

8. Exhibition programs should give special attention to works by artists not represented by a commercial gallery. Museums should also sponsor the production and exhibition of such works outside their own premises.

9. Artists should retain a disposition over the destiny of their work, whether or not it is owned by them, to ensure that it cannot be altered, destroyed, or exhibited without their consent.

B. UNTIL SUCH TIME AS A MINIMUM INCOME IS GUARANTEED FOR ALL PEOPLE, THE ECONOMIC POSITION OF ARTISTS SHOULD BE IMPROVED IN THE FOLLOWING WAYS:

1. Rental fees should be paid to artists or their heirs for all work exhibited where admissions are charged, whether or not the work is owned by the artist.

2. A percentage of the profit realized on the resale of an artist's work should revert to the artist or his heirs.

3. A trust fund should be set up from a tax levied on the sales of the work of dead artists. This fund would provide stipends, health insurance, help for artists' dependants, and other social benefits.

The extent to which each "member" agrees with each "demand" fluctuates to the point where structural fluidity of the organization itself is unavoidable. The AWC has as many identities as it has participants at any one time (there are no members or officers and its main manner of fund-raising is a "Frisco Circle" at meetings), and the number of participants varies as radically as does their radicality, according to the degree of excitement, rage, guilt, generated by any given issue. It has functioned best as an umbrella, as a conscience and complaint bureau incorporating, not without almost blowing inside out, groups and goals that are not only different, but often conflicting. Advocates of a tighter structure, of a real dues-paying union situation, have reason but not reality on their side. Nobody, inside or outside the Coalition, has illusions about its efficiency; the difference is that everyone outside thinks it could be done better another way and from the inside that looks impossible.

At the first few open meetings of the Coalition there was a terrific atmosphere of aesthetic and economic mistrust. Eventually basic dislike of organizations, innate snobbism about which artists should or could be associated with one, the reluctance to waste time, and revulsion for yelling, rhetoric, and opportunism (not unique to the AWC) broke down in favor of common excitement and, finally, even affectionate tolerance for some of the more therapeutically oriented participants. Nobody thought it was ideal; and nobody had ever seen New York artists come on any other way, either. Despite the heterogeneous composition, during the winter and spring of 1969 the AWC became a community of artists within the larger art community. The honeymoon period centered around plans for the open hearing and publication of its record and, later, around the "alternatives committee," whose search for alternative structures ran the gamut between a trade union complete with dental care, a massive takeover of the city's abandoned Hudson River piers for studio and exhibition space (that is now being done by the establishment itself), and an information center complete with Xerox machine, ending comfortably, if a little wearily, as a discussion group covering the highest tides of idealism and philosophical foam, with which New York art is very much at home. The weekly general meetings consisted of about sixty people, sometimes one hundred; the committees were much smaller. Both were characterized by reversals and arguments and endless bullshit (usually defined as somebody else talking), naïveté, commitment, and lack of knowledge about how to implement it, a high evangelical pitch reached in the bar after meetings, not to mention the endless phone calls that plague a small organization with no efficient communication channels, all backed up by an excited realization that MOMA was, for some inexplicable reason, afraid of us.

This period culminated in intramural quarrels surrounding the problem of what to do about the Museum of Modern Art's "blackmail" of First Generation New York School artists (which I consider one of our most important endeavors) and problems of structure, now that the Coalition was getting big with what sometimes seemed a false pregnancy. These most often concerned the point of whether or not the general meetings should have veto power over the hard-working committees or special interest groups, including the usually controversial "action committee," where the militants and the Guerrilla Art Action Group were focused. Kestutis Zapkus' antiveto "Proposal," circulated in the summer of 1969, stated, among other things: "There is no reason why the AWC should model itself on the procedures of conventional bureaucratic organizations. The development of special interests must not be dissipated by a less involved majority."

The most controversial aspect of the AWC among artists and establishment has been its so-called politicization of art, a term usually used to cover the black and women's programs as well as demands that museums speak out against racism, war, and repression. On May 4, 1969, Hilton Kramer of *The New York Times* left-handedly complimented us by saying that the Open Hearing proposed, "albeit incoherently . . . a way of thinking about the production and consumption of works of art that would radically modify, if not actually displace, currently established practices, with their heavy reliance on big money and false prestige." He had "the vivid impression of a moral issue which wiser and more experienced minds have long been content to leave totally unexamined." But as the AWC gathered steam (or power), we became less attractive; his second article (January 18, 1970) ended with a plea to all those nice people "who believe in the very idea of art museums—in museums free of political pressures—to make our commitments known, to say loud and clear that we will not stand for the politicization of art that is now looming as a real possibility." We wrote a lengthy reply which was published with his third article on the subject (February 8, 1970). In it we said that if by the "politicization of art" he meant "political art" he should be made aware that the AWC has never offered any opinions on the content or form of art, which we consider the concern of individual artists alone"; also, that "Mr. Kramer ignores the fact that what radical critics are opposed to is the present conservative politicization of the Museum. . . . If the men now controlling the Museum of Modern Art are not politically involved, who the hell is?" The AWC did not begin as a political group, but its models were clearly the black and student movements of the 1960s, and by the time of the Open Hearing it was obvious that nonart issues would assume, if not priority, a major rhetorical importance. Though the Black Panthers, the Chicago Seven, and other radical causes have been supported; though we have protested by telegram and testimony ecological catastrophes, budget cutbacks to museums, expressways, etc., and once gave half the treasury (some £300 from sales of the books) to a Biafran woman who delivered a particularly stirring plea at a meeting, the AWC, like its predecessor and sometime colleague, the Artists and Writers Protest, has concentrated its political energies on Peace, as did the May 1970 Art Strike. On the first Moratorium Day (October 15, 1969) the AWC managed to get the Modern, the Whitney, and the Jewish museums and most of the galleries to close, and (with the crucial help of the participating artists) the Metropolitan to postpone the opening of its big American painting and sculpture show till a more auspicious date, though the museum itself stayed open and, with the Guggenheim, was picketed.

The bitterest quarrel the AWC has had with the museum (aside from the "blackmail" issue) was over joint sponsorship of the Song-My massacre protest poster—a ghastly colored photograph of the event from *Life* captioned, "Q: AND BABIES? A: AND BABIES," which was vetoed by the president of the Board of Trustees after an initial, though unexpected, executive staff acceptance of the proposal. We picketed and protested in front of *Guernica*, published fifty thousand posters on our own and distributed them, free, via an informal network of artists and movement people; it has turned up all over the world. Our release read, in part: "Practically, the outcome is as planned: an artist-sponsored poster protesting the Song-My massacre will receive vast distribution. But the Museum's unprecedented decision to make known, as an institution, its commitment to humanity, has been denied it. Such lack of resolution casts doubts on the strength of the Museum's commitment to art itself, and can only be seen as bitter confirmation of this institution's decadence and/or impotence." Via this and other experiences we discovered that semi-private institutions are unable to buck their trustees, particularly when the issue is one that presents the trustees with a direct conflict of interest. (As Gregory Battcock said at the Open Hearing: "The trustees of the museums direct NBC and CBS, *The New York Times*, and the Associated Press, and that greatest cultural travesty of modern times—the Lincoln Center. They own A. T. & T., Ford, General Motors, the great multibillion-dollar foundations, Columbia University, Alcoa, Minnesota Mining, United Fruit, and AMK, besides sitting on the boards of each other's museums. The implications of these facts are enormous. Do you realize that it is those art-loving, culturally committed trustees of the Metropolitan and Modern museums who are waging the war in Vietnam?") We also discovered that one thing museum administrators can't seem to realize is that most of the art workers lead triple (for women, often quadruple) lives: making art, earning a living, political or social action, and maybe domesticity too. When the museum official gets fretful about our distrust of long dialogues and our general inefficiency (irresponsibility, he calls it), he forgets that he is being paid a salary for "caring for" work and issues that his opposite number on the picket line produces in return for no financial assurances whatsoever, and that the Coalition itself has to beg time from the "real" world to get anything done at all.

The AWC will be powerful only in the art field, where artists have power, and it seems to me that if an artist is more involved in the Peace Movement than in artists' rights he should be working directly for the movement. What anyone can do via the AWC for the Panthers or for peace or for Welfare mothers or trees can be done a hundred times better within those organizations specializing in each of those fields. As an artist, however, he can exert his influence on those institutions which depend on him for their life, to make them speak up and influence others. The fact that these institutions are run by people running other areas of the larger world makes artists' actions as artists all the more important. What is sad is how few artists will even acknowledge their political burden, how many seem to feel that art, and thus their own art, is so harmless that it needs no conscience. At least I don't hear that doubtful statement "My art is my politics" quite so often since Art Strike and other recent developments. It's how you give and withhold your art that is political. Your art is only your politics if it is blatantly political art, and most of the people who say that are blatantly opposed to political art. The Coalition is neutral; it has always been a nonaesthetic group involved in ethics rather than aesthetics. For the most part, however, the artist's dilemma: Is this the kind of society I can make art in? What use is art in this or any society? Should it have no use, even morally? remains unsolved in or out of the AWC.

The ethical role of the Coalition infuriates people. It is frequently criticized for not representing enough of the art community to be listened to; we in turn frequently criticize the rest of the art community for not speaking up, with *or* against us. The Coalition is out there working and occasionally accomplishing something; where do those guys get off resting smugly on a nest egg of their *own* compromises and preferring to fight us rather than the common enemy? In June, 1969, during an exchange with artists who had (we charged) been subjected to blackmail by donating works to MOMA for a "historical" show that just incidentally had to come from the museum's collections, we wrote: "Our actions should not be mistaken for those of the community as a whole, but rather as a 'conscience' in regard to the existing system. We represent the present membership [of the AWC] and, by default, the passive element in the art community. Anyone who does not speak for himself will be spoken for by us until he does take a position on the various issues. . . . The AWC does not begrudge the success of the artists in this show, to whom we all owe a major aesthetic debt, nor are we judging the aesthetic content of the exhibition. We are all too aware of the conditions in which these artists have existed for years under the present system, and it is this system we would like to change. We have no intention of letting the 'watchdog' ghost of Ad Reinhardt lie. In the 1960s large sections of the world's population have realized what Reinhardt realized in the art world long before, that sins of omission and commission, crimes of silence and rhetoric, are equally indefensible."

The crux of the matter is, of course, that no artist, in or out of the AWC, wants to be told anyone else is thinking for him. Nor does anyone like to be reminded that he is a pawn of the system. It comes harder to more successful artists than to those who are just beginning. The artist is a person who has chosen a life of "independence" from the conventional structures. He is by nature unequipped for group thinking or action. He has also made certain sacrifices in order to have the advantages of "freedom." However, he prefers to bitch to (and about) his fellow artists about the gallery system, museums' ignorance of art and artists' lives, how critics "use" him and his art, than to do anything about it. And this is, I suspect, because if he admitted to himself how far up against the wall he has been driven, life would be pretty unbearable. The illusion of freedom is of the utmost importance to a person for whom society does nothing else. Even if he is successful (and some of the aesthetically and ethically unhappiest artists in the city, the ones that act like cornered rats when talking to members of the Coalition, are the most successful socially and financially), even then, if he measures his success against his compromises, he is asking for a downer. It's pleasanter not to be aware of the issues than to feel nothing can be done about them. Ad Reinhardt and Carl Andre, two artists who have had the courage to expose publicly the contradictions inherent in their own situation, have come in for far more mudslinging than their weaker colleagues who have accepted to wallow in suspect patronage, than the artist who is content to be waterboy to a critic or mascot to a collector.

The real value of the AWC is its voice rather than its force, its whispers rather than its shouts. It exists both as a threat and as a "place" (in people's heads, and in real space as a clearing house for artists' complaints). Its own silent majority is larger than is generally realized. More important than any of our "concrete" achievements is the fact that whether or not we are popular for it, the Coalition has brought up issues that American artists (since the 1930s) have failed to confront together, issues concerning the dignity and value of art and artist in a world that often thinks neither have either. If the American artist looks with increased awareness at his shows, sales, conferences, contracts as an autonomous and independent member, even mover, of his own system, the AWC has made sense. But if aesthetic differences are a barrier even to a successful artist's understanding or working with equally successful colleagues, as artists for artists' rights, maybe there's no ball game. Maybe artists will have the unique distinction of being the only vocation in the world that can't get together long enough to assure their colleagues of not suffering from their mistakes. Maybe sweetness, light, idealism and personal integrity, conventionally presumed to characterize art, have been bred out of it by this brutal age. Maybe the Coalition is about not thinking so, even if the odds look bad.

THE ERUPTION OF ANTI-ART

by Ursula Meyer

In this article Ursula Meyer traces the origins of Anti-Art and, quite naturally, credits the Dadaist activists with some of the earliest Anti-Art provocations. The author links Anti-Art with political art and cites Herbert Marcuse and Emory Douglas (Culture Minister for the Black Panther Party) to illustrate her discussion of "desublimination" of cultural values.

Finally, Ms. Meyer accepts the difficulties in the labeling and classification of authentic Anti-Art (now) and observes: "If Anti-Art exists at all, it has to be redefined in terms of its temporariness."

Ursula Meyer is editor of Conceptual Art *and her articles have been published in* Art News, Arts Magazine, *and* Women in Art. *She teaches at Herbert H. Lehman College of the City University of New York. "The Eruption of Anti-Art" has been excerpted from her comprehensive study* Political Art: Past and Present.

The Dada mind took delight in the irony of paradoxes inherent in bourgeois assumptions. The notion of Anti-Art, applicable to antiestablishment art, ridiculed *l'art pour l'art* pretensions. Calling attention to its shopworn mores and pious clichés, Dada attacked the bourgeoisie with satirical images and spoofs and in a decidedly unorthodox manner pursued political goals by means of aesthetics.

> The activity of Dada was a permanent revolt of the individual against art, against morality, against society. The means were manifestos, poems, writings of various kinds, paintings, sculptures, exhibitions, and a few public demonstrations of a clearly subversive character.
>
> However the implication of the movement went beyond literature and art. It aimed at the liberation of the individual from dogmas, formulas and laws, at the affirmation of the individual on the plane of the spiritual; it may even be said that the movement liberated the individual from the mind itself, placing the genius in the same rank as the idiot.[1]

Dada was a state of mind, undogmatic and radicalized. The term *Dada* was adroitly chosen precisely for its total absence of meaning. As Jean Arp put it: "What interests us is the Dada spirit and we were all Dada before Dada came into existence."[2] Tristan Tsara commented that Dada was useless and unpretentious "as life should be." He declared Dada as "the point where the yes and the no and all the opposites meet . . . very simply at streetcorners like dogs and grasshoppers."[3]

At the eve of World War I, Duchamp coined the term *Anti-Art*, implying his disdain for the establishment's inept practices in art and politics. The Readymades were sarcastic jibes against an elitist art world, museums, dealers, status seekers, collectors. Duchamp confronted the bourgeoisie with the irony of

[1] Georges Ribemont-Dessaignes, "History of Dada," from *The Dada Painters and Poets*, ed. by Robert Motherwell (New York: George Wittenborn, Inc., 1967), p. 102.

[2] *Ibid.*

[3] Tristan Tsara, "Lecture on Dada" (1922), from Motherwell, p. 251.

its erroneous assumptions. Affixing the moustache on *Mona Lisa* ridiculed bourgeois reverence for a classical Renaissance while "drawing attention to a sexual ambiguity in Leonardo's work and life."[4] The letters *L.H.O.O.Q.*, captioning the *Mona Lisa*, make an obscene pun when pronounced in French "*Elle a chaud au cul.*" Duchamp's Anti-Art denigrates *l'art pour l'art* mystification as much as the establishment that promotes it. He felt that art did not belong in a civilization bereft of all but commercial values. The notion of Anti-Art was more of an antiestablishment quip than a derision of art. According to Hans Richter, the meaning of Duchamp's *Fountain* was that he was pissing on the establishment's aesthetic values, which supposedly determine what is, and what is not, art.[5] Duchamp rebelled against the pervasive object cultus, typical of the commerce culture. His "aesthetic rebellion" was, however, politically quite ineffective. After the initial shock wore off, the bourgeoisie "loved" Duchamp's Anti-Art, bought and collected it like other *objets d'art*, much to Duchamp's dismay and annoyance. In 1920, he surprisingly announced that he had changed from "anti-artist" to "engineer." (The shift coincides with Duchamp's adoption of the pseudonym Rose Sélavy.)

The German contingent of Dada could not very well afford a freewheeling political attitude matching the bravado anarchism of the Dadaists of the Allied Nations. The Germans had experienced a rotting empire, a disastrous war, and misery and famine in its wake.

[4] William S. Rubin, *Dada, Surrealism and Their Heritage* (New York: Museum of Modern Art, 1968), p. 19.

[5] Hans Richter, "In Memory of a Friend," *Art in America*, July/August, 1969.

The social distress following the Kaiser's military adventures eventually hit home and German Dada reflected the collapse of the bourgeoisie. "Dada is German Bolshevism. The bourgeois must be deprived of the opportunity to 'buy art for his justification.'"[6] The German Dadaists saw themselves as *Kunstkommunisten* who put the demands of the Party ahead of aesthetic involvements. They called for the eradication of all nationalistic values, vigorously depreciating German culture: "What is German Culture? (Answer: Shit.)"[7] The uprising of 1918–1919 in Berlin involved Dada in violent revolutionary activity: "Dada spontaneously offered its services to the proletariat and went down into the streets . . . it incited to revolt by means of good-humored or cruel allusion. . . ."[8] The strength of the German Dada movement was its ferocious sense of humor matched by intense political commitment.

George Grosz and John Heartfield, collaborators since 1915, were active members of the Union of Communist Artists of the KPD (*Vereinigung Kommunistischer Kuenstler der KPD*), the so-called *Rote Gruppe*, of which Grosz was the chairman. Both artists were founders of the German Dada movement. Grosz commented on Dada:

> In Germany since decades Dadaism was the only relevant artistic movement. Do not smile—compared to this movement all "isms" in art have become little

[6] Richard Huelsenbeck, "En Avant Dada," from Motherwell, p. 44.

[7] Rubin, p. 42.

[8] Georges Hugnet, "The Spirit in Dada Painting," from Motherwell, p. 142.

> studio-problems of yesterday. Dadaism was not by any means an "organized" movement, but an organic product which developed as a reaction against the "cloud wanderer tendencies" (*Wolkenwanderertendenzen*) of the so-called hallowed art whose followers thought about cubes and gothic, while the generals painted with blood. Dadaism forces artists to show their colors.[9]

In 1923, Malik published George Grosz' portfolio *"Hintergrund"* ("Background"), containing seventeen drawings prepared for Piscator's theatrical production *Schweijk.* Some of these drawings alarmed the authorities. For example: *Be Obedient to the Rulers* portrays two military men, a judge, and a priest balancing a cross on his nose. *The Outpouring of the Holy Ghost* depicts a churchman spewing bombs and grenades. *Shut Up and Serve* (*Maul halten und Weiterdienen*) shows the crucified Christ muzzled with a heavy gas mask. On account of these three drawings George Grosz was indicted for "defamation of God" (*"Gotteslästerung"*). The process, which took three years, became a *cause célèbre* in Europe. When Grosz incorporated the drawing *Shut Up and Serve* into the litho series entitled *Ecce Homo,* he was indicted again for defaming God. Appearing in his own defense, the artist told the court: "The moralist I am can finally choose no better word than 'Ecce Homo'! For Christ is the embodiment of man and the opposite of what has been demonstrated here." [10]

[9] From the catalogue of the exhibition "George Grosz/John Heartfield," Württembergischer Kunstverein, Stuttgart, Germany, 1969, p. 14. (Quote from George Grosz, Wieland Herzfelde, *Die Kunst ist in Gefahr.*)

[10] *Ibid.*, p. 24. (Quote from excerpts of the stenographic court record of February 16, 1924. Reprinted in *Tagebuch,* February 23, 1924, s. 240–48.)

During World War I, George Grosz and John Heartfield's aversion to the pretenses of Teutonic patriotism were already explicitly manifested, not only in the artist's work but also in certain actions and antiestablishment gestures. For instance, the famous World War I slogan "May God Punish England" so provoked Heartfield, that he decided to anglicize his name, changing it from Helmut Herzfeld to John Heartfield. By the end of the war his brother, Wieland Herzfelde,[11] performed one of the first political art actions. He continued to wear his disgustingly filthy uniform in order to dishonor it. Pretending to have a skin disease, he shaved only one cheek. Thus he paraded in the streets of Berlin in order to emphasize the horrors of war. And George Grosz marched in Berlin wearing a skull and carrying a sign: "*Dada Über Alles.*" In a sense, these "guerilla actions" reveal more of the spirit of Anti-Art than work that later could be absorbed into the body of establishment art.

John Heartfield's design arrangements and mannequins substituted political for aesthetic content. His collages treated bourgeois morality and aesthetics with equal irreverence. From the ceiling of an exhibition room he hung the figure of a German officer whose partly opened visor revealed a pig's head. The medium of photomontage proved most suitable to Heartfield's particular forte, that was, the "desublimation" (as Marcuse called it four decades later) of the adversary's symbols and metaphors which were ridiculed by means of "literary" interpretations and illustrations. For instance, Goering's famous *dictum* "Iron

[11] Wieland Herzfelde added the *e* to Herzfeld after Else Lasker-Schüler misspelled his name in *Aktion* in 1914.

has made the country strong, butter and lard make people fat" is illustrated by a family at the dinner table devouring parts of ironware with gusto. This montage is boldly imprinted with the caption: "*Hurrah, die Butter ist Alle!*" ("Hurrah, no butter left!"). Heartfield's montage *We Are Praying to the Power of the Bombs* shows a church which is constructed of bombs and with a swastika, a dollar sign, and a pound sign atop its steeples. His collage *Whether Black or White, United in the Struggle* (1931), the earliest image of the black fist and the white fist clenched in the revolutionary salute, was created in response to the miscarriage of justice in the Scottsboro case.

The awareness of the insidious encroachment of power politics on the fabric of human life is necessary for the understanding of political art which is essentially a response to this predicament. Cognizant of the political potential of art to reflect and influence events, Herbert Marcuse investigated the interrelation of art and politics. Observing the ever accelerating change in styles of contemporary art, he comments in *An Essay on Liberation:*

> The radical character, the "violence" of the reconstruction in contemporary art, seems to indicate that it does not rebel against one style or another, but against "style" itself, against the art-form of art, against the traditional "meaning" of art. The great artistic rebellion in the period of the first World War gives the signal.[12]

The obliteration of style after style, the revulsion against the image, is significant for an art that has lost

[12] Herbert Marcuse, *An Essay on Liberation* (Boston: Beacon Press, 1969), p. 40.

its identity. A sense of arbitrariness prevails, which allows for trying anything, while being committed to nothing. Herbert Read calls this phenomenon the "corruption of consciousness." The avant-garde has chosen to concern itself with experimental innovation and occasional gimmickry. The much lamented demise of the "high arts of painting and sculpture" apparently reflects the malaise of the culture. It is not usual, however, that in times of social distress art drops to a "lower level." [13] The surging trends for democratization and social equalization deflate the "higher" accumulated cultural values, which now cease to relate to societal needs. A particular art form, then, is perceived as comatose when it persists in its commitment to the past. It becomes an exercise in pretense without much relevance to the present. *L'art pour l'art* sensibility does not correspond to a society in turmoil. As Nietzsche pointed out, "*L'art pour l'art* means: let morality go to the devil." Endless stylistic innovations and fads fail to come to terms with issues located at a level that cannot be reached by variations of the same.

According to Herbert Marcuse, the culture finds itself in a process of "desublimation." The sublime, the beautiful, the orderly, the segregated, and the harmonizing have suddenly lost much of their assumed meaning and hallowedness. Through the "ingression of the esthetic into the political," [14] cultural

[13] Gustave Courbet suggested that art should be put on a "lower level," since it was pretentious and insensitive to societal needs. The Academy blamed him for his "contempt of idealism." (Arnold Hauser, *The Social History of Art* [New York: Vintage Books, reprint of 1951 Alfred A. Knopf edition], p. 248.)

[14] Marcuse, p. 36.

meanings are changed, reversed, "desublimated." For instance the meaning of "Flower Power" is that the beautiful and natural is far more powerful than coercive force. Illustrating this contention, young girls put flowers into the barrels of the guns of the National Guards during the Pentagon demonstration. Marcuse gives another example of "desublimation": Familiar obscenities, hurled at government officials by radicals, undermine the self-understood status decorum essential to the smooth functioning of the governmental machinery.

> . . . a . . . subversive universe of discourse announces itself in the language of the black militants. Here is a systematic linguistic rebellion, which smashes the ideological context in which the words are employed and defined, and places them into the opposite context —negation of the established one. Thus, the blacks "take over" some of the most sublime and sublimated concepts of Western civilization, desublimate them and redefine them.[15]

In a footnote Marcuse states a hypothetical case: If, for example, high executives, presidents, and governors were to be addressed Pig X and Pig Y instead of President X and Governor Y, and if their speeches were translated "Oink, oink," their cultural status would indeed be "desublimated."

Marcuse's example might have been drawn from the illustrations by Emory Douglas, culture minister of the Black Panther Party. Douglas' cartoons, which appear in *The Black Panther* newspaper, transform the civic arena into a political zoo, populated by pig-police-

[15] *Ibid.*, p. 35.

men, vulture-businessmen, and rat-politicians. Twisting the status symbol beyond recognition, Emory Douglas is a master of cultural desublimation.

The desublimation of culture is basic to all revolutionary art. It typifies Anti-Art. But not all desublimating art is necessarily Anti-Art. For instance, the art of Emory Douglas desublimates culture, but it is not representative of Anti-Art. Douglas is not concerned with the issue of anti-aesthetics, an issue which is at the core of Anti-Art. Addressed to the black masses, the "Other Culture," and not to the white establishment, his eloquent work is free from the aesthetic conflict that has come to haunt the work of the avant-garde.

Marcuse describes desublimated art and Anti-Art as a liberating force in the struggle for freedom. The aesthetic dimension is not merely perceived in its formal and decorative aspects but in terms of its functional affinity to freedom. Not simply limited to what is considered "art," aesthetics embraces every human activity, a viewpoint that life-style artists, guerilla-art-action performers, and other radical artists share with Marcuse. In this sense, the diffusion of aesthetics deflates the importance allotted to art: "Then, art may have lost its privileged, and segregated, dominion over the imagination, the beautiful, the dream."[16]

In Marcuse's sense, aesthetics and morality eventually merge.

> The aesthetic morality is the opposite of puritanism. It does not insist on a daily bath or shower for people

[16] *Ibid.*, p. 48.

> whose cleaning practices involve systematic torture, slaughter, poisoning. Nor does it insist on clean clothes for men who are professionally engaged in dirty deals. But it does insist on cleaning the earth from the very material garbage produced by the spirit of capitalism and from this spirit itself. And it insists on freedom as a biological necessity: being physically incapable of tolerating any repression, other than that required for the protection and amelioration of life.[17]

The untapped potentialities of art at the revolutionary threshold are visualized: disruptive art, Anti-Art, prepares the stage, "where society's capacity to produce may be akin to the creative capacity of art, and the construction of the world of art akin to the reconstruction of the real world—union of liberating art and liberating technology.[18] The culmination of Marcuse's "aesthetic ethos" is the idea of "society as a work of art." [19] It was this utopian vision that inspired students during the Paris May Rebellion, 1968. Expounding a new consciousness, the students found that creative activity is immanent in each man and that the work of art or the artist happens to be "moments of this activity." [20] The Anti-Art spirit is revealed in these moments and does not lay any claim on permanence. And these moments must not be paralyzed by a social system "which makes the work or the man into a monument." [21]

The art of the May Rebellion exemplified this spirit: spontaneous and expendable statements desublimat-

[17] *Ibid.*, p. 28.
[18] *Ibid.*, p. 48.
[19] *Ibid.*, p. 45.
[20] *Ibid.*, p. 48.
[21] *Ibid.*

ing bourgeois assumptions. Affecting the whole environment, graffiti, posters, and guerilla theatre actions played a significant role in catalyzing the revolutionary impact, confirming Marcuse's dictum: "The revolution must be at the same time a revolution in perception which will accompany the material and intellectual reconstruction of society, creating the new aesthetic environment." [22]

The Paris Rebellion affected student rebellions everywhere, setting the tone for both the efficacy of student power and the style of "playing at the revolution." The buoyant spirit of the students succeeded in enlisting vast popular support: workers, clerks, shopkeepers, artists, etc. There was no time for aesthetic inbreeding: the urgency of the political purpose dominated the moment. Revolutionary life-style endorsed a life and a joy affirming radicalism, a far cry from the dead-serious dogmatism of Party politics: "And the young also attack the esprit de sérieux in the socialist camp: miniskirts against aparatchiks, Rock 'n' Roll against Soviet Realism." [23] The students were inspired by Marcuse's notion of creative freedom and not by Party stratagems, which had become unattractive.

> Revolution, like life, is an art, and it is up to each of us to live it like an artist. To elevate the paving-stone into a work of art, as some actually did, is to place oneself in the tradition of Marcel Duchamp rather than that of Lenin. To conceive revolution as a liberating festivity, as a sort of gigantic happening, demanding the participation of everyone and snatching the actors from the

[22] *Ibid.*, p. 37.
[23] *Ibid.*, p. 26.

> passivity and glumness of the commonplace, is to be an artist practicing the art of changing the world, by changing life and this is fairly far removed from the classic Marxist model.[24]

> "The most beautiful sculpture in the world is the paving-stone, the heavy paving-stone thrown in a policeman's face."[25]

The May rebellion rediscovered the importance of the urban play with students and artists, and the police as protagonist. Overnight the city became a giant theatre with barricades, burning buildings, torn-up pavements. Police actions against rebellious students almost like medieval passion plays, and guerilla theatre actions, performed by artists and students, acquired surrealistic overtones. The dream of creative freedom overwhelmed a repressive reality. Jean Jacques Lebel's "Capture of the Odéon" was an event, bigger and better than any other Happenings of European or American vintage. It made them look like Boy Scout exercises by comparison.

In contrast to the drama unfolding in the streets, the individual artist's "studio efforts" seemed to lag behind time:

> If only the artist can realize that most of his output stamps him as a man of the past, an anachronism, this will be a great step forward. All he will then have to do is find out how he can become a man of the future. Or

[24] Raymonde Moulin, "Living Without Selling," from *Art and Confrontation*, ed. by New York Graphic Society (New York: New York Graphic Society, 1970), p. 133.

[25] André Fermigier, "No More Claudels," from *Art and Confrontation*, p. 62.

simply a man of the present which would be an improvement.[26]

The May Rebellion created its own image with posters, slogans, and graffiti, scribbled hastily on the walls of buildings, public and private, inside and outside: *CULTURE IS DEAD—CREATE! IMAGINATION AU POUVOIR*. The emphasis was on the moment of action: *VIVRE AU PRÉSENT!*

That the Paris May Rebellion posters and graffiti were eagerly consumed by dealers and collectors does not change the fact of their past revolutionary impact.[27] The rebellion was a French problem and did not trouble American museums,[28] which a few months later exhibited the revolutionary propaganda. Up against the wall of New York museums the revolutionary spirit was barely perceptible, the radical impact as good as lost.

The revolutionary posters designed to be given away freely became collectors' items. Thereafter, the more popular posters were commercially printed and sold inexpensively.[29] In either case, the posters ceased to be free and ceased to be revolutionary.

[26] Michel Ragon, "The Artists and Society," from *Art and Confrontation*, p. 28.

[27] The Museum of Modern Art exhibition, "Paris, May, 1968, Posters of the Student Revolt," November, 1968.

[28] The Jewish Museum exhibition, "Up Against the Wall: Protest Posters," December, 1968.

[29] The Paris May Rebellion Posters have been published by: Editions Tchou, *Mai 68 Affiches;* Usines Universités union, Paris, 1968, *Atelier Populaire présenté par lui-même. 87 Affiches de mai-juin;* Verlag M. Du Mont Schauberg, *Das Politische Plakat und der Aufstand der französischen Studenten;* London: Dobson; New York: Bobbs-Merrill, *Atelier Populaire*, 1969.

Theodore Roszak reports that Marcuse himself had become "hot feature material" for the American and European press in the wake of the 1968 European student rebellions. Though Marcuse was chagrined with this situation, it was but another example confirming his conception: "At the same time it is a beautiful verification of my philosophy, which is that in this society everything can be co-opted, everything can be digested."[30] With the same zeal with which the press collected Marcuse items against his wishes, collectors collect art that had been specifically designed to be free. Collectors *must* collect. The acquisitive urge overcomes all sorts of obstacles, satisfied with nothing but more. In exchange for patronage, artists have traditionally been expected to enhance the patron's prestige and to exalt the existing power structure. In a state of decadence, however, the establishment appears quite eager to catch up with the rebellious expression and to purchase the latest slap.

In his article "Marcuse and Anti-Art," the critic Gregory Battcock presents the following definition of Anti-Art:

> In order for a statement to be awarded the "Anti-Art" label, such a statement must, in some way, demand (require) a change in the prevailing receptive capabilities. Therefore, it must not only be difficult to accept as art, but *it must be unacceptable as art.* The assumption is that only the work that is unacceptable is capable of forcing a readjustment, a change, a disruption, a revolution of those capacities and faculties that ultimately

[30] Theodore Roszak, *The Making of a Counter Culture* (New York: Doubleday-Anchor Books, 1969), p. 71.

> determine the meaning and effectiveness for the individual of all information received.[31]

At first glance it would appear that the criterion of *unacceptability* is well chosen. Battcock's definition apparently comes to terms with the commodity status of the art object.

Nonetheless, on closer inspection, a definition based on *unacceptability* does not work. There is no form of art that cannot be absorbed by a voracious art market. Classifying recent styles in terms of being more or less *unacceptable*, Battcock finds Earth Art "*unacceptable*," for it can be neither collected nor merchandised and hence places itself outside of the gallery and museum business. Within a couple of years, however, Earth Art acquired a super-commodity-status, going into large-scale investments, land transactions which appealed to the culture-taste of the super-rich. According to Battcock, Conceptual Art, which can no longer be defined "as a commodity or even a physical fact of any commercial value," [32] is the most *unacceptable* art form. Battcock proposes to dub it "Outlaw" art. (One might be tempted to argue with a romantic terminology suggestive of virile strength and stamina when applied to an *oeuvre* predominantly intellectual and without physical presence.) After a few years, however, Conceptual Art also has been successfully assimilated by the international art market in the form of books, statements, photos, and Xeroxed and teletyped diagrams.

[31] Gregory Battcock, "Marcuse and Anti-Art," *Arts Magazine*, Summer, 1969.

[32] *Ibid.*

John Cage's definition of radical art, which Battcock mentions in his article, merits attention: ". . . the radicality of art is defined not in terms of its form, but in terms of its disruptive function within a given social, political, economic, or psychological framework." According to Cage's definition, the radicality of form within the art context is politically ineffective. Battcock's definition of radical art is couched in terms of aesthetic rather than political radicalness. He does not deal with the elusiveness of Anti-Art. Marcuse calls attention to this phenomenon.

> . . . the eruption of anti-art has manifested itself in many familiar forms: destruction of syntax, fragmentation of words and sentences, explosive use of ordinary language, compositions without score, sonatas for anything. And yet, this entire de-formation is Form: anti-art has remained art, supplied, purchased and contemplated as art.[33]

In Duchamp's sense, the term *Anti-Art* applied more to aesthetic than to political radicalness. (The degree to which his Anti-Art upset the establishment, however, clearly bordered the political.) Convinced that the importance of political issues dwarfed the concern with aesthetics, the German Dadaists—particularly George Grosz and John Heartfield—used their art to amplify political issues. But in spite of their intentions, their political art (as well as Duchamp's Anti-Art) is *now* perceived only as art in terms of aesthetic criteria. Evidently the means for liberating art from the encroachment of the establishment are

[33] Marcuse, pp. 41–42.

not contained within the art object. The radicalness of Anti-Art does not change the system but is merely absorbed by it.

The elusiveness of Anti-Art raises the question whether the continued use of the term serves any further purpose. It has been frequently argued that there is no such thing as Anti-Art. Everything turns into art anyway. Objects become collector's items and Anti-Art is victimized by the acquisition compulsion. The ingenious establishment devises ways to collect art whose very essence is to defy acquisition. In opposition to the artists' intention the work of Anti-Art is obscenely transformed into an art object for sale. If the further use of the term *Anti-Art* makes any sense, it has to be redefined as rebellious, desublimating art that negates notions of quality and permanence and hence cannot be collected.

Herbert Marcuse's *Essay on Liberation* resuscitated the concept of Anti-Art, radicalizing it substantially by extending it into the purely political arena. In contrast to Duchamp, Marcuse places Anti-Art in streets and marketplaces and not in galleries and museums. For Marcuse, desublimating Anti-Art becomes a means for catalyzing and expressing revolutionary consciousness.

The art of the Paris May Rebellion established that Anti-Art existed only at its inception when it spilled its guts. Within a couple of months or sooner, the revolutionary Anti-Art became harmless. It had then the shock value of a polar bear rug spread in front of a four-poster. In a discussion of the May Rebellion art at the Guggenheim Museum, New York City, 1969, Marcuse commented on its Anti-Art characteristics, a comment he later disowned at a meeting with Gregory Battcock in Cabris, France, July, 1970.[34] Understandably so. What had been perceived as Anti-Art at its creative moment had been transformed into art objects exhibited in museums and galleries. Yet, the elusiveness of Anti-Art is precisely what it is about. If Anti-Art exists at all—not only in terms of an art historical (Duchampian) oddity, but in the context of a revolutionary present—it has to be defined on the basis of its temporariness. When the time factor is taken into consideration, Gregory Battcock's criterion of *unacceptability* is applicable to its definition. The disruptive function of Anti-Art manifests itself only at the crucial moment when it spends itself in an eruption of furious energy.

[34] Recounted by Gregory Battcock.

IT'S ONLY WORDS *

by John Perreault

Elsewhere in this book Harold Rosenberg observes that the existence of Conceptual Art "... depends entirely on words." John Perreault goes a step further when he points out that "If Conceptual Art is not photogenic, certainly the artists themselves are." Perreault (as well as Rosenberg, though for different reasons) sees Conceptual Art as an inevitable and logical development that lies well within the mainstream of the history of modern art: "Conceptual Art takes Constructivist-Dada Minimalism one step further. . . ."

In considering the larger cultural and technological ambience for vanguard art Perreault asks: "Is it so surprising that in a time when postindustrial ephemeralization is rampant, when information bits are speedier and more important than . . . face-to-face contact, when we are bombarded with message units, when time is so precious it almost has become a substance, when space is at a premium, when history forces us to dematerialize, that artists everywhere should come up with Conceptual Art?" In short, Perreault combines the thinking of Fuller with the terminology of McLuhan; he notes, "Conceptual Art is a symptom of globalism. . . ."

Perreault has been art critic for The Village Voice *for years. His "performances" have been presented all over,*

* Reprinted from *The Village Voice*, May 20, 1971.

including such places as The Whitney Museum, St. Mark's Church, and the Architectural League. A recent work, "Oedipus, A New Work," was performed in Greenwich Village in 1971. He is the author of Andy Warhol.

It has been established by now that Conceptual Art is a legitimate art form, as legitimate as painting or sculpture. It should not be confused with either. In Conceptual Art the idea is paramount and the materials are immaterial. Well, almost.

Throughout my wanderings, however, here and in the hinterlands, the question that pops up most is one of categories. Is or isn't Conceptual Art poetry? I answer that in most instances the verbal format used is inglorious, workaday, transparent prose. Besides, let's not worry about categories. If an artist places anything, even his dirty underwear, in an art context, then it's art, good, bad, or indifferent art, but still art. This approach is Duchampian but workable.

I for one never doubted that Conceptual Art was legitimate, but then I have a reputation for being notoriously open-minded. That is my role as an art critic, particularly since there are already so many art critics of the opposite approach who somehow feel that there is something precious to be guarded, some religious standard of high art to be maintained.

On some deep level I am a romantic. We all are. Even Puritanism is romantic. I am insatiable. I am never content with what is or with what has been. I always want something else, something more. It is not a bad habit. It is my character. I was born restless and hungry and a little bit angry.

Museums recently have tended to beat the galleries

to the punch. There have already been several museum shows in New York of Conceptual Art: the controversial "Information" show at the Modern and the Conceptual show at the New York Cultural Center, which, by the way, has neatly taken the place of the Jewish Museum in terms of new art. The strongest works in the ill-fated "Software" show at the Jewish were Conceptual in nature. This is not to mention numerous shows, fully or partly Conceptual, across North America recently (in Ohio, in Seattle, and in Vancouver) and worldwide (in Argentina, Switzerland, London, etc.).

I am not saying that everyone should or can appreciate this new art form. A lot of it I myself find pointless or unintelligible. Bad writing and/or fuzzy thinking placed in an art context can only be bad art, the context notwithstanding.

From one point of view, Conceptual Art takes Constructivist-Dada Minimalism one step further by virtually eliminating the object. A good case can be made for the reductionist model that tries to describe changes in art in terms of the process of elimination. The pun is intended.

On the other hand, it must be recognized that art takes place not only in a historical context but in a cultural and sociological one as well. Is it so surprising that in a time when postindustrial ephemeralization is rampant, when information bits are speedier and more important than heavy matter or face-to-face contact, when we are bombarded with message units, when time is so precious it almost has become a substance, when space is at a premium, when history forces us to dematerialize, that artists everywhere should come up with Conceptual Art? Conceptual Art is a symptom of globalism and it is the first—Surrealism almost was—really international art style.

Conceptual Art, in case you care, has already been assimilated, at least at the top half of the art pyramid. Only recently did Earth Art make a big, picture-spread splash in the pages of *Esquire.* That's at least a three-year gap between the art-magazine house organs and the slickest of the slicks. There's an even bigger gap between *Esquire* and *The Village* ("expect the unexpected") *Voice.* The structure is destructive. Sociology is as much a part of art as sex. It will take a similar amount of time for Conceptual Art to seep below the top half of the art pyramid. I am using *pyramid* metaphorically and literally because art in many ways is a tomb.

It will be interesting to see how it all turns out, for certainly Conceptual Art is not as photogenic as Robert Smithson's masterful Salt Lake spiral jetty or Heizer's desert trenches, which were pictured in *Esquire.* That these Earth Art works are photogenic is not a point of criticism. That they happen to be photogenic merely adds another level of communication.

In three years or maybe less, I suspect we *Esquire* readers will be treated to two-page photo spreads of the Conceptual artists themselves, with captions by Bruce Jay Friedman or whoever else happens to be hanging around Elaine's. (Kurt Vonnegut or Tom Wolfe would have been less tasteful but better as art critics.) Joe Kosuth at his typewriter, in the act of creation! The Art & Language group, conferring! Douglas Huebler loading his camera! Ian Wilson uttering! Mel Bochner measuring! Robert Barry thinking! Gilbert and George actually dancing! If Conceptual Art is not photogenic, certainly the artists themselves are. All is not lost.

The Dwan Gallery, home of many Conceptual and Earth Artists, has closed. The party, however, is not over. John Weber will take care of most of the Dwan artists in his new downtown emporium.

(Recently I asked someone how I could get tickets to Andy's play *Pork* and my friend said, "Oh, just go to the box office and say you are in Andy's party." "I don't think that will work," I answered, "because everybody is in Andy's party.")

I am bored with the art world hysteria. The grapevine has it that all the galleries are closing. You name the gallery and I can play you a telephone tape of some recent conversation that contains the information that it is closing. Who cares? They can all close and we would still be ahead. Other merchants or wingdings needing tax write-offs or glory are eagerly in the wings. All reports have been delivered to me with fiendish glee. The tone of voice is always "I told you so, the towers of Babylon are falling." Who cares? Nixon? Art is not as delicate as it appears to be. Art is alive and well and not living in Argentina, or Brazil.

The really great art-gallery people are shrewd merchants and have to be. Since I prefer the company of artists, who are infinitely more amusing, to the company of merchants, I have never had anything to do with the splendid dealer heads who have to make a living off of living artists. The relationship is reciprocal, ideally.

The fact of the matter is that amidst all this chaos, which I consider healthy and corrective, Castelli, certainly one of the top galleries, has taken the Conceptual plunge, and with incredible taste. Barry, Kosuth, and Huebler are all having shows.

FOUR INTERVIEWS *

by Arthur Rose

The four artists who respond to questions from Arthur Rose have been working in the Conceptual area longer than most; in some ways they may be considered "originators" of the movement. This frank and concise exchange contains observations that focus, in a general way, on many aspects of the Conceptual aesthetic.

Douglas Huebler states, ". . . I really don't care about precise or exhaustive documentation. The documents prove nothing. They make the piece exist. . . ." In explaining how he arrived at his present views, Joseph Kosuth says, "I began to realize . . . that the intelligent and sensitive people in my environment had experiences with nonart portions of their visual world that were of such quality and consistency that the demarcation of similar experiences as art would make no appreciable difference." He concludes the thought with these words: ". . . perhaps mankind was beginning to outgrow the need for art on that level." In discussing his art, Lawrence Weiner remarks, "One could say the subject matter is materials, but its reason to be goes way beyond materials to something else, that something else being art."

* Reprinted from *Arts Magazine*, 43, no. 4.

ROBERT BARRY

Q: How did you arrive at the kind of work you are now doing?

BARRY: It's a logical continuation of my earlier work. A few years ago when I was painting, it seemed that paintings would look one way in one place and, because of lighting and other things, would look different in another place. Although it was the same object, it was another work of art. Then I made paintings which incorporated as part of their design the wall on which they hung. I finally gave up painting for the wire installations (two of which are in the show). Each wire installation was made to suit the place in which it was installed. They cannot be moved without being destroyed.

Color became arbitrary. I started using thin transparent nylon monofilament. Eventually the wire became so thin that it was virtually invisible. This led to my use of a material which is invisible, or at least not perceivable in a traditional way. Although this poses problems, it also presents endless possibilities. It was at this point that I discarded the idea that art is necessarily something to look at.

Q: If your work is not perceivable, how does anyone deal with it or even know of its existence?

BARRY: I'm not only questioning the limits of our perception, but the actual nature of perception. These forms certainly do exist, they are controlled and have their own characteristic. They are made of various kinds of energy which exist outside the narrow arbitrary limits of our own senses. I use various devices to produce the energy, detect it, measure it, and define its form.

By just being in this show, I'm making known the existence of the work. I'm presenting these things in an artistic situation using the space and the catalogue. I think this will be less of a problem as people become more acclimated to this art. As with any art, an interested person reacts in a personal way based on his own experience and imagination. Obviously, I can't control that.

Q: Exactly what kind of energy do you use?

BARRY: One kind of energy is electromagnetic waves. There is a piece in the show which uses the carrier wave of a radio station for a prescribed length of time, not as a means of transmitting information but rather as an object. Another piece uses the carrier wave of a citizens' band transmitter to bridge two distant points in New York and Luxembourg several times during the run of the show. Because of the position of the sun and favorable atmospheric conditions during January—the month of the show—*this* piece could be made. At another time, under different conditions, other locations would have to be used. There are two smaller carrier-wave pieces which have just enough power to fill the exhibition space. They are very different in character, one being AM, the other being FM, but both will occupy the same space at the same time—such is the nature of the material.

Also in the show will be a room filled with ultrasonic sound. I've also used microwaves and radiation. There are many other possibilities which I intend to explore—and I'm sure there are a lot of things we don't yet know about which exist in the space around us, and, though we don't see or feel them, we somehow know they are out there.

DOUGLAS HUEBLER

Q: How does the work "enter the mind" as you have put it?

HUEBLER: Through a system of documentation which includes the use of maps, drawings, photographs, and descriptive language. The documents are not intended to be necessarily interesting, that is, *they* are not "art." What I want is to use the documents to create a condition of absolute coexistence between "image" and "language." For example, the "image" of my *New York Variable Piece #1* is a description of space made from the location of "points" that are either static or move vertically and horizontally in a random disposition. There is no possible way in which this piece can be experienced perceptually. It can be totally experienced through its documentation.

Q: Can any of your works be experienced as physical presence?

HUEBLER: None can—so far at least—and yet they do possess material substance. The area of a "site sculpture" is immense and the sites are located by very small markers that, no doubt, will soon enough actually disappear. The material of a duration piece does disappear during the period of time that it is made. Nonetheless, it actually exists in present time through its documentation.

Q: Do you attach any significance to the sites in your pieces?

HUEBLER: None. When I go to the site to document it—to "mark it"—I think "here it is" and that's all. As a matter of fact, I consider it important that it is no different from the next ten feet or next block or whatever. It's very much like seeing the border of a state. Both the sites selected and the shape that they describe are "neutral" and only function to form "that" work. In effect, no privileged value is assigned to the elements that form the work over those other possible things that are not chosen. In a similar way I would point out that "duration" works do not necessarily "complete" the destiny of the material used within the specific situation. A period of time is chosen and whatever happens to the situation is documented. In some works "logical" chronology is the structure and in others the sequence is scrambled after the documentation is complete.

Q: That leads me to ask if all this documentation is complete, precise, or logical.

HUEBLER: In the same sense that I don't care about specific appearance I really don't care about precise or exhaustive documentation. The documents prove nothing. They make the piece exist and I am interested in having that existence occur in as simple a way as possible. Where a thing is located involves everything else and I like that idea much more than how I "feel" about it or what it looks like.

JOSEPH KOSUTH

Q: For the last few years all of your work has been subtitled "Art as Idea as Idea." Why and how did you arrive at this and what does it mean exactly?

KOSUTH: Well, a few years ago I became increasingly aware of the fact that the separation between one's ideas and one's use of material, if not wide at the inception of the work, becomes almost uncommunicatively wide when confronted by a viewer. I wanted to eliminate that gap. I also began to realize that there is nothing abstract about a specific material. There is always something hopelessly real about materials, be they ordered or unordered.

I began to realize, as well, that the intelligent and sensitive people in my environment had experiences with nonart portions of their visual world that were of such quality and consistency that the demarcation of similar experiences as art would make no appreciable difference; that perhaps mankind was beginning to outgrow the need for art on that level; that he was beginning to deal with his world aesthetically. It was the feeling I had about the gap between materials and ideas that led me to present a series of photostats of the dictionary definition of water. I was interested in just presenting the *idea* of water. I had used actual water earlier because I liked its colorless, formless quality. I didn't consider the photostat a work of art; only the idea was art. The words in the definition supplied the *art information;* just as the shape and color of a work could be considered its art information. But I wanted complete art and wanted to remove even entertainment as a reason for its existence. I wanted to remove the experience from the work of art. In this series I went from presenting an abstraction of a particular (water, air) to abstractions of abstractions (meaning, empty, universal, nothing, time).

Q: Would you discuss what you are doing now?

KOSUTH: My current work, which consists of categories from the thesaurus, deals with the multiple aspects of an idea of something. And, like the other work, it's an attempt to deal with abstraction. The largest change has been in its form of presentation—

going from the mounted photostat to the purchasing of spaces in newspapers and periodicals (with one "work" sometimes taking up as many as five or six spaces in that many publications—depending on how many divisions exist in the category). This way the immateriality of the work is stressed and any possible connections to painting are severed. The new work is not connected with a precious object—it's accessible to as many people as are interested: it's nondecorative—having nothing to do with architecture; it can be brought into the home or museum but wasn't made with either in mind; it can be dealt with by being torn out of its publication and inserted into a note-book or stapled to the wall—or not torn out at all—but any such decision is unrelated to the art. My role as an artist ends with the work's publication.

Q: Why do you think the—as you put it—"art of our time" cannot be painting and sculpture?

KOSUTH: Being an artist now means to question the nature of art. If one is questioning the nature of painting, one cannot be questioning the nature of art; if an artist accepts painting (or sculpture) he is accepting the tradition that goes with it. That's because the word *art* is general and the word *painting* is specific. Painting is a *kind* of art. If you make paintings you are already accepting (not questioning) the nature of art. One is then accepting the nature of art to be the European tradition of a painting-sculpture dichotomy. But in recent years the best new work has been neither painting nor sculpture, and increasing numbers of young artists make art that is neither one. When words lose their meaning they are meaningless. We have our own time and our own reality and it need not be justified by being hooked into European art history.

Nothing being done could be done without the accumulated knowledge we have at our disposal, obviously. One can never completely escape the past, but to look in that direction intentionally and blatantly is creative timidity. The academic and conservative mind always craves historical justification: a sort of homogenization of ancestor worship and cravings for parental approval. One should learn about the past but not from it, so that one can find out what was real then and what one doesn't want to do now.

Q: Won't the difficulty of the work, and its use of language rather than colors, bore people?

KOSUTH: Inherent in the artist's intentions are his ideas, and the new art is dependent on language not much less than philosophy or science. Obviously the shift from the perceptual to the conceptual is a shift from the physical to the mental. And where an intellectual interest doesn't exist on the part of the viewer, a physical (sight or touch) one is desired. Nonartists often insist on something along with the art because they are not that excited by the idea of art. They need that physical excitation along with the art to keep them interested. But the artist has that same obsessed interest in art that the physicist has in physics and the philosopher in philosophy.

Q: But if one accepts your idea of art, and the artist no longer adds to man's visual world, what will be art's future?

KOSUTH: I'll pass on that by first pointing out something. The major philosophical tendencies of this century show a complete rejection of traditional philosophy. It just isn't possible to make conclusions about the world in the way it once was. Among the educated and the youth, religion as well has lost its meaning.

The assumption of traditional philosophy and religion are unreal at this stage of man's intelligence. If philosophy (and religion) is finished, it is possible that art's viability may be connected to its ability to exist as a pure, self-conscious endeavor. Art may exist in the future as a kind of philosophy by analogy. This can only occur, however, if art remains "self-conscious" and concerns itself only with art problems, changing as those problems may be. If art does become a "philosophy by analogy" it will be because its intellectual rigor (in terms of the artist's ability to "create") is equal in quality to the intensity of the best thinking of the past. If proper philosophy cannot be in our time, then obviously art posing as philosophy would be equally meaningless. But an art concerned with the special issues related only to art may fill that gap in man's thought in our time.

LAWRENCE WEINER

Q: When you did your early pieces, which consisted of paint being applied directly on the floor or wall (I am thinking of "the spray on the floor for so many minutes" pieces—one of which was reproduced in *Arts Magazine* last October—the paint thrown on the wall piece, and the paint poured on the floor piece), what did you have in mind?

WEINER: Making art.

Q: It has been said that some of the "Antiform" artists have been influenced by the look of some of your work. Is this true, and what is the primary difference between their work and yours?

WEINER: I can't imagine how, as they are primarily

concerned with making objects for display—which has nothing to do with the intent of my work.

Q: An integral aspect of your work is the existence of a receiver. The receiver—as I understand it—decides whether you will build the piece, have the piece fabricated, or not build it at all. Why?

WEINER: Because it doesn't matter.

Q: What doesn't matter?

WEINER: The condition of the piece. If I were to choose the condition, that would be an art decision which would lend unnecessary and unjustified weight to what amounts to presentation—and that has very little to do with the art.

Q: What is your interest in removing as an art process.

WEINER: I'm not interested in the process. Whereas the idea of removal is just as—if not more—interesting than the intrusion of a fabricated object into a space, as sculpture is.

Q: What role does time play in your work?

WEINER: As a designation of quantity.

Q: What is the subject matter of your work, would you say?

WEINER: Materials.

Q: You state that the subject matter of your work is materials, yet you claim that you are not a materialist—how does this follow?

WEINER: Material*ist* implies a primary involvement in materials, but I am primarily concerned with art. One could say the subject matter is materials, but its reason to be goes way beyond materials to something else, that something else being art.

ART AND WORDS *

by Harold Rosenberg

Elsewhere in this volume appears a quotation taken from a Rosenberg article that predates the piece printed here. Referring to recent problems in some avant-garde exhibitions, Rosenberg wrote: "The museum seems unaware how precarious it is to go as far out from art as it has on no other foundation than its simple-minded avant-gardism. In the direction it has taken, nothing awaits it but transformation into a low-rating mass medium." In the article that follows, Rosenberg examines characteristics of some recent trends and notes, "Every modern work participates in the ideas out of which its style arose."

With this thought in mind, the writer advances the idea that new directions in Conceptual and Antiform art are related to Abstract-Expressionist trends and specifically to so-called Action Painting. He observes, "No matter how completely paintings and sculptures succeed in purging themselves of subject matter, they continue to resent the essential subject matter of art's own self-conscious history."

This article is one of the first to appear that deals with the broader problems inherent in the aesthetic of a new type of art existing without many of the traditional properties heretofore associated with the art ob-

ject itself. The author views the general aesthetic of Conceptual Art in its historical perspective. As might be expected, Rosenberg sees the history of art as a major link between the new trends and other modern art. He concludes with a note of despair: "The current attempt in art to allow either the words or the materials to have their own way sacrifices the advantage of concrete thinking in behalf of an apparently irresistible tendency further to rationalize the practice of art."

Rosenberg sees a particular link between new art which communicates via explication and documentation and Abstract-Expressionist painting: "Art communicated through documents is a development to the extreme of the Action Painting idea that a painting ought to be considered as a record of the artist's creative processes rather than as a physical object."

Harold Rosenberg, one of the most distinguished and respected American art critics, is art critic for The New Yorker *magazine. His books include* The Tradition of the New *and* The Anxious Object.

A contemporary painting or sculpture is a species of centaur—half art materials, half words. The words are the vital, energetic element, capable, among other things, of transforming any materials (epoxy, light beams, string, rocks, earth) into art materials. It is its verbal substance that establishes the visual tradition in which a particular work is to be seen—that places a Newman in the perspective of Abstract Expressionism rather than of Bauhaus design or mathematical abstraction. Every modern work participates in the ideas out of which its style arose. The secretion of language in the work interposes a mist of interpretation between it and the eye; out of the quasi-mirage arises the prestige of the work, its power of survival, and its ability to extend its life through aesthetic descendants. The art-historical significance conferred by Duchamp and by Duchamp commentators on a bicycle wheel has induced the repeated resurrection of this object as if it were an *Annunciation*, an image indispensable to contemporary spiritual life. Its latest rebirth is *The Perpetual Moving Bicycle Wheel of Marcel Duchamp*, drawn by the kinetic artist Takis and shown at the Howard Wise Gallery in February.

In the last century, it was believed that the exclusion of subject matter (landscapes, people, family scenes, historical episodes, symbols) from painting would disentangle the image on the canvas from literary associations and clear the way for a direct response of the eye to optical data. In becoming more and more abstract, art is supposed to have attained, or been reduced to, speechlessness. The "Art of the Real" exhibition at the Museum of Modern Art last year described its selections as chunks of raw reality totally liberated from language; the black paintings of the late Ad Reinhardt aspired to be material equivalents of the silences of his Trappist friend, the late Thomas Merton. The common view was recently summed up as follows: "Modern art has eliminated the verbal correlative from the canvas." Perhaps. But if a work of today no longer has a verbal correlative, it is because its particular character has been dissolved in a sea of words. Literary language has been banished; a painting is no longer conceived as the metaphor of an experience available to both words and paint. But the place of literature has been taken by the rhetoric of abstract concepts.

An advanced painting of this century inevitably gives rise in the spectator to a conflict between his eye and his mind; as Thomas B. Hess points out in the February *Art News*, the fable of the emperor's new clothes is echoed at the rebirth of every modernist art movement. If work in a new mode is to be accepted, the eye-mind conflict must be resolved in favor of the mind; that is, of the language absorbed into the work. Of itself, the eye is incapable of bringing into the intellectual system that today distinguishes between objects that are art and those that are not. Given its primitive function of discriminating among objects in shopping centers and on highways, the eye will recognize a Noland as a fabric design, a Judd as a stack of metal bins—until the eye's outrageous philistinism has been subdued by the drone of formulas concerning breakthroughs in color, space, and even optical perception (this, too, unseen by the eye, of course). It is scarcely an exaggeration to say that paintings are today apprehended with the ears. Miss Barbara Rose, one of the promoters of striped canvases and aluminum boxes, confesses that words are essential to the art she favors when she writes, "Although the logic of Minimal Art gained critical respect, if not admiration, its reductiveness allowed for a relatively limited art experience." Recent art criticism has reversed earlier procedures; instead of deriving principles from what it sees, it teaches the eye to "see" principles; the writings of one of America's influential critics often pivot on the drama of how he failed to respond to a painting or sculpture the first few times he saw it but, returning to the work, penetrated the concept that made it significant and was then able to appreciate it. To qualify as a member of the art public, an individual must be tuned to the appropriate verbal reverberations of objects in art galleries, and his receptive mechanism must be constantly adjusted to oscillate to new vocabularies.

Since the eye and the analogies it discovers in common-sense experience cannot be trusted, the first rule in discussing modern art is that a painting or sculpture must never be found to resemble (or to be) an object that is not a work of art; a sculpture consisting of a red plank must under no circumstance be identified as a red plank, a set of Plexiglas cubes as a type of store fixture. When Theodore Roosevelt observed at the 1913 Armory Show that Duchamp's *Nude Descending a Staircase* reminded him of a "Navajo rug," he committed the archetypal critical *faux pas.* Art is the product of an etiquette, and to neglect its conceptual framework and reduce it to its physical data is an act of barbarism, like using a prayer shawl for a cleaning rag; the point of the emperor story is that it was a child ignorant of the rules who announced that the emperor was naked. As a sculpture, a painted plank is not only its material substance but the crystallization of a moment in the continuous debate on the nature of art—an intellectual element missing from planks in lumberyards. Injected into this discourse, the plank, or one of Christo's packages, becomes an item of our aesthetic culture, though not necessarily a profound or desirable item. The ban against saying what a painting or sculpture "really is" arises out of the verbal aspect of modern art, and to keep art intact the power of words in it needs to be constantly augmented. By segregating the object it accredits as a painting or sculpture from all other objects in nature, language sustains the sacred or mythical status of art without the need for religion or myth. The taboo against assimilating the description of a painting into the general rhetoric of visual experience, against describing a striped canvas and a striped tablecloth in the same terms, is a twentieth-century version of the outlawing of blasphemy. For more than a century, radical art movements have been demanding the "desacralization" of art and the dissolution of all barriers between art and life. Such efforts are bound to fail as long as the word *art* continues to refer to a special category of objects. Regardless of the Anti-Art character of modern paintings, their verbal ingredient separates them from images and things merely seen and removes them to a realm founded on the intellectual interrelation among works of art. No matter how completely paintings and sculptures succeed in purging themselves of subject matter, they continue to present the essential subject matter of art's own self-conscious history. Without this invisible content, art would no longer exist, though individuals, among them two-year-olds, grandmothers, and automobile designers, might continue to satisfy the impulse to make things attractive through form and color.

To the consternation of art critics, the materials-words composition of art has become an explicit theme in the newest modes of painting and sculpture displayed this season. With comic literalism, "Earthworks" sculpture attempts to overcome the separation of art from nature by acting on a segment of the landscape—in short, by treating nature itself as art material. An artist makes circular tracks on a snowfield or shapes a contour in the desert; another cuts a trench across a driveway. Art that reshapes the terrain was once known as landscape architecture or landscape gardening. The terms are, however, strenuously resisted by contemporary Earthworkers, whose aim is not an eye-delighting prospect but the realization of a concept. Art that is part of nature represents a hyper-materialization that overcomes the limits of specialized art materials and even of man-made materials generally (since everything, from foam rubber to magnets, has now been incorporated into art's stockpile). Earthworks also avoid placing creations in art galleries and so surmount the segregation of art on the social plane, though Earthworks art does get into art galleries by informational means—photographs, models, diagrams, maps, statements by the artist (for example, the current exhibition of moss and algae, chemical, and mold pieces by Peter Hutchinson at the John Gibson Gallery). Ironically, Earthworks materialism produces in practice an effect opposite to the intended fusion of art and the physical world, for, like "Art of the Real," its existence as art depends entirely on words (the announcement of the Hutchinson show cites his articles on earth and plant art in leading art magazines). Since the Earthwork is usually not transportable—it may not even be perceptible as a unit or during a particular time—all that is available to the spectator is its documentation, and this, according to one site-modifier, "creates a condition of absolute coexistence between 'image' and 'language.'"

Art communicated through documents is a development to the extreme of the Action Painting idea that a painting ought to be considered as a record of the artist's creative processes rather than as a physical object. It is the event of the doing, not the thing done, that is the "work." Logically, the work may therefore be invisible—told about but not seen. The sculpture Oldenburg made to be buried underground has become an influential work through hearsay. In the same spirit, a sculpture by Bruce Nauman consists of a flat slab said to have a mirrored surface on the underside, and an item by Richard Artschwager at the Whitney Annual was made up of a hundred pads of varied substances inconspicuously scattered around the gallery (because it used the Annual as its environment, the Artschwager could never "take place" again). One step further and the work of art need not even be made; the creative act can consist of a proposal for a work. Not long ago, Kienholz exhibited a score of framed sheets describing projects he was prepared to execute. This is, intellectually, a more rarefied gesture than sending diagrams to a factory and delivering finished products to an art gallery. Two young artists in Latin America contrived a Happening that was reported in detail in the press but never took place, so their "work of art" consisted of their own news releases and the resulting interviews, accounts, and comments. Given the mythical status of art conferred by words, uncreated art is the myth of a myth. An artist whose current medium is space bought in newspapers put it another way: "Art may exist in the future as a kind of philosophy by analogy."

In his exhibition at the Dwan Gallery last month, Robert Smithson, a sculptor who is also the author of arcane meditations and satires, attempted to combine the conceptualization of the invisibilists with the rugged materiality of the earthshapers. His "nonsites" consisted of containers of rocks, gravel, and lumps of asphalt selected and arranged according to a recondite system of formal correspondences, geological information, stone-collecting trips to the country, and interpretations of the recent history of sculpture. For spectators incapable of mastering Smithson's rationale or unwilling to take the trouble, the visual actuality of his exhibition consisted of stones in differently shaped and painted bins (some cut out on top to match the profile of the terrain, others shaped in the chic mode of mathematically patterned floor sculpture), plus diagrams, photomaps, documents, and framed statements on the wall. Here, as in "Art of the Real," aesthetic metaphor was replaced by the "real thing"—what can be more real than raw rocks, piles of gravel, maps, and documents?—but the real thing proved once again to be art as an excrescence of theory. An interviewer writes that Smithson "reads Worringer, Hulme, Ehrenzweig, Borges, Robbe-Grillet on the subject of art," and, mentioning also Empson and Wittgenstein "on the subject of linguistics," he concludes that Smithson's pieces are "not primarily sensual or even, visual [but] are reconstructions of thought processes"; Smithson, like the artist of newspaper inserts, believes that art today must become "speculative philosophy."

In an apparent move away from verbalized or conceptualized art, experiments are being made to produce paintings and sculptures through letting materials "speak for themselves" with a minimum of formal ordering by the artist. Allowing paint, scattered scraps of paper, or flung bits of metal to arrange themselves as they will belongs to the traditional ruse of the art of this century employed to bring forth unknown energies out of its mediums in order to silence the directives of aesthetics and art history. The reduction of the arts to their material components corresponds to an awareness of the decomposition of inherited art forms—an awareness that keeps growing more acute. The composer Morton Feldman states the proposition that "sound *in itself* can be a totally plastic phenomenon, suggesting its own shape, design, and poetic metaphor." Equivalent ideas are presented in literature by practitioners of "concrete poetry." They stem from the conviction that existing forms in painting, poetry, and music inevitably distort experience, and that it is necessary to start afresh with the raw matter out of which a poem or painting is made. The medium itself becomes the "mind" that, to Feldman, "suggests its own shape, design, and poetic metaphor." In sum, it delivers its own substance as its "message."

The idea of art as the action of the artist's materials complements the idea of art as the act of the artist. The retrospective of the paintings and drawings of Willem de Kooning at the Museum of Modern Art is the record of thirty years of experiment in fusing these forms of action into a synthesis of will and chance. In de Kooning's laboratory, the animated paint takes its form from the artist's personality, while the artist discovers the changing form of his personality in the physical potentialities of his medium. The Action paintings of Jackson Pollock, a large selection of whose works in black-and-white will be on view at the Marlborough-Gerson Gallery through this Saturday, also represent a union of the artist's action with that of his pigment. Pollock's handling of paint has, however, been misinterpreted as a version of automatic writing, and this has led to distortions concerning the self-activation of materials and the part of materials in the creation of art.

The reputation of Helen Frankenthaler, currently seen in a retrospective at the Whitney Museum, rests on her adaptation of Pollock's "liberated" fluid pigment on unprimed canvas; *No. 26* (1951), at the Marlborough, is a particularly good example of the Pollock originals. Frankenthaler's paintings have the immediate attractiveness of tastefully matched colors and, in some of her later canvases, bold design. Unfortunately, the favorable first impression does not hold up, for reasons I shall go into later. At the point of diminishing response, however, words intervene to remove this artist's paintings to a plane other than the visual. In the opening sentences of the exhibition catalogue, Professor E. C. Goossen, who also arranged the "Art of the Real" exhibition, credits Miss Frankenthaler with having "invented an original method for applying paint to canvas. Known as the soak-stain technique, it was instrumental in making a new kind of color painting possible." Here materials find a corollary in art-historical verbiage (the alleged significance of Frankenthaler's influence on Noland and Louis)—a magical combination sufficient to give the artist a retrospective at forty and a public advantage over such superior contemporaries as Joan Mitchell and Lester Johnson, both of whom stem, like Frankenthaler, from Action Painting. (Johnson's show at the Martha Jackson Gallery in February was the most powerful exhibition of new paintings by a younger artist this year.) Regardless of the accuracy of attributing the "invention" of soak-stain to Frankenthaler (one thinks of it as customary procedure in watercolor, and of Georgia O'Keeffe painting with absorbent cotton), the notion that a new way of using materials can be inherently significant and even progressive is another instance of the overpowering of the eye by words. Writing in the February *Arts* of an exhibition at the Castelli warehouse gallery of the new "Anti-Form" art, which calls upon the expressive powers inherent in sheets of rubber, felt, chicken wire, and lead pellets, Mr. Grégoire Müller declares that the works under consideration are often of "greater intellectual than visual interest." Since the intellectual interest lies not necessarily in the artist's own ideas but in the debate and polemics into which his paintings fall, Mr. Müller's judgment may be applied also to Miss Frankenthaler's self-expressive paint. It is weak visual matter in an envelope of aggressive critical language. The early paintings in her retrospective, with their borrowings from Pollock, Gorky, Kandinsky, and other occasional stainers, are sensitive, but more timid than sensitive. In her middle period, she attempts to detach herself from more patent influences and her work falls into a confusion of blots, stabilized at times by hints of the rectangle. Later, the transparency of acrylics cooperates with her uncertainty by permitting forms to blot visibly over one another without compelling the artist to select among them. In her canvases of the past three years, large, simplified torn shapes communicate an appearance of assurance, but *Flood* (1967) is a relapse into vague spongings.

In the Action paintings of Lester Johnson, the action emanates from the artist in a decisive locking of forms, lyrical rhythms, tension between image and scale, compression of surface by color. With Frankenthaler, the artist's action is at a minimum; it is the paint that is active. The artist is the medium of her medium; her part is limited to selecting aesthetically acceptable effects from the behavior of her color. Apparently, Miss Frankenthaler has never grasped the moral and metaphysical basis of Action Painting, and since she is content to let the pigment do all the acting, her compositions fail to develop resistances against which a creative act can take place. The result is a distressing flabbiness, an effect (emphasized by the huge dimensions of her Whitney canvases) of too little out of too much. The soaked-in pigments, which keep the surface flat regardless of the number of veils of color, spread the eye across an expanse as characterless as the sheen of a photograph. In a photograph, the gaze is arrested by the subject; in the Frankenthalers, apart from patches of lively color, there is nothing to see. In their lack of purpose, her runs and blots often touch the edge of the absurd, and paintings such as *Interior Landscape*, *Buddha's Court*, and *Small's Paradise* are over the edge. Presented one or two at a time, the Frankenthalers are often pleasing for their color. Massed in a retrospective and featuring the biggest, they are decorative bombast sustained by dubious art history.

Paul Jenkins, whose canvases were shown in March at the Martha Jackson Gallery and in his Broadway studio, also sets in motion transparent veils of pigment, but his paintings are haunted by a vocabulary that differs from the art-historical dogmas of the Frankenthaler circle. Jenkins is an occultist with fantasies of action at a distance. His process art collaborates with his psychic detachment to produce an image that is like the chemical flowering of ice or rock. In several of the new mammoth canvases, mountainous flaunts of gray on gray sweep into distances of pure white that solicit silence as intensely as the black squares of Reinhardt.

The animation of materials in no matter how random a way cannot be dissociated from the artist's aesthetic aims, which are in turn related to his state of being (Müller speaks of the "occasional lapses into sentimentality" of one of the Anti-Form arrangers of rubber and plastic) and his general outlook. An artist's choice of material is inevitably expressive; the stained burlap sacks the Italian artist Burri used as his medium in the forties while he was an American prisoner of war represented an emotional universe different from that of the elegant substances to which he turned after he had become internationally known. But in addition to representing feelings, materials, even the rawest, have become conceptualized; as Valéry stated it, "The modern world is being remade in the image of man's mind." There is no turning back to the organic astuteness of the traditional craftsman, nor will surrendering to his medium liberate the artist from the obsessions of thought. The words of art will continue to speak to the artist either from behind, directing him without his being aware of them, or in the form of conscious problems to be confronted and modified. If, as the sculptor Clement Meadmore recently declared, "the current question seems to be 'Is the material, left to its own devices, capable of performing as a work of art?,'" the answer is a categorical "No," not because chance or "the natural behavior of different materials" is incapable of producing significant combinations but because no material can, properly speaking, be "left to its own devices." Given the present degree of aesthetic self-consciousness, even the most haphazard scattering of debris, if carried out in the milieu of art, has become purposive through the fact that it is by now a fifty-year-old technique for creating art. Today, chance itself cannot prevail against the potency of aesthetic recollections. In art, ideas are materialized, and materials are manipulated as if they were meanings. This is the intellectual advantage of art as against disembodied modes of thought. The current attempt in art to allow either the words or the materials to have their own way sacrifices the advantage of concrete thinking in behalf of an apparently irresistible tendency further to rationalize the practice of art.

ON EXHIBITIONS AND THE WORLD AT LARGE: A CONVERSATION WITH SETH SIEGELAUB *

by Seth Siegelaub

During the last two years Seth Siegelaub has acted as a dealer and exhibition organizer to assist and present the activities of those artists to whose ideas he has felt committed. Rather than attempt to push this art along the channels through which art is customarily given currency, he has established situations suggested by the radically different nature of the art itself. Exhibitions have recently tended to be dominated by prestigious objects. Siegelaub has been principally concerned with artists for whom work does not necessarily result in the creation of anything visible or discrete. More energetically and more imaginatively than any other defender of the conceptual in art he has worked to provide new conditions of exhibiting and publishing whereby the ideas of the artists may be made as widely available as possible without the risk of spurious identities attached to them.

Several of the earliest exhibitions dealing with Conceptual Art were organized by Seth Siegelaub. One of these, called "0 Objects, 0 Painters, 0 Sculptures," was held in New York in January, 1969.

Siegelaub has published several books and catalogues that were pioneering documents within the

* Reprinted from *Studio International*, December, 1969.

field of Idea Art. In October, 1970, he participated in the Halifax conference of Conceptualists and in 1970 authored (with lawyer Bob Projansky) the Artists' Reserved Rights Transfer and Sale Agreement, *which protects and defines artists' rights.*

CHARLES HARRISON: Do you think exhibitions affect looking at art?

SETH SIEGELAUB: They can. But usually pejoratively. In a large sense, everything is situation. In an exhibition situation the context—other artists, specific works—begins to imply, from without, certain things about any artwork. The less standard the exhibition situation becomes, the more difficult to "see" the individual work of art. So that an exhibition with six works of one artist and one of another begins to bring to bear on the art pre-exhibition values that prejudice the "seeing" process. All choices in the predetermination of the exhibition hinder the viewing of the intrinsic value of each work of art. Themes, judgmental criticism, preferences for individual artists expressed by differences in the number of works, all prejudge art.

CH: Can exhibitions ever serve the intentions of the artist, and if so, how?

SS: When artists show together their art shares a common space and time. This situation makes differences more obvious—if only by proximity. If all the conditions for making art were standard for all artists—same materials, size, color, etc.—there would still be great artists and lesser artists. The question of context has always been important. The nature of the exhibition situation begins to assume a "neutral" condition as one standardizes the elements in the environment in which art is "seen." I think exhibitions can function to clarify or focus in on certain dominant interests of an artist. As we know now, things that look alike are not necessarily alike. Certain exhibitions present differences better than others. Most exhibitions stress similarities, at the expense of the individual works.

CH: If the responsibility of the organizer is to standardize, what sort of choices can he take upon himself?

SS: The choice of specific artists and of the environment in which their work is to be placed.

CH: What conditions these decisions?

SS: The personal sensibility of the organizer, obviously. We're all critics, the most important criticism being "yes" or "no." After that his decisions should be in the realm of the practical and logistical, not the aesthetic. The organizer should have as little responsibility as possible for the specific art.

CH: Have the conditions for exhibitions changed as art has changed, and if so, how?

SS: Until 1967, the problems of exhibition of art were quite clear, because at that time the "art" of art and the "presentation" of art were coincident. When a painting was hung, all the necessary intrinsic art information was there. But gradually there developed an "art" which didn't need to be hung. An art wherein the problem of presentation paralleled one of the problems previously involved in the making and exhibition of a painting: i.e., *to make someone else aware that an artist had done anything at all.* Because the work was not visual in nature, it did not require the traditional means of exhibition but a means that would present the intrinsic ideas of the art.

For many years it has been well known that more people are aware of an artist's work through (1) the printed media or (2) conversation than by direct confrontation with the art itself. For painting and sculpture, where the visual presence—color, scale, size, location—is important to the work, the photograph or verbalization of that work is a bastardization of the art. But when art concerns itself with things not germane to physical presence, its intrinsic (communicative) value is not altered by its presentation in printed media. The use of catalogues and books to communicate (and disseminate) art is the most neutral means to present the new art. The catalogue can now act as primary information for the exhibition, as opposed to secondary information *about* art in magazines, catalogues, etc., and in some cases the "exhibition" can be the "catalogue." I might add that presentation—"how you are made aware of the art"—is common property, the same way that paint colors or bronze are common property to all painters or sculptors. Whether the artist chooses to present the work as a book or magazine or through an interview or with sticker labels or on billboards, it is not to be mistaken for the "art" ("subject matter"?).

CH: The organizer's response to an art "idea" is still primary. Where no other information is available, the man who takes responsibility for making someone else aware that an artist has done something can still make his own response absolutely intrusive; a kind of filter between the work and everyone else.

SS: It's a question of where an artist will give up his choice. This is a vitally important difference between the new work and what has preceded it. Whereas painters have generally never specified how much light their paintings should be seen by, what size wall they should be hung on—they have left it up to you *implicitly*—this new body of work *explicitly* denies any responsibility for presentation. All you need to see a painting is light. This new work doesn't even conern itself with that. The question of what environment you see the work in has nothing to do with what has been done. If it is made clear that the presentation of the work is not to be confused with the work itself, then there can be no misreadings of it. If an audience is made aware of an artist's work and he knows that *how* he is made aware is not within the artist's control or concern, then its specific presentation can be taken for granted.

CH: How do you make it clear?

SS: The standardizing of the exhibition situation begins to make the specific intentions of the artists clearer.

CH: Do you feel that this new work cannot, by its very nature, be misused as earlier work has often been in mixed exhibitions?

SS: No. By selection you could choose ideas between artists that parallel each other, just as you could pick up fifty stripe paintings and make them look more alike than they really are. You could load any exhibition situation in the same way. Orienting a show is not any more or less possible than it was when painting was painting and sculpture was sculpture. You can still make anything look like what you want it to. Figures don't lie; accountants do.

CH: So how has your function as an exhibition organizer been different from anyone else's?

SS: By keeping the exhibition situation as uniform as possible for each and all of the artists in the exhibition and not relying on outside verbal information like catalogue introductions, thematic titles, etc., I've tried to avoid prejudicing the viewing situation.

CH: This holds good as long as no one can begin to identify a "house style" in what you do.

SS: True. Failure is imminent. Unfortunately over a period of twenty exhibitions one begins to *become* the theme and the cement; which begins to be as offensive as prefaces, thematic titles, etc.

CH: Do you think then that every exhibition organizer has only a limited time before his activity becomes harmful to the artist?

SS: Only if he's successful. Yes. Because his opinions begin to become more important than what his opinions are about.

CH: Important for whom?

SS: For the people who are aware of the exhibitions he is doing.

CH: Do you think the development of this situation can affect the artists?

SS: It can only be detrimental to the artists for the same reasons.

CH: Do you think this now means that it is dangerous for artists to be associated with you?

SS: I don't know. Certainly right now it is. I may be a total bind. I don't really know. There are certain artists who interest me right now who would conceivably be the focus for some interests of mine. I feel my dilemma now is to be able to deal with art generally but not get involved specifically with specific artists. Everyone's pushing artists; which is OK, but I want to move away from that.

CH: Is there anything to move into?

SS: I don't know. I'm still interested in distributing art and art information. I personally value my network of booksellers and my mailing list throughout the world as a very important aspect of what I do. I am concerned with getting art out into the world and plan to continue publishing in multilingual editions to further this end. This is a very important communications consideration. American museums, with typical chauvinism, never publish in more than one language —just English.

CH: This implies that despite being a New Yorker, you are interested in decentralization.

SS: I think that New York is beginning to break down as a center. Not that there will be another city to replace it, but rather that where any artist is will be the center. International activity. It is more important to send artists to exhibitions than to send art. Art centers arise because artists go there. They go there because of (1) geographic and climatic factors, (2) access to other artists, (3) access to information and power channels, and (4) money. These factors are now becoming balanced throughout the world. To be part of this changing situation interests me very much.

CH: Do you think the new art has forced a new relationship between artists and those involved in art in a secondary capacity—dealers, critics, exhibition organizers, etc.?

SS: Yes, very definitely. I doubt whether artists have ever been so articulate about what they're doing as they are right now.[1]

[1] "What I say is part of the artwork. I don't look to critics to say things about my work. I tell them what it's about"—Douglas Huebler.

CH: So what's the nature of the new relationship?

SS: There are really two types of people: artists and everyone else.

CH: Artists have art and everyone else has relative amounts of power to manipulate or promote art. So where's the relationship and what's new about it?

SS: The need for an intermediary begins to become lessened. The new work is more accessible as art to the community: it needs fewer interpretive explanations.

CH: Do you think art ever needed interpretive explanations?

SS: I don't know anything about history, but the art we're talking about seems to be much more self-explanatory than any other. It just goes from mind to mind as directly as possible. The need for a community of critics to explain it seems obviously superfluous right now.

CH: Is this perhaps because they have fewer specifics to deal with?

SS: Yes. I think a basic underlying tendency in all art today is the ability of the artist to set general limits and not care about being specific. The tendency in practically all art today is toward generality about how things look rather than what specific things look like.

CH: How can this be made explicit in exhibitions?

SS: By organizing exhibitions in which the general conditions are proposed to the artists and the decisions about specifics are left entirely to them. Artists are the best judges of their own work. The general feeling one got from Harald Szeemann's show "When Attitudes Become Form" [2]—the nonchalance of it—did much to

[2] "When Attitudes Become Form" was first shown at the Kunsthalle, Berne, in March–April, 1969, and has also been seen in Krefeld and at the ICA in London (August–September, 1969).

enhance the viewing situation for individual works.

CH: Maybe the most important thing a critic or organizer or whatever can do is to draw attention to what is art by isolating what is not and acting to devalue it.[3]

[September, 1969]

[3] "I want to remove the experience from the work of art." – Joseph Kosuth.

DOCUMENTATION IN CONCEPTUAL ART *

Four Conceptual artists—Lawrence Weiner, Daniel Buren, Mel Bochner, and Sol LeWitt—were asked by the editors of Arts Magazine *to submit any document not exceeding one printed page in length for the April, 1970, issue of the magazine. These pages have been included in this anthology to serve as examples of several types of art documentation frequently utilized by Idea artists.*

The following documentations introduce serious questions concerning the function of an art magazine in a Conceptual Art environment. They seem to threaten the continuing vitality of traditional art criticism and the role of art illustration.

Texts about art, and reproductions of artworks, are what art magazines are all about. The relationships between the two are clearly defined. However, the texts submitted by these four artists are apparently intended to be evaluated as art rather than as criticism, aesthetics, or reportage even though they certainly contain something of all three.

The texts themselves have become the art, and the traditional device of using photographic reproductions in art magazines has been mocked. After all, in this instance, the artworks are not reproductions; the pages that follow are the works of art. There are no more reproductions. There is no more criticism. No more aesthetics. Only art.

* Reprinted from *Arts Magazine*, April, 1970.

Thus the major contribution to art offered by these four artists is that they have further blurred the traditional borders between literature criticism, theory, and reproduction—and nowadays anytime you subvert an established boundary, that's good.

By reducing the necessity (and questioning the validity) of using photographic illustrations of artworks, these artists have provided yet another positive contribution to the ultimate and long overdue reidentification of the medium of the art magazine. They have strengthened the integrity of the typographic medium and, as a result, what was previously a mere communicative vehicle can now become an independent form of enormous potential.

LAWRENCE WEINER

1. The artist may construct the piece
2. The piece may be fabricated
3. The piece need not be built

Each being equal and consistent with the intent of the artist the decision as to condition rests with the receiver upon the occasion of receivership

DANIEL BUREN

It Rains, It Snows, It Paints

Back there in the distance, within the realm of stupidity, the battle still rages, and it takes all the desperate efforts of the merchant class (critics, galleries, museums, organizers, avant-garde magazines, artists, collectors, art historians, art lovers) to keep reports of the combat on the front pages of today's paper.

Panic strikes the art establishment as its members begin to realize that the very foundation on which their power is established—art itself—is about to disappear. Faithful to their archconservative or arch-avant-garde positions, they continue to champion art versus Anti-Art, form versus Anti-Form, creating today's news so as to have something to talk about, to analyze, to sell tomorrow. Black and/or white, hot and/or cold, pop and/or op, pro and/or con, object art and/or conceptual art, subjective and/or objective, maximum and/or minimum are their stock in trade, their way of thinking, their way of dividing to conquer. But their conquests now are at an end, for the question of art, which is the only question, cannot be contained within their confusing and archaic frame of reference, their primitive dualism of pro's and con's.

"Art-and-Anti-Art" now constitute a single unit, defining limits within which art is continually bounced back and forth. What finally happens is that the notions of art and Anti-Art cancel each other out, and all our cherished beliefs: art as affirmation, art as a protest, art as the expression of individuality, art as interpretation, art as aestheticism (art for art's sake), art as humanism, are stripped of all significance. The artist's task is no longer to find a new form of art or counter art with a new anti-form; either pursuit is henceforth totally pointless.

Why then, even as it is about to disappear, when its existence has lost all justification, "*does art appear* for the first time to constitute a search for something essential; what counts is no longer the artist, or his feelings, or holding a mirror up to mankind, or man's labor, or any of the values on which our world is built, or those other values of which the world beyond once held a promise. Yet art is nevertheless an inquiry, precise and rigorous, that can be carried out only within a work, *a work of which nothing can be said, except that it is.*"[1]

We cannot hope to answer this question here. In any case it seems to us less remarkable as a question than as an observation of what is occurring, of an inevitable tendency.

"A work of which nothing can be said, except that it is"; there's the crux of the issue, the nucleus, the central tension around which all activity falls into place. Painting will henceforth be the pure visuality of painting; it will create a means, a specific system not to direct the viewer's eye, but simply to exist before the eye of the viewer.

This central tension has many implications. We will deal here with only one, which follows from what has been said, i.e., the neutrality of a work, its anonymity or, better still, its *impersonality.* By that we do not mean the anonymity of the person or persons who put out or produce the work. For them to remain anonymous would be a cheap solution to a problem demanding much more: the neutrality of the statement—painting as its own subject—eliminates all style and leads to an anonymity which is neither a screen to hide behind nor a privileged retreat, but rather *a position indispensable to the questioning process.* An anonymous, or rather, *impersonal* (the word is less ambiguous) "work" offers the viewer neither answer nor consolation nor certainty nor enlightenment about himself or the "work," which simply exists. One might say that the impersonal nature of the statement cuts off everything we habitually call communication between

[1] Maurice Blanchot, "L'Avenir et la Question de l'Art," *L'Espace Littérature* (*Collection Idées*), Paris: Ed. Gallimard, p. 295. Italics mine.

the work and the viewer. Since no information is offered, the viewer is forced to confront the fundamental truth of the questioning process itself.

The producer of an anonymous work must take full responsibility for it, but his relation to the work is totally different from the artist's to his work of art. Firstly, *he is no longer the owner of the work* in the old sense; he takes it upon himself, he puts it out, he works on common ground, he transforms raw material. He carries on his activity within a particular milieu, known as the artistic milieu, but he does so not as an artist, but as an individual. (We find it necessary to make this distinction because, particularly at this time, the artist is increasingly hailed as art's greatest glory; it is time for him to step down from this role he has been cast in or too willingly played, so that the "work" itself may become visible, no longer blurred by the myth of the "creator," a man "above the run of the mill." This impersonal effort, without style, inevitably produces a result poor in, if not totally lacking, form. Such form, as ineffective as it may be, is none the less essential, for it is the work *simply being* and not the image of something or the negation of an object. *This form is the object questioning its own disappearance as object.* It is not the result or the reply to the question. It is the question, the question endlessly being asked. Let us also make it clear that if an answer does exist, it is understood *a priori*—lest any illusions remain, lest the act of questioning itself become a comfortable pose—that one possible answer to the question is that the question—as to the essence of art and its theoretical formulation—ought not to have been asked. Moreover, no solutions to enigmas are to be expected; the fundamental question does not necessarily imply an answer, whatever it may be. Form, art's quest throughout the centuries, obliged to incessantly renew itself to keep alive, becomes a matter of no interest, superfluous and anachronistic. Of course then art is bound to disappear, at least its traditional mainspring is. Creating, producing, is henceforth of only relative interest, and the creator, the producer, no longer has any reason to glorify "his" product. We might even say that the producer-"creator" is only himself, a man alone before his product; his self is no longer revealed through his product. Now that he is "responsible for" an impersonal product, he learns, putting out the product, that he is "no longer a 'somebody' at all." His product, devoid of style, could by extrapolation have been put out, that is to say, made, by anyone. This possibility neither adds to nor detracts from the product itself. It is simply another implication of the impersonal nature of the product, not a way of affirming that the product is neutral/anonymous. While putting out a product is not at all the same, as we have seen, as "creating a work of art," the person responsible for the product does have a certain form of attachment to his work. His relation to his product is similar in nature to the relation between a demonstrator and the product he is demonstrating. His function in relation to the product is purely a didactic one.

The impersonal or anonymous nature of the work/product causes us to be confronted with a fact (or idea) in its raw form; we can observe it only without a reference to any metaphysical scheme, just as we observe that it is raining or snowing. Thus we can now say, for the first time, that "It is painting," as we say, "It is raining." When it snows we are in the presence of a natural phenomenon, so when "it paints" we are in the presence of a historical fact.

MEL BOCHNER

No Thought Exists Without a Sustaining Support

Mel Bochner

No Thought Exists Without a Sustaining Support

at / in

over / in

/ in

at / out

THEORY OF BOUNDARIES: (#1–4) BROWN PIGMENT ON WALL

THE STATEMENT OF THE SET OF UNDERLYING PRINCIPLES
A LAYING BARE OF ... BEHIND THE RELATIONSHIPS
(APPARENT RELATIONSHIPS — THIS IS
WHAT DIFFERENTIATES IT FROM
HYPOTHESIS OR SPECULATION)

OF THE SURFACE (AS FILM) TO ITS BORDER (BORDER
BEING THE ARBITRARY ENCLOSURE
IMPOSED)

THE FIRST TERM OF THE
LANGUAGE FRACTION REFERS
TO THE
CONTINGENCY OF THE FILM
TO THE BORDER

SECOND TERM OF FRACTION
REFERS TO POSITION OF FILM
AS REGARDS THE
SENSE OF ENCLOSURE ( )

ENCLOSURE CONSIDERED NOT AS BOUNDARY
BUT AS CONDITION OF POSITION

SOL LEWITT

I wanted to do a work of art that was as two-dimensional as possible.

It seems more natural to work directly on walls than to make a construction, to work on that, and then put the construction on the wall.

The physical properties of the wall, height, length, color, material, architectural conditions and intrusions, are a necessary part of the wall drawings.

Different kinds of walls make for different kinds of drawings.

Imperfections of the wall surface are occasionally apparent after the drawing is completed. These should be considered a part of the wall drawing.

The best surface to draw on is plaster, the worst is brick, but both have been used.

Most walls have holes, cracks, bumps, grease marks, are not level or square, and have various architectural eccentricities.

The handicap in using walls is that the artist is at the mercy of the architect.

The drawing is done rather lightly, using hard graphite so that the lines become, as much as possible, a part of the wall surface, visually.

Either the entire wall or a portion is used, but the dimensions of the wall and its surface have a considerable effect on the outcome.

When large walls are used the viewer would see the

drawings in sections sequentially, and not the wall as a whole.

Different draftsmen produce lines darker or lighter and closer or farther apart. As long as they are consistent there is no preference.

Various combinations of black lines produce different tonalities; combinations of colored lines produce different colors.

The four basic kinds of straight lines used are vertical, horizontal, 45° diagonal left to right, and 45° diagonal right to left.

When color drawings are done, a flat white wall is preferable. The colors used are yellow, red, blue, and black; the colors used in printing.

When a drawing is done using only black lines, the same tonality should be maintained throughout the plane in order to maintain the integrity of the wall surface.

An ink drawing on paper accompanies the wall drawing. It is rendered by the artist while the wall drawing is rendered by assistants.

The ink drawing is a plan for but not a reproduction of the wall drawing; the wall drawing is not a reproduction of the ink drawing. Each is equally important.

It is possible to think of the sides of simple three-dimensional objects as walls and draw on them.

The wall drawing is a permanent installation, until destroyed.

THE DECLINE AND FALL OF THE AVANT-GARDE *
by Robert Hughes

and LES LEVINE REPLIES: TWO VIEWS ON ADVANCED ART

Elsewhere in this volume Joseph Kosuth claims "The 'purest' definition of Conceptual Art would be that it is inquiry into the foundations of the concept art." *And Kosuth goes on to suggest that "... art may possibly be one endeavor that fulfills what another age might have called 'man's spiritual needs.'" Robert Hughes gives several reasons why he would not agree.*

In this essay Hughes claims that "For all the pretense of entering the world out there ... Conceptual Art remains inexorably culture-bound." New trends in art that bypass the traditional aesthetic of the object reveal an inherent purposelessness that becomes "... a real liability in one area; conceptualism." Thus according to Hughes the very existence of Conceptual Art "... hinges on the privileged status

* Reprinted from *Time*, December 18, 1972.

of art itself . . ." and not on a new and more democratic approach to reality.

Hughes cites the works of Schwarzkogler, Nitsch, and Rainer as indicative of the artist "having nothing to say and nowhere to go" and he criticizes the popular conceptualist notion of art as information as ". . . the shibboleth of the seventies." The avant-garde as principle is no longer viable in new art because "To be ahead of the game now seems pointless, for the game—under its present rules—is not worth playing."

The strong and critical views on advanced art offered by Hughes are widely held. However, one exception is writer/Conceptual artist Les Levine who has prepared some frank and personal comments concerning the negative claims made by Hughes and the Formalist critics; they appear here immediately following "The Decline and Fall of the Avant-Garde."

Robert Hughes is art editor for Time Magazine. *Les Levine is a well-known Conceptual artist who has exhibited very extensively in North America and Europe. He too has published many articles on contemporary art.*

THE DECLINE AND FALL OF THE AVANT-GARDE

Art is in bad shape. Advanced art, that is. The diagnosis: condition feeble. The prognosis: poor. The avant-garde has finally run out of steam, whether in Munich or Los Angeles, Paris or New York; the turnover of styles and theories that gave the 1960s their racketing ebullience (Abstract Expressionism, Minimalism, Op, Pop, and so on) has been followed by a sluggish descent into entropy. There seems to be no escape from that spiral.

Dealers continue to exhibit their pet trends as though nothing had happened, but recent art criticism has taken on a glum, apocalyptic tone: "The art currently filling the museums and galleries is of such low quality generally that no real critical intelligence could possibly feel challenged to analyze it . . . There is an inescapable sense among artists and critics that we are at the end of our rope, culturally speaking."

The writer is not some reactionary fogy whose predictions have finally come true, the way a stopped clock is right twice a day. She is a leading modernist critic, Barbara Rose, and her strictures would not have been made in the sixties, when American art seemed to inhabit an endless summer. Then New York believed in its manifest destiny; it had become the new Paris, or even Imperial Rome. The "mainstream" ran through New York. And it seemed by mid-decade that virtually everyone with something to invest was blundering about in its turbid flood like a shark, snapping up artworks. The culmination of this process was "Henry's show," a huge and partial exhibition called "New York Painting and Sculpture: 1940–1970" that Henry Geldzahler organized at The Metropolitan Museum of Art. If ever an exhibition broke the back of a decade, it was this one. It declared the union of new art, capital, and official power to be indissoluble, and crystallized the dissatisfactions that many artists felt with the interlocking, market-based system. It seemed to proclaim the end of an era.

The era was of great significance. It still seems true that American painting and sculpture during those thirty years reached a level of quality and invention that it never had before and may not soon regain. But creative periods do not last forever, and the desire to invent does not guarantee them. By 1970, few serious artists were untroubled by the exploitation of art. And one remedy that was proposed with increasing frequency was the abolition of the art object itself—anything that could be bought or possessed. This was not a new idea. Unfortunately, when used as a principle of art activity, it caused an eddy—even a vacuum—in which the avant-garde is immobilized today.

"Advanced" art—whether Conceptual Art, Process Art, video, Body Art, or any of their proliferating hybrids—avoids the object like the plague. The public has retreated, in turn, from it. This is a worldwide phenomenon, and what now exists is not simply a recession of interest (and talent) but a general weariness—a reluctance to believe in the avant-garde as principle. To be ahead of the game now seems pointless, for the game—under its present rules—is not worth playing.

Why did this happen? Those interested in the fate of the avant-garde should reflect on a Viennese artist named Rudolf Schwarzkogler. His achievement (and limited though it may be, it cannot be taken from him; he died, a martyr to his art, in 1969 at the age of twenty-nine) was to become the Vincent Van Gogh of Body Art. As every moviegoer knows, Van Gogh once cut off his ear and presented it to a whore. Schwarzkogler seems to have deduced that what really counts is not the application of paint, but the removal of surplus flesh. So he proceeded, inch by inch, to amputate his own penis, while a photographer recorded the act as an art event. In 1972, the resulting prints were

Hermann Nitsch: *O. M. Theatre* (orgies-mysteries theatre). Performed at the Everson Museum of Art, Syracuse, New York, November 16, 1972. Photograph by A. Chelz.

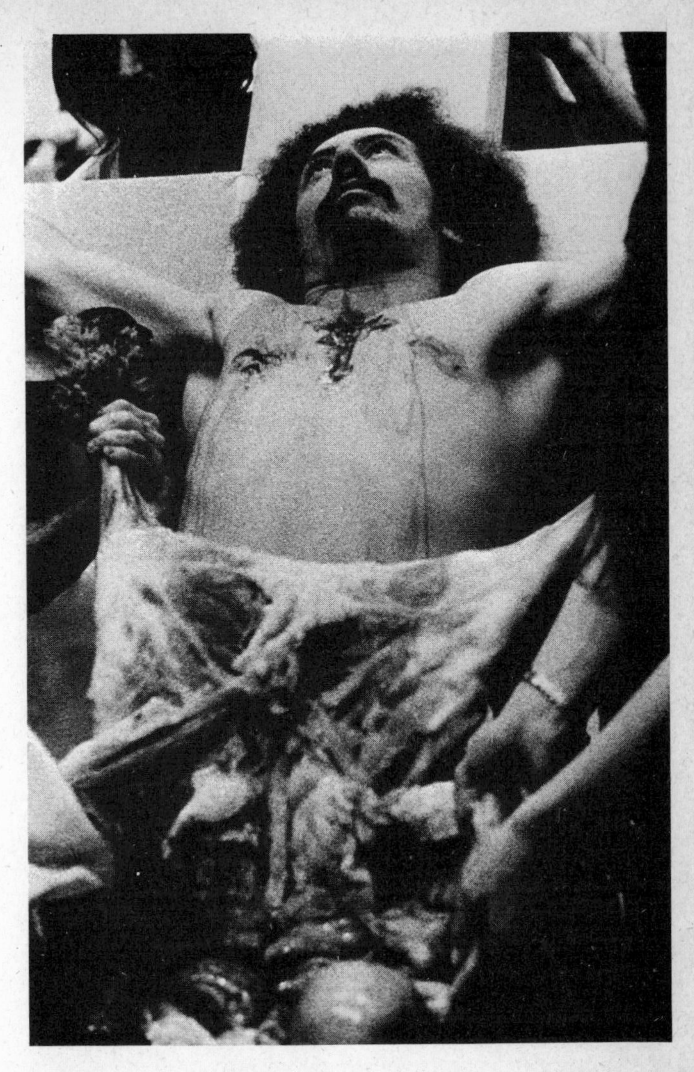

Hermann Nitsch: *O. M. Theatre* (orgies-mysteries theatre). Performed at the Everson Museum of Art, Syracuse, New York, November 16, 1972. Photograph by A. Chelz.

reverently exhibited in that biennial motor show of Western art, "Documenta 5" at Kassel. Successive acts of self-amputation finally did Schwarzkogler in.

Resurrected though incomplete, Schwarzkogler has entered the pantheon along with such living eminences of the Viennese imagination as Hermann Nitsch (whose ritual, the *Orgies-Mysteries Theatre*, performed in New York in 1972, consists of covering himself, a room, and everyone in range with animal blood and guts) and Arnulf Rainer (whose act is to truss himself, like a plucked hen, in thongs and twine, have photos taken, and smear the prints with black paint).

No doubt it could be argued by the proponents of Body Art (a form of expression whereby the artist's body becomes, as it were, the subject and object of the artwork) that Schwarzkogler's self-editing was not indulgent but brave, taking the audience's castration fears and reducing them to their most threatening quiddity. That the man was clearly as mad as a hatter, sick beyond rebuke, is not thought important: wasn't Van Gogh crazy too? But Schwarzkogler's gesture has a certain emblematic value. Having nothing to say, and nowhere to go but further out, he lopped himself and called it art. The politics of experience give way to the poetics of impotence. *Farewell, Jasper; hullo, Rudolf!*

The idea of an avant-garde art was predicated on the belief that artists, as social outsiders, could see further than insiders; that radical change in language (either oral or visual) could accompany, and even help cause, similar changes in life. To keep renewing the contract of language, so that it could handle fresh and difficult experience—such was the hope of the avant-garde, from Gustave Courbet to André Breton and beyond. And the hope needed certain conditions of nourishment. First, there had to be something to say, some proposition about experience, and this entailed a rigorous sense, among artists, of the *use* of their art. Art needed to be a necessary channel of information. Otherwise, why should changing it matter? Second, art required a delicate, exact sense of its own distance from society, so as not to be co-opted. And third, there had to be a strict faculty of judgment about one's responsibilities to language. Newness for its own sake lay on the periphery, not the center, of the avant-garde.

These are not, to put it mildly, the conditions that govern what passes for advanced art today, especially in New York. The Avant-Garde Festival, held in 1972 on a boat moored at the South Street Seaport in Manhattan, was a fair example of the problem: a confusion of irresolute trivia, ranging from a cabin full of autumn leaves (which, at least, the kids enjoyed throwing around), through numerous video pieces, to Charlotte Moorman—who enjoys a fame of sorts as the world's only topless cellist—playing her instrument under water. It was all so affably amateurish, like a transistorized rummage sale, that one gave up expectation.

A besetting problem for experimenters is that people no longer expect to get their necessary information from art; it was this gap that the artist-made video tape promised to close. But an event does not automatically gain aesthetic meaning because it is recorded, hand-held, on half-inch tape. Too many video pieces are either bald documentaries or hermetic diaries. Watching a tape of some artist making funny faces at himself has as many *longueurs* as gazing into the painted eye of a Landseer spaniel.

The inherent purposelessness of anti-object art becomes a real liability in one area: conceptualism. The basic claim of Conceptual Art is that making objects is irrelevant. The artist's duty is to reveal and criticize the attitudes by which art is made. In fact, painting and sculpture have always done this; every authentic creation is also a criticism, but criticism is not its sole subject. Instead, as art critic Max Kozloff pointed out in a trenchant essay on art-as-idea, we get "deliberately undigested accretions of data, documentations without comment, the purveying of information for its own sake, and the measuring of meaningless quantities."

And so a thicket of verbiage protects, and supports, the most banal propositions. Recently, an artist named Jannis Kounellis showed (among other things) a live macaw, sitting on a perch that projected from a steel plate. "The parrot piece," Kounellis explained, "is a more direct demonstration of the dialectic between the structure and the rest, in other words, the nature of the parrot, do you see? The structure represents a common mentality, and then the sensuous part, the parrot, is a criticism of the structure, right?" Stripped of its jargon, this is a not very surprising revelation that parrots are not perches. But at least one could scratch the parrot, which is not the case with more conceptualized works like Mel Bochner's recent piece at the Sonnabend Gallery: *The Seven Properties of Between, 1971–72.* It consisted of leaves of paper on which were laid stones, labeled A, B, X, and Y, with such observations written below as "If X is between A and B, A and B are not identical." What, one wonders, are such minimalities doing in an art gallery rather than in a child's primer of logic? Gallery space is not, in fact, necessary: one of Robert Barry's Conceptual efforts required that the door of his gallery be locked and adorned with this notice: "For the exhibition, the gallery will be closed."

There are no aesthetic criteria for dealing with such works. If some artist shows a clutch of Polaroids of himself playing table tennis, this is called "information." But who is informed, and about what? "Information" has become the shibboleth of the seventies, a vogue word, as "flatness" was in the sixties and "gesture" was in the fifties. Information is somehow opposed to "culture." For all the pretense of entering the world out there, however, Conceptual Art remains inexorably culture-bound. Its very existence hinges on the privileged status of art itself, a status drilled into the world audience by decades of institutional art worship. No matter how nugatory an event or object seems, it is nevertheless special, being art. And within this protective box, the Conceptual artist—as sculptor Robert Smithson acerbically put it—disports himself "like a B. F. Skinner rat doing his 'tough' little tricks."

These matters do not afflict Body Art to the same degree, even though the atmosphere of suspension and privilege peculiar to the recent avant-garde remains. But the trouble with most Body pieces is that they are either so small in conception as to be negligible—for instance, Dennis Oppenheim slowly tearing off a section of his fingernail—or so grotesque in their implications, as with poor Schwarzkogler, that they amount to overkill. Triviality or threat: take your choice.

There is something indubitably menacing about the

work of people like Vito Acconci, one of whose recent pieces was to build a ramp and crawl around below it, masturbating invisibly; or the young Los Angeles artist Chris Burden, who had himself manacled to the floor of an open garage, between live wires and buckets of water, so that (in possibility) anyone who cared to might kick over the pails and electrocute the artist. The sight of such gratuitous risk is a vulgar *frisson* for the spectators, and unlikely to appeal to those who believe that art and life interact best at a distance from one another. At least the psychodramas of Body Art connote a desperate involvement that is missing from the other, and colder, latitudes of conceptualism. If Conceptual Art represents pedagogy and stale metaphysics at the end of their tether, Body Art is the last rictus of Expressionism.

But faced with the choice between amateur therapy and finicky, arid footnotes to Duchamp, the mind recoils. In fact, the term *avant-garde* has outlived its usefulness. The hard thing to face is not that the emperor has no clothes; it is that beneath the raiment, there is no emperor.

LES LEVINE REPLIES

TO THE READER: The italicized phrase preceding each of the points in Mr. Levine's essay below identifies the passage in Mr. Hughes's essay being discussed by Mr. Levine.

". . . that gave the 1960s their racketing ebullience . . ."

1. In the sixties, the art market was booming and Formalism felt secure that it had control of that market. Anti-Formalism was not a threat. Now that Formalism feels threatened, the avant-garde has been revived to provide a scapegoat.

'. . . *no real critical intelligence could possibly feel challenged . . .*"

2. A. In the same way that art has lost its potency, so has criticism. Critics are confused and have begun to write about themselves. Most are annoyed that advanced art has damaged old markets and not created new ones.

B. Robert Hughes has often followed leads provided by Barbara Rose.

". . . *when American art seemed to inhabit an endless summer.*"

3. American art now self-consciously looks like "American art," the way French art did in the thirties. This must be recognized as a decaying factor. Art only succeeds when it breaks ritual down into knowledge. It ceases to be art when it develops its own ritual.

". . . *blundering about in its turbid flood like a shark, snapping up . . .*"

4. In a society that has a supermarket in each home, it would seem natural that art would become just another consumer product and develop the problems that all consumer markets face eventually: how to keep customers happy and coming back for more of the same.

"*artworks. The culmination of this process was 'Henry's show' . . .*"

5. Here the point is, "I'm in with the in-crowd, I go where the in-crowd goes."

"*. . . increasing frequency was the abolition of the art object . . .*"

6. The art object supports a system that is in serious trouble, and the contemporary artist would be rendered impotent if he made no attempt to reflect this.

"*. . . caused an eddy—even a vacuum—in which the avant-garde . . .*"

7. Conceptual Art, art that exists as ideas rather than as objects, was not only important, but totally necessary, to reexamine an art world that had lost its way in the boom of the mid-sixties.

"*. . . the object like the plague. The public has retreated . . .*"

8. The term *avant-garde* made sense only before McLuhan forced us to understand media. Painting and sculpture had to do with pre-electronic understanding of media. Now that we know what media is we must make media matter.

"*. . . a reluctance to believe in the avant-garde as . . .*"

9. The alchemy of the avant-garde was "lead time." The assumption that a favored individual or group would have access to information or sensibilities not readily available to anyone else. Higher technology and mass production have made it possible for everyone to know and sense as much as anyone else now.

"*To be ahead of the game now seems pointless, for . . .*"

10. Why blame art for all it has become. The artist responds to a subliminal demand from society to act out for them their anxieties and desires. The public

must accept responsibility partially for what they elicit from their artists. The war in Vietnam almost made the game of life not worth playing.

"Why did this happen? Those interested in the fate of . . ."

11. It happened in part because art insisted on existing for art's sake only. Or it didn't happen. The art world merely reflected a lethargy of moral integrity pervading the culture in general.

". . . Schwarzkogler. His achievement (and limited though it . . ."

12. Why pick Rudolf Schwarzkogler as an example? Why not pick Mark Rothko, the important abstract painter and demigod of the Greenberg Formalist School, who slashed his wrist to end his life one year earlier. Surely, a similar frame of mind about art caused his death. Freaks make better scapegoats than Formalists.

". . . As every moviegoer knows, Van Gogh . . ."

13. Every magazine reader knows that dead art's better than living art, and that there's only one thing better than a good artist and that's a dead artist.

". . . the application of paint, but the removal of surplus flesh. . . ."

14. Why bring up painting? What has that to do with this madness, other than to imply that all art emanates from paint, which is not true.

". . . he proceeded, inch by inch, to amputate his own penis, while . . ."

15. Sounds like a line from a pornographic novel. Would be interesting as reader excitement in a detec-

tive story also or a stock market report or a women's fashion magazine or even *Popular Mechanics.* After all, who wants to write about advanced art when you can write about penis amputations and call them advanced art.

"*. . . self-amputation finally did Schwarzkogler in. . . .*"

16. The avant-garde comes out of the cultural closet to self-amputate itself, while Formalism shouts, "Look where the sins of anti-Formalism lead to!"

"*. . . New York in 1972 . . .*"

17. Hermann Nitsch also performed four years ago in New York, but at that time Formalism was too busy making money to worry about Hermann's esoteric and out-of-mainstream performance.

"*. . . Arnulf Rainer (whose act is . . .*"

18. Another example of a relatively innocuous art form being presented as mainstream to ridicule advanced art by association and to imply that it is happening everywhere, not just America.

"*. . . the subject and object of the artwork) that Schwarz- . . .*"

19. Wrong definition, there is no object in Body Art. It is the body, its systems and behaviors that are under consideration.

"*. . . nothing to say, and nowhere . . .*"

20. Well, he certainly said, "I don't want to live in this world anyway."

"*. . . to go but further out, he lopped himself and called it art. . . .*"

21. He called it art, but we don't have to call it art. It could easily be the pressures of a society that de-

mands more all the time, which causes such desperate attempts for attention as Jim Morrison masturbating before an audience, or Janis Joplin and Jimi Hendrix pushing off on heroin.

"*. . . impotence.* Farewell, Jasper; hullo, Rudolf!"

22. No one who has even the most rudimentary knowledge of contemporary art would compare Rudolf Schwarzkogler to Jasper Johns, let alone imply that Rudolf has replaced Jasper. Here, the media are trying to make their own messages.

"*. . . could handle fresh and difficult experience . . .*"

23. It is the artist's job to mold the world into a sphere; to show us the shape of what we've got and how it works.

"*. . . necessary channel of information. . . .*"

24. Has Formalist painting and sculpture been a necessary channel of information in recent years? The answer is no, the public is no longer willing to consider seriously an art that is constantly talking about itself and to itself.

"*. . . its own distance from society, so as not to be co-opted. . . .*"

25. Good art has always been co-opted by society eventually. If it's worth co-opting, society will take it over and use it.

"*. . . one's responsibilities to language. Newness for its own sake . . .*"

26. People reject new ideas because they feel they own the old ones, and the new ones belong to someone else. Protect your property! There is still no superior quality for a work of art to have than genuine newness.

"*. . . York. The Avant-Garde Festival . . .*"

27. The Avant-Garde Festival has never been anything more than an art aside. To be surprised at this point, that it amounts to "irresolute trivia," is almost the same as being surprised that *Time* is a magazine and not a clock.

"*. . . transistorized rummage sale, that one gave up expectation.*"

28. Many gave up expectation years ago and merely considered this event as the art world's day off, a sort of Beau's art ball. To set it up as an example of advanced art, so one can knock it down as a "rummage sale," is negligent reportage.

"*. . . longer expect to get their necessary information from art . . .*"

29. Neither do they expect to get it from any other source. After ten years of saturation media coverage of Vietnam, how many Americans know what it's all about?

"*. . . was this gap that the artist-made video tape promised . . .*"

30. Video artists made no such promise. It was not an alternate channel, but an additional channel.

"*. . . painted eye of a Landseer spaniel.*"

31. Or for that matter watching the innumerable talk shows that are on TV, where the sole purpose seems to be for the guests to compliment one another. Now that we know what media is we know that its magnets are not even making it matter. Nobody in the world knows what to do with TV.

"*. . . a real liability in one area . . .*"

32. Anti-object art is not a real liability. It's a deficit in an object market.

". . . artist's duty is to reveal and criticize the attitudes by which art . . ."

33. It is also the duty of an artist to impose his sensibilities on interpreting existing social systems, which are changing and affecting our lives at a more rapid pace than we can finesse our culture to cope with them.

". . . Kozloff . . ."

34. Max Kozloff is another Formalist art critic who could certainly be expected to respond negatively to advanced art. So what's the point to quote him, when it's clear ahead of time, he doesn't like it?

". . . But at least one could scratch the parrot . . ."

35. Animal art: another freak element implying a similar kind of information that monkey art did in the period of Abstract Expressionism.

". . . logic? Gallery space is not, in fact, necessary: one . . ."

36. Logic is not a fair exchange for understanding.

". . . 'the gallery will be closed.' "

37. This work is almost an exact copy of Marcel Duchamp's *Relage*, a work in which Duchamp closed the theatre for the evening and put *relage* on the doors. So one could say it's following a tradition, and hardly advanced.

"There are no aesthetic criteria for dealing with such . . ."

38. There are criteria for dealing with this art. However, methinks the critics do protest too much. Using

logical references to previous art, it may be difficult, but it is the critic's job to develop the new channels of criticism necessary.

". . . who is informed, and about what? . . ."

39. The reason artists do things for society is to find out why society would want them done in the first place. Also it is necessary to define the difference between information and knowledge more clearly.

". . . opposed to 'culture.' For all the pretense . . ."

40. Information is not opposed to culture, for information is culture. Information is opposed to mindless creativity, however, that appears to have no constructive value other than to titillate esoteric taste.

". . . 'tough' little tricks."

41. One of the tricks no doubt would be putting rocks in metal bins or mirrors by the seashore.

". . . take your choice."

42. Truth or consequences?

". . . masturbating invisibly . . ."

43. The artist may be offering a heavily masturbating society to do just that: masturbate.

". . . electrocute the artist. The sight of such gratuitous risk is a . . ."

44. The artist may be trying to alleviate self-guilt about needless killing in Vietnam. "I offer you the choice to kill me so that you can realize that this choice is being made on your behalf every day. If you have no qualms about killing Vietnamese, why should you care about killing me or you?"

". . . frisson *for the spectators, and unlikely to appeal to those . . ."*

45. French word, means thrill. Any serious art critic given the choice between "frisson" and thrill is going to use the word *frisson* to imply worldliness and avoid the possibility of cheap thrill.

"*. . . arid footnotes to Duchamp, the mind recoils. In fact . . .*"

46. Formalist critics refuse to be informed about the anti-Formal art that has happened since Duchamp. Even to use Duchamp in this reference at this late stage amounts to a misapprehension of his work. For if his *Urinal* were in a museum today, no doubt, someone would urinate in it.

". . . avant-garde *has outlived its usefulness. The hard . . .*"

47. Yes, ten years ago, so why consider it so seriously now? Why not look at painting and sculpture and find out why that's so constipated?

"*. . . emperor has no clothes; it is that . . .*"

48. The public loves to be told that art is a sham, that, after all, art is no better than the worst of them. Trying to frighten the public back to painting and sculpture, that no longer have any meaning, will only scare them further away from all art.